BEAUTY
DIES

For Gay—

BEAUTY
DIES

Melodie Johnson Howe

A Claire Conrad/Maggie Hill Mystery

Melodie Johnson Howe

VIKING

VIKING
Published by the Penguin Group
Penguin Books USA Inc., 375 Hudson Street,
New York, New York 10014, U.S.A.
Penguin Books Ltd, 27 Wrights Lane,
London W8 5TZ, England
Penguin Books Australia Ltd, Ringwood,
Victoria, Australia
Penguin Books Canada Ltd, 10 Alcorn Avenue,
Toronto, Ontario, Canada M4V 3B2
Penguin Books (N.Z.) Ltd, 182–190 Wairau Road,
Auckland 10, New Zealand

Penguin Books Ltd, Registered Offices:
Harmondsworth, Middlesex, England

First published in 1994 by Viking Penguin,
a division of Penguin Books USA Inc.

10 9 8 7 6 5 4 3 2 1

PUBLISHER'S NOTE
This is a work of fiction. Names, characters, places, and incidents either are the
product of the author's imagination or are used fictitiously, and any resemblance
to actual persons, living or dead, events, or locales is entirely coincidental.

LIBRARY OF CONGRESS CATALOGING IN PUBLICATION DATA
Howe, Melodie Johnson.
    Beauty dies : a Claire Conrad / Maggie Hill mystery / Melodie
Johnson Howe.
        p.   cm.
    ISBN 0-670-85449-2
I. Title.
    1. Private investigators—New York (N.Y.)—Fiction.   2. Women
detectives—New York (N.Y.)—Fiction.   I. Title.
PS3558.O8926B4   1994
813'.54—dc20   94-10343

Printed in the United States of America
Set in Adobe Minion
Designed by Virginia Norey

To Bones Howe, Kathleen Boddicker,
Erica Marlette, and Geoffrey Howe

You will put on a dress of guilt
and shoes with broken high ideals.

—Roger McGough

ACKNOWLEDGMENTS

I want to thank my agent, Chuck Verrill, for believing Maggie and Claire would rise again; Pam Dorman for her support; my dear friend Lenore Salzbrunn; and a special thanks to T. E. D. Klein.

One

"Wanna buy a diamond ring, lady? Check it out."

The man's dark angry face glistened with sweat in the cold spring morning light. He thrust his hand at me. I stared at a chunk of rhinestone as big as a glass eye.

"Diamond ring, lady. Twenty bucks."

Diamonds are forever, I thought. Neil's ring had slipped on so easily and it had taken me forever to get it off.

"Check it out, twenty bucks."

As I turned away from the man, our shoulders collided.

"Fuck you," he said in low voice.

That's exactly what Neil had said to me when I left him. Only he had added my name, Maggie Hill. My *maiden* name.

It was Tuesday, my last day in New York City, and I could hardly wait to get back to the isolation and uneasy separation that was Los Angeles. I hadn't thought about my ex-husband for two whole weeks. That's because I was a new woman with a new job.

I moved quickly up Madison, tightening my grip on the package Claire Conrad had sent me to pick up. It contained two pairs of kid gloves made specially for her. One black pair, one white pair. She wore gloves not because she was a lady. She wore them because she was a private detective and didn't want to leave her fingerprints around to confuse the cops.

Claire and I had met only a few weeks before in Los Angeles, where my previous employer had blown his head off. My new position consisted of secretarial duties and running errands. In other words, I was her assistant. Also, because I hold the dubious distinction of having once written and published a novel, I was chronicling Claire Conrad's exploits—including how she had proven my employer's suicide was really murder, and how her extraordinary intelligence, her unnerving perceptions, and my help had solved the crime. I was writing slowly. I wanted this job to last. At thirty-five, I was getting a little too old for temp work. A little too old even to be a new woman.

I hoofed it past store windows displaying antique pillows, men's silk bathrobes, and the ubiquitous thin mannequins adorned in spring suits as white as a little girl's First Communion dress. The store windows reflected my own image back at me: the dark brown hair, questioning dark brown eyes, defiant chin, and sharp straight nose that dipped slightly down, as if it were trying to call attention to my mouth. In contrast to these rather pointed features, my lips were full and sensual. Men had a tendency to look at them instead of my eyes.

I stopped in front of my favorite shoe store. There they were. A pair of black and white spectator pumps. I longingly admired how the black shiny patent curved around the pristine white leather. I delighted at the little holes punched along the edge of the patent so the white leather peeked through. I appreciated the sexy curve of the heel.

In college I had read a play by Odets. A character described his feelings for a woman by comparing her to a pair of black and white wingtips, shoes that he could never afford, shoes far beyond his reach. It had never occurred to me to try to be that unobtainable woman. She belongs with the perfect man. I just wanted the shoes, *spectator* shoes. Think of the possibilities. If I slipped my feet into them, what would I observe? Witness? As usual I didn't go into the store, didn't ask the price, and didn't try them on. I just longed for them. It does the soul good to yearn for something.

I turned right on Sixty-third and sauntered toward the Parkfaire Hotel.

"Miss?"

A young woman with wasted blue eyes stepped quickly in front of me. A greenish yellow bruise spread across her left cheek.

"Miss?" She wiped her runny nose on the sleeve of her cheap red jacket.

I veered right, but she stayed with me. I moved to my left. So did she.

"Miss?" Her hair was bleached brittle blond.

I kept walking toward the hotel. The doorman, who minus legs would have been perfectly square, was looking toward Park Avenue where little green buds heralded new life on the trees in the center island. The young woman reached out her hand toward me with new hope. Ah, spring.

"Miss?"

"Look," I said, stopping and confronting her. "It's only nine o'clock in the morning and I haven't even had my coffee and I've already been told to fuck off. I left all my money in my hotel room. Go try somebody else."

"She didn't kill herself," she said, doggedly scuffing alongside me in red cowboy boots.

I was at the hotel.

"Cybella didn't kill herself."

The doorman turned toward us, his long beige coat flapping in the breeze. Cool eyes peered from his bright red face, sizing up the young woman.

"Good morning, Miss Hill," he said, stepping between the girl and me. "I hear you're leaving us today."

"That's right, Frank." We spoke to each other as if she didn't exist.

I pushed through the revolving door into the white marble lobby. It wasn't much bigger than your average-size Beverly Hills living room. I stood for a moment brushing my hair from my face, then turned and looked back.

Frank was waving his stubby arms at the young woman —she was maybe twenty-three—forcing her to cross the street. She flipped him off, then stood on the opposite sidewalk, arms folded against the wind, defiantly staring at the hotel. She wore a short, skintight, white leather skirt. Red fishnet stockings boldly defined her long thin legs. Her gaunt pale face was mean with determination.

"We had to throw her out of the lobby this morning." Desanto, the manager of the Parkfaire, came up to me all decked out in tails and pin-striped trousers. He looked like an officious groom waiting for a bride who was too smart to show up. "She wanted to see Claire Conrad," he said with a sniff.

"What about?"

"I didn't bother to find out."

I turned away from the revolving door and the image of the young woman. Leave it alone, Maggie, I told myself. Soon you'll be back in L.A. I headed toward the elevators.

Desanto half-closed his eyes, drew his head so far back that his chin looked ingrown, and marched along beside me. It was difficult to take a walk alone in this town.

"You will be checking out at noon?"

"That's what I told you, Mr. Desanto." I pushed the elevator button. Desanto was used to dealing directly with

Claire, and now he had to deal with me. I guess he thought it was a step down.

"I just wanted to make sure. Mr. Orita is coming in this evening and I told him he could have the Conrad Suite. It's his favorite."

Desanto's eyes darted from me to a heavily carved table in the middle of the room. An Oriental vase the size of a small child held an enormous bouquet of dangerous-looking flowers. Bony stems and petals as sharp as long red fingernails twisted upward to the ceiling, jabbing at an old, gracious crystal chandelier. A woman in a black uniform was methodically replacing some of the dead flowers. Desanto watched her every move with a busy intensity. He suddenly pulled in his chin again and rushed to greet the Bovine Lady, as I called her, who was just settling down into her usual chair by the marble fireplace at the end of the lobby. She was a plump, middle-aged woman laden with jewelry. Her face was long and sad, her eyes big and blue. She looked as though her wealthy husband had put her out to pasture. I thought of the young girl with her thin arms folded against the morning cold. Not everybody was put out in the same pasture. Leave it alone, Maggie.

The elevator door opened. I stepped aside, letting out four men and one woman in business suits with briefcases. Four to one, not a good ratio. The elevator shot me up to fifteen.

At the end of the hall a brass plate on the door identified the Conrad Suite. I gave the special knock: two quick taps, three long ones. Boulton let me into the black-and-white marble foyer, looking every inch the English butler in his gray jacket, vest, and dark pin-striped trousers.

"Did madam enjoy her morning stroll?" he asked, bowing slightly. His jacket was opened and I could see the butt of the gun in his shoulder holster.

"I wouldn't exactly call it a stroll," I said.

Boulton's chestnut brown hair was swept back from his high, intelligent forehead. His lips, in repose, were somber, almost sad. I liked them.

"Where's Claire?"

"Madam's in the drawing room," he said in his formal English accent.

"To me it will always be the living room," I said.

A slight smile.

"What kind of mood is she in?" I asked.

"Depressed as always when she finishes a job. Especially insurance fraud cases. Tread lightly. By the way I took the liberty of packing for you."

"Thanks."

"If you'll forgive me, I thought you were the type of American woman who wore those athletic-looking under-garments. The see-through, white lace bra was a pleasant surprise. Breakfast will be served momentarily." He turned crisply on his heels and headed down the short hallway to the dining room.

I loved observing Boulton. I loved how he moved. I loved the grace of his lean compact body. Where I had trouble with him was up close. Then his grace and intelligence had a coolness, a steeliness that disturbed me. My ex-husband is an LAPD detective. I know about macho men and their guns. Boulton may have been English and looked like he'd just stumbled out of *Masterpiece Theater,* but these men are all the same. I think a woman should try once in her life to desire a man who doesn't carry a gun. I was keeping my distance.

I opened the double doors to the living room and tried to dismiss the image of Boulton alone in my room, his hand cupping my bra. Claire Conrad was enthroned in her Queen Anne chair. Not the one she had in Conrad Cottage in L.A., but her New York chair. Covered in white linen, it had the same bowed legs, clawed feet, high straight back, and sides that winged out. I had the feeling there were Queen Annes in hotel suites all around the world waiting for the famous detective's backside to nestle onto their downy cushions.

It was Claire's day to dress in black. It fit her mood. She wore black slacks, a black silk shirt, and a black wrap jacket. Her ebony walking stick leaned against her chair like a faithful dog.

"Your gloves," I said, placing them on a small table next to her. In response she stared at the tips of her shoes.

I sat down at my desk. It was a gray lacquered affair and had better legs than I did. The room was done in various shades of white. Two sofas covered in grayish white silk faced one another in front of a gray marble fireplace. The coffee table was glass with an iron base. Windows, which looked down on Park Avenue, were graced with ecru damask.

"Breakfast will be served momentarily," I said.

Her penetrating dark blue eyes found me. Silvery white hair folded back like the wings of a bird from her refined, handsome face. Deep lines ran across her forehead and down the corners of her lips, enhancing her elegance instead of detracting from it. As her biographer I should have known her age, but I didn't. I guessed her to be in her fifties. One of these days I was going to have to ask her. For a moment I thought she was going to speak, but she just stared at me. The sound of car horns and sirens filtered through the large windows, gently disturbing the silence in the room. Between the street and the fifteenth floor the traffic noise had lost its anger. Amazing what money can do.

I looked down at my list and checked off the gloves. Next came the Bentley. I had to call the rental company so they would be sure to have someone at the airport to pick it up. Then I had to call Graham Sitwell, the CEO of New York

Insurance, to tell him Claire considered the fraud case closed and to please send the money. Just as I reached for the phone, Boulton appeared.

"Breakfast, madam," he announced.

Claire stood and stretched her lean six-foot frame, then followed him out of the room. I took up the rear. We made a somber procession down the hallway to the dining room. It was small, with mirrored walls and pale gold carpet. Crystal sconces, with silk lampshades that never stayed straight, offered an expensive glow.

Claire sat at the head of the table. I sat on her right. Boulton placed *The New York Times* next to her and began to serve the coffee. Gerta, carrying two plates, pushed open the swinging door from the small galley kitchen.

"Good morning." She served us caviar and sour cream omelets.

"How are you, Gerta?" I asked. "It's nice to talk to somebody."

"We go home," she said in her thick Hungarian accent. She looked at Claire, sighed heavily so we could all hear it, then looked back at me. "I hope a job will be waiting for her when we get to L.A. Then all this gloom will disappear."

Gerta pushed the swinging door with her heavy hip and returned to the kitchen, followed by Boulton.

Claire picked up the newspaper and began to read. We ate our omelets and drank our coffee in silence. The only sounds came from the tinkling of crystal and china and the rustle of *The New York Times.* Very cosmopolitan.

Claire leaned back in her chair. Her shrewd eyes came to rest on me. "Beauty dies, Miss Hill." Her voice was edged with melancholy.

"I beg your pardon?"

"It's interesting how many other qualities die with beauty.

Style, grace, elegance, hope. Society puts a great deal of hope, of promise, in beauty. Hope dies, too."

I gave this some thought, then said, "It was just an insurance fraud case. And, if you don't mind me saying so, you earned a ton of money having that poor old accountant arrested. He's the one who should be depressed, not you."

"I? Depressed? What *are* you talking about?"

"What are you talking about?"

"Cybella."

I put down my coffee cup. She tossed me the paper folded to the obituaries.

"Cybella." I repeated the name.

The page was filled with the accomplishments of old white dead men and very young dead men, the letters *AIDS* looming over their successes. In the bottom of the left-hand corner of the page was a photograph of a woman of great beauty. The caption read: BEAUTY DIES, CYBELLA DEAD AT 53. The photograph had been taken when she was around my age, mid-thirties. She had a long graceful neck, dark hair setting off high cheekbones, and a strong chin. Her mouth was lush but not soft. Dark haunting eyes stared into mine. She had the kind of beauty that seemed to come from the ages—not from two minutes on MTV.

The gist of the obituary was that Cybella, *née* Nancy Grange from Buffalo, New York, had been *the* top model in the sixties. Later she had tried acting, but her cool beauty had turned to ice on celluloid. Suffering from depression, she had jumped from the tenth floor down the stairwell of her Manhattan apartment building. She left one daughter, named Sarah Grange, a model.

I thought of the girl standing outside the hotel. I also thought of another young girl, me, standing in front of my bathroom mirror trying to suck in my cheeks and extend my neck so I could look like Cybella. I had forgotten her name, but not her face.

"I saw her only once, Miss Hill, many years ago, at a reception given in my honor in Paris," Claire said. "She was the guest of the minister of culture, a randy old thing. When Cybella walked in you could feel a change in the room. A frisson. Beauty had entered."

I looked at Claire. "She didn't kill herself."

"You deduced that from this innocuous obituary? Maybe I should write about you."

"No, no." I was on my feet. "Just a minute. I'll be right back."

I ran out of the dining room, down the hall. I pounded on the elevator button till the doors pulled open.

As I shoved the revolving door around, the cold wind hit my face. She was across the street smoking a cigarette, waiting for me. I squeezed between two limos parked at the curb, checked the traffic, and darted across.

"Okay," I began, "three questions. How did you know Claire Conrad was staying at this hotel?"

She reached into the pocket of her jacket and handed me a crumpled newspaper clipping. A picture of Claire, Boulton, and me coming out of the Parkfaire was captioned: THE ELUSIVE CLAIRE CONRAD IS IN TOWN. The name of the hotel could be seen in the background. Boulton and I were not mentioned.

"Even I can read the *Daily News*," she said.

"How do you know Cybella didn't kill herself?"

"You got a VCR?"

"Yes."

"Then I have proof." She took a videocassette from her plastic purse.

"What's your name?" I asked.

"Jackie."

"Jackie what?"

"Jacqueline Kennedy Onassis Murphy. My mother had dreams."

"I can take you up to see Claire Conrad, but she'll probably throw you out."

"I'll never live it down." She flicked her cigarette into the street.

Let it go, Maggie, I told myself once more. Soon we'll all be in Los Angeles, I'll be driving my Honda, the car radio my only contact with the outside world and the sun warm on my arms and face. Let it go.

Oh, hell. Her mother had dreams.

Two

Boulton opened the door.

"Jackie, this is Boulton," I announced. "He's going to search you. Where's Claire?"

"Drawing room." He stepped between Jackie and me, moving her against the wall of the foyer. His hands moved efficiently, expertly down her body.

"Hey, what the fuck's going on here?" she demanded.

I closed the living-room doors behind me.

Claire was back in the Queen Anne, long legs extended, observing the tips of her black loafers.

"There's a young woman who says that Cybella didn't kill herself. Here's the proof." I held up the video.

Her gaze moved slowly from her shoes to the cassette. I could tell by her expression she found her own footwear more interesting.

"I'm walking back to the hotel," I explained quickly, "and this girl appears out of nowhere and says, 'Cybella didn't kill herself.' I think she's just another crazy. I come up here and read about Cybella's suicide."

I gestured toward the door. "The girl's in the foyer."

"The only thing you were supposed to bring back with you were my gloves, Miss Hill."

"All you have to do is listen."

I opened the doors. Boulton, a firm grip on Jackie's arm, guided her into the room.

"Do you always have your clients body-searched?" she demanded, trying to squirm out of his grasp.

Claire's eyes riveted on me. "Client? Client!"

At least I had her full attention. "You spoke about Cybella so eloquently." I picked my words carefully. "Remember how the room changed when Cybella walked in? I remember when I was eight years old and how I wanted to look like her. She affected us both. Isn't that worth the time it takes to look at this tape?"

"No!" snapped Claire.

"Maybe just for once a beautiful woman didn't die by her own hand."

"Miss Hill, we have a plane to catch."

"She didn't kill herself," Jackie said.

"Be quiet!" I barked.

"Don't tell me to be quiet. Who the fuck do you people think you are, anyway?"

Boulton tightened his grip on her arm and Jackie sucked in her breath. Claire leaned back in her chair and closed her eyes. When Claire closes her eyes, she's either listening carefully to those around her or pretending they no longer exist. I didn't have to guess which it was today.

"Show your video to the police," I said to Jackie.

"The police? What world are you living in?"

"Come on."

Boulton began to pull her back toward the foyer.

"No!" She dug in her heels and struggled in his grip. "If you jump down a stairwell, you don't fall in a straight line. You bounce off the railings, the walls, until you finally hit the floor."

Claire opened her eyes and held up her right hand. The

chunk of lapis she called a ring shimmered darkly on her forefinger. Boulton released Jackie.

"You saw her being pushed over the railing?" Claire asked.

"I'm not saying I saw it happen."

"What's your name?" Claire asked.

"Jackie."

"Jackie what?"

I held my breath.

"Jacqueline Kennedy Onassis Murphy."

"Her mother had dreams," I added quickly.

"A firm grasp on reality might have been more helpful." Claire studied Jackie. "If you didn't witness Cybella's death, then how did you know she was dead?"

"I read about it in the paper."

"And how did you know where to find me?"

"She read that in the paper too," I said. Jackie took the clipping out, waved it, then shoved it in her purse.

"What do you do, Miss Murphy?" she asked.

"I'm an actress. I perform at Peep Thrills. Private booth. Just me and the customer. White blondes are special." She tilted her head back and fluffed her dried bleached hair with her fingers as if she were in a Clairol commercial gone terribly wrong.

"And I'm not being a racist," she added. "Let's face it, there's no fuckin' equality in sexual fantasies." She looked evenly at Claire, giving her time to absorb this observation. Claire peered back at her: sage to sage.

"Just to look at me costs a token," Jackie continued, her hands on hips, back slightly arched, breasts proud. "For another token the customer can talk to me on the telephone while I perform. Tell me what he wants me to do, what he wants me to be. Or what he'd like to do to me while I'm doing what it is he wants me to be. Like I said, I'm an actress."

"How did you become acquainted with Cybella?" Claire asked.

"I met her last week. We had coffee. She wanted to know why her daughter did this video."

"Her daughter?" Claire leaned back in her chair. "I will regret this. Play the tape, Miss Hill."

Jackie sat on the sofa, Boulton standing behind her. I opened the armoire, put the tape in the VCR, then sat back down at my desk and hit the remote control. The television screen flickered gray and then went to color. I blinked. The camera was very close-in on something round and pinkish. Slowly, I realized the pinkish mound was flesh. Soft flesh. Female flesh. The camera jerked back, revealing Jackie's breasts, barely covered by a red evening dress. Sitting next to her on a bed was a lovely brunette about Jackie's age. She had a wide sculpted face with high cheekbones and coffee-brown, passionless eyes. She wore black stockings, garter belt, panties, and bra. Legs crossed, the two women looked into the camera as if they were waiting to be asked to dance.

"That's me in the red!" Jackie pointed to her image. "I got to wear the dress. It was so pretty."

Claire grumbled, "The young woman next to you is Cybella's daughter, Sarah Grange?"

Jackie nodded, never taking her eyes off herself.

The camera shoved in on the two women. Acting her part with gusto, Jackie unfastened Sarah's bra, slowly slipping it from her small, firm breasts. Sarah was passive, her expression inappropriately aloof for being in a porno film. A disdainful smile formed on her lips as she slowly turned and began to remove Jackie's red dress.

Female flesh merged. Breasts on breasts. Tongues licked.

Hands grabbed. Fingers stroked. Jackie groaned dramatically. The camera closed in on Sarah's face as she moaned in forced ecstasy. I decided it was best for my new career not to look at Claire.

Jackie leaned forward on the sofa, watching herself with a narcissistic intensity. Boulton's eyes met mine in a look of strangely ambivalent sexuality. You cannot view pornography without becoming a part of it, even if it repels you. Its power is to make you the voyeur, the needy person in the dark peeking through windows, through parted curtains, through the crack of a half-open door. In other words, it makes you feel like an assistant to a detective.

I turned back to the TV. The camera lurched in on wet nipples, blond hair, an elbow, black-stockinged legs, thighs, buttocks, Sarah's wet lips. I could hear Claire muttering while Jackie and Sarah did everything to each other except discuss women's liberation. Suddenly the tape flickered to gray. I hit the remote control.

Claire did a slow turn, glared at me, then turned back to Jackie. "My dear young woman, your video makes no connection between Sarah Grange and Cybella's death."

"Do you know who Sarah Grange is? She's one of the top models in New York. She's worth millions. You find out why she did this video and you'll have your connection."

Claire leaned back, tapping the toe of her shoe with her walking stick. Jackie fell silent. Mucus ran from her nose onto her upper lip.

"Give her some Kleenex, Miss Hill."

I took a box from my desk and handed it to Jackie. She blew her nose.

"Allergies," she said, turning demure.

"Do not insult my intelligence, young woman," Claire said. "Who set up the video?"

"What do you mean?"

"Who told you to be in the video? Who held the camera? Who paid you? I assume you were paid?"

"The money was just there for me in the room." She appeared confused by the barrage of questions.

"Not that I am a connoisseur, but this is obviously not a professional porno video. Who shot it?"

"I don't know." Her fingers nervously twisted the silk fringe of a pillow.

"Was it the person who struck you?"

The fingers moved quickly to her bruise. "He loves me."

"Of course." Claire sighed. "Tell me about your meeting with Cybella."

Jackie wiped her nose, then pulled a crumpled pack of cigarettes from her jacket pocket and lit one, cupping her hand around the match as if she were still standing outside in the wind. Her eyes avoided Claire. "I never met Cybella. I just said that so you wouldn't throw me out."

"Why are you really here, Miss Murphy?"

"I think I'm being followed."

"Who is following you?"

"If I knew that, I wouldn't need you, would I?"

"Maybe it's a customer, Jackie," I said.

"No. I think it's because I did this video. And now Sarah Grange's mother is dead. They say it's suicide, but it really isn't, see what I mean? I could be next."

Claire stood. "Give her fifty dollars and her tape, Miss Hill. We leave for Los Angeles at the appointed time."

I got the tape and handed it to Jackie.

"What's the problem?" she demanded.

"Jackie," I pointed out, "you have no proof that Cybella was murdered."

"Well, I'm not the detective, am I? That's her job." She gestured toward Claire, who was making a quick exit from the room.

"I'm sorry, Jackie," I said.

"I knew she wouldn't believe me. Here." She tossed the video onto the cushion of the Queen Anne. "Something to remember me by."

We rode down in the elevator in silence. The doors slipped open and we stepped out into the lobby. I handed her the fifty dollars.

"This make you feel better?" she asked snidely.

"No."

She took the money. "I've been in better hotels than this one." Giving the opulent decor a disdainful glance, she strolled across the lobby. Cowboy boots scuffed at the marble floor. She paused in front of the revolving door and adjusted her red jacket, arched her back, and squared her hips. Her tough street sexuality back in place, she pushed the door around and disappeared.

Back in the suite, I tried not to think of her. Around eleven o'clock Boulton stacked the luggage in the foyer and went to the garage, which was a block away, to bring the Bentley around. I called for two bellboys. Restless, Claire stalked from room to room.

As I packed my portable computer, she prowled near the living-room window. A pigeon, tottering on the sill, eyeballed her like a drunken sailor. No matter how much money you have in this city, you can't rise above the pigeons. She swung her walking stick at the window. The pigeon flew.

"Filthy little beasts." She turned on me. "There was nothing I could do for that girl. And you, Miss Hill, must not go around picking prospective clients off the street. It's unseemly."

"I didn't pick her. She picked you. And one of these days you're going to break that window."

"Nonsense. I know exactly where to strike so that the pigeon flees and the glass remains intact."

The doorbell rang. Gerta let in two bellboys. They arranged the luggage on their carts. As we followed them out of the suite, I tried not to look at the cassette on the Queen Anne chair. Oh, hell, maybe Mr. Orita could figure it out.

Looking as if we were going on safari instead of back to L.A., we made it down to the lobby. Desanto waited by the elevators, bowing and scraping his way alongside Claire as our procession headed out to the street.

I instinctively looked for Jackie but she was gone. Boulton pulled up in the black Bentley and got out. Desanto was still oozing around Claire while the bellboys and Frank loaded the luggage into the car. Boulton's voice cut sharply through Desanto's slobbering words.

"Across the street, Miss Conrad."

Jackie stood holding on to a wrought-iron railing. She stumbled off the curb, the red cowboy boots dragged and scuffed against the pavement. She walked through the traffic as if invulnerable. Her blond hair, like a frayed halo, blew in thin wisps around her head. Boulton moved toward her, but she staggered past him toward me, hands out in front of her like a toddler learning to walk. I took hold of her, guiding her to the sidewalk. Her mouth opened. A bright red bubble formed, slid down her chin, and popped. Another bubble took its place. She collapsed at my feet. A woman entering the hotel screamed. Desanto flapped around, commanding the bellboys. I kneeled, squeezing her hand. Again her mouth opened. I leaned close, but heard only the gasping fight against death. Claire knelt next to me. Jackie went limp. Her eyes, still mean with determination, stared into mine.

"I've called the police," the doorman said.

"We've got to get her into the lobby," I said.

"Don't you dare!" Desanto cried.

"Stab wounds in her abdomen," Claire noted.

"No, no, I won't have this," Desanto wailed.

"We can't leave her on the street," I said.

"Two, to be exact," Claire observed. "One appears shallow. The other deep."

Gerta offered her traveling blanket. "Here, keep her warm."

"It's too late for that, Gerta," Claire said, feeling for a pulse.

The bellboys returned, carrying two large Chinese screens, which they hurriedly placed around us.

Boulton peered behind the screens. "I found her purse across the street. You had better take a look at it." He beckoned Claire.

She followed him. I stayed, holding Jackie's hand. I could hear the howl of sirens like trapped animals. Claire reappeared and kneeled next to me.

"The newspaper clipping of us leaving the hotel. Where was it?"

"In her purse."

"And the money?"

"Same."

"Both are gone."

"Let go of her, Maggie." Boulton's voice.

I looked at my hand. Her blood was as sticky as cotton candy on my fingers.

Let it go, Maggie. Let it go.

Slowly I released her hand. It lay on my palm. Her chewed

fingernails were painted a rosy pink. I looked up at the screen. Chinese ladies, delicately carved of rosewood, peeked discreetly down at Jackie from behind their mother-of-pearl fans.

"Have the luggage returned to our rooms, Boulton. We're extending our stay," Claire announced.

Three

It was a perfect martini.

The police were gone and I sat at the small bar just off the hotel's lounge. All tweed and leather, the room was very subtle, very masculine. It was like being surrounded by a country gentleman's embrace.

I took another sip, trying to get my emotions under control. An hour earlier I had told the police that I didn't know Jackie, that we'd been leaving for the airport when she staggered toward us and died. The police had found some blood in the basement stairwell of the apartment house across the street. The building was empty, waiting to be renovated. There were no witnesses. There was no wallet or any kind of identification in her purse. There was no money and no newspaper clipping of Claire Conrad. The police assumed Jackie had died in a mugging, a dope deal, or a trick gone wrong. Take your pick. She had a lot of options. They took our names and addresses as a matter of course, put her in a body bag, and carted her off. Desanto had the screens removed and the sidewalk washed down.

Now it was twelve-thirty and I held a chilled crystal cocktail glass. I looked at the bill. My martini cost eight dollars and ninety-five cents. It was perfect. Everything was perfect in this hotel. Everything was perfect if you had the money. Everything was perfect if you weren't a dead young woman named Jackie.

I turned on the bar stool and looked at two fashionably dressed men, drinking expensive water, sitting at a table overlooking Park Avenue. Gold watches shimmered on their broad wrists. Jackie's mother had dreams. The two men looked at each other, very satisfied, as if they'd just made a great business deal or just had great sex. Whatever it was, it was perfect, and it made me angry. Why did I always go for the anger instead of the sadness?

Across Park were two churches with a brownstone nestled between them. The Presbyterian church spiraled its steeples with Puritanical restraint toward the Manhattan sky and God. The Church of Christ, Scientist, round like a giant belly, appeared too fat and too weighted to Park Avenue to even bother to reach toward the heavens. Maybe if I believed, I'd be able to feel sadness instead of anger. I carry my grandmother's rosary in my purse, but that's only because she gave it to me, because she believes, and because I love her. My mother believes with a vengeance. She uses holy water like some women use Chanel No. 5. Still, that brownstone squeezed between the two churches did look protected. I hoped a young woman lived there, a woman who had dreams.

"Miss Hill!" Desanto's voice made me jump. He hurried toward me, rubbing his hands together like Lady Macbeth.

"This is unacceptable," he said in a high-pitched tone.

"I agree. No martini should cost eight dollars and ninety-five cents."

"I don't mean the martini. I talked to the floor maid. She said Miss Conrad is back in her rooms."

"That's right, we're extending our stay."

"You can't do that. You know I promised the suite to Mr. Orita."

"Give him another one."

"He wants the Conrad Suite. He loves to sit in the Queen Anne chair."

"Sorry."

"How long are you staying?"

"As long as it takes."

I raised my glass to him and finished off my drink. He jerked his head back and his chin did its disappearing act. His lips twitched with anger.

"If you weren't with Claire Conrad, I'd order you out of this hotel right now," he said, trying to keep his voice down.

"If I weren't with Claire Conrad, I wouldn't be in this hotel right now," I retorted.

He took a deep breath. "Try to understand. I've got Mr. Orita." His breath came out in one long desperate sigh. "What's one more dead whore to Claire Conrad?" he blurted.

The two men at the table turned from their water and peered at Desanto.

"I'll tell you, Desanto, what one more dead whore is. She's one more dead woman." I didn't bother to keep my voice down. My anger was in full bloom. Now the two men stared at me, their satisfied faces pinched with annoyance. I was feeling better.

Desanto's eyes narrowed till he looked like one of the rosewood Chinese ladies peeking over her fan. He tucked in his chin and marched out of the room. The two men paid and left. I stared at the churches and the brownstone. There was a plaque on the big fat church. In the two weeks I'd been here I'd never bothered reading it. I slid off the stool and peered out the window. I could just make out the word *lepers,* the word *dead,* and another word: *rinse.* Rinse? Rinse the lepers. Rinse the dead? Couldn't be. But then I didn't know much about the Christ Scientist Church. Maybe they believed in a good rinsing. I was sitting back at the bar when Boulton came in.

"Are you all right, Maggie?" he asked, taking the stool next to me.

"Yes."

He called the bartender over and ordered a brandy.

"Miss Conrad's been looking at the video. She wants you to buy some of those fashion magazines such as *Vogue* and *Bonton.*"

"We should've helped Jackie."

The bartender served Boulton his drink. He waited for the barman to leave before he spoke.

"Even if Miss Conrad had taken the case, Jackie still would've walked out of the hotel and been murdered. Nothing could have prevented that, Maggie." He took a long swallow of brandy.

"I know. But at least she would've known that for once somebody had taken her seriously." I studied the sharp line of his aquiline nose. He studied my lips. "How do you adjust to it?"

"To what?"

"Murder. Death."

"You learn to separate yourself from it. You become an observer."

"A spectator?"

"In a way."

"Like wearing a pair of black-and-white shoes."

"How many martinis have you had?"

"Only one."

He smiled. It was a lovely warm smile. I liked him sitting next to me. I had to restrain myself from resting my head on his big broad shoulder.

"Have you ever been in love with a woman, Boulton?"

The smile disappeared. He stared at me for a moment as if he were debating something within himself, then sighed as if he had lost the debate.

"I have had great passion for women. I have had great respect for women. I have even felt passion and respect for the same woman. But I have never been in love."

"I knew that."

"You have probably been in love many times." The watchful brown eyes took me in. "We're perfect for one another."

We smiled, knowing we were deeply attracted and that we weren't perfect for one another. Distance, Maggie. I turned and looked out the window. "Can you read that plaque on the church?"

He walked over to the window. "Something about to raise the lepers, to raise the dead." He took his place next to me.

"Of course. Raise the dead."

"That's the one thing even Miss Conrad will agree she can't manage," he said with a slight grin. "But she can find Jackie's killer." He tossed off the rest of his brandy. "She's waiting for those magazines." The English butler was back. Our intimate moment was over.

I made it down to a little shop off Park that sold magazines and newspapers from as far away as Croatia. I could never find an *L.A. Times* in the place. I guess that was too far away for New Yorkers. I bought the April editions of *Vogue* and *Bonton* and asked the woman behind the counter if she had any left over from a couple of months ago. She went in the back and came out with the February and March issues of *Bonton*.

I made two other stops. One was to a nearby Catholic church. The great thing about this city is that there is a church of your choice on practically every corner. It's kind of like gas stations in Los Angeles. I lit a candle for Jackie.

The last time I had lit a candle, I was sixteen years old. It was for my father. I had sat in the back of the church and watched the priest, a Scotsman with gin-colored eyes, snuff my candle out. When I'd confronted him, he informed me that he was saving money. There were only a few candles and so many sorrows, and my father was going to die anyway. My father did. Religion has a practical side to it.

Jackie's flame was tiny and I could almost feel its warmth.

My last stop was the shoe store. The black and white spectator pumps. I just looked. Observed.

Back in the suite Claire was in her chair, her eyes bright with the intensity of thought. Claire was at her best when she was working on a case, and a murder gave her the kind of glow usually reserved for women in the first stages of a love affair. I handed her the magazines and sat down at my desk. Jackie, in the red dress, was freeze-framed on the screen. Boulton kneeled on one leg before her image, like a man about to propose marriage. Except he had his camera and was taking a picture of her image.

"It'll be a bit grainy," he commented, "but serviceable."

"Fine." Claire tilted her elegant head toward me and pointed her ebony walking stick at the TV. "What do you see, Miss Hill?"

"Jackie in a red dress."

"Look again."

"A red dress that's a little too large for her."

"Yes. And?"

"But even not fitting properly, the dress looks great. Expensive."

"Couture. I would say three or four thousand dollars'

worth. Jackie couldn't afford such a gown. Where did it come from?"

"The model Sarah Grange?"

"Odd. Very odd."

"We can move on to the next," Boulton said.

Claire clicked the remote control. Sarah came into view. Sultry anger showed in her eyes. Claire clicked the remote and Sarah stopped moving. Boulton began taking his pictures.

"Something is disturbing me." Claire stood and began to pace methodically. "The killer had to have followed Jackie to our hotel. Why not kill her before she'd made contact with you, Miss Hill? Or at least when you left her standing outside the hotel? Why wait until she'd spoken to me?"

"Are you saying you think it was a mugging? She said she was being followed."

"I'm saying that the killer did not seem concerned with the fact that Jackie had talked to me."

"Maybe the killer didn't know you were staying in the hotel."

"Then why take the newspaper clipping?" Boulton observed.

"Exactly." Claire leaned one elbow on the top of the Queen Anne, and rested her chin in her hand.

Boulton stood. "I'll take the film down to one of those fast photo places. They can have it developed in about an hour."

"Take the photo of Jackie to Bergdorf Goodman," Claire instructed me. "Go to the designer section. See if they recognize the dress, if they know who the designer is."

"All right."

"Tonight, Boulton, I want you to take the photographs to Peep Thrills. See what you can find out about Jackie."

"Wait a minute," I said. "He gets Peep Thrills and I get

Bergdorf's? That is the most sexist delegation of work I've ever encountered."

"Sexist? Miss Hill, you know I detest such words. They clutter the language. They impede any rational thinking. Why do you persist in using them?"

I knew she detested words ending with *ist* and *ism,* except the word *elitist,* of course, but it was my only weapon against her. I didn't want to stay here running errands and writing. I wanted in on this one. I had a candle burning.

"I use those words because you persist in making reactionary decisions," I said pompously, then leaned back in my chair for an even more obnoxious affect. I got a grimace.

"My decision is not based on any reactionary polemics, Miss Hill. It is based on reality. You will not be accepted at Peep Thrills."

"I'll be accepted because I'm a woman. The girls there will talk to me. They'll identify with me. You think they trust men?"

Claire stalked my desk. "Miss Hill, the women performing at Peep Thrills will not identify with you. Quite the contrary, you will be the only woman there who isn't being manipulated by male sexual fantasies. Therefore, you will be a threat to both the men and the women, hardly conducive to obtaining information."

I turned on Boulton. "I suppose you agree?"

"I do. Except I'm not so sure who is manipulating whom."

"Look, we all feel guilty about Jackie's death," I said.

"Guilty?" Claire spoke the word as if she'd never heard it before. "I *expose* the guilty, Miss Hill. I don't feel guilty."

"All right, *I* feel some kind of responsibility. And running around picking up gloves and magazines and going to Bergdorf's is not helping you solve this murder. The women at Peep Thrills will accept me."

Claire and Boulton shared a knowing look. Claire spoke: "You have this middle-class fantasy that it is your God-given right to be accepted by anybody and everybody. Life, Miss Hill . . ."

"Now we're making class distinctions," I said doggedly. I knew I had her.

She sighed, then looked at Boulton. "The thought of an evening with her in this suite as she rages on about feminism, sexism, elitism, guilt, and class distinctions fills me with dread. Take her with you."

"But, madam, I don't think that's wise."

"Alas, my decision is based on self-preservation, not wisdom, Boulton."

"Quite. I'll have these developed," he said stiffly, and walked out of the room. Claire slouched into her chair.

"It is times such as this that I wonder how I could have possibly hired you, Miss Hill. Was it an unguarded moment of compassion for all those future employers you would torture? Or just a moment of insanity?"

"It was my charm." I smiled.

"All the charm of a cobra in a basket."

"Sexism and feminism aside, I'm surprised you're not going yourself."

Her dark blue eyes came to rest on mine. The lapis shimmered. "I have never liked the smell of Lysol mixed with the smell of sex. It lacks humanity."

Four

Two hours later, holding a photo of Jackie in a manila envelope, I stood in front of Bergdorf's. I pushed through the revolving door and found myself in the cathedral-shaped room of the cosmetics section. The circular glass counters, displaying creams, oils, and pretty packages of makeup, shimmered with all the promise of an engagement ring. Too many perfumes, which had no business mingling, reminded me of when my four aunts came to visit. The air in our living room would thicken with unspoken anger and the battle of their fragrances.

Women, some still clutching their winter coats around their shoulders, stared into the display cases, an obsessive look in their eyes. It was the same look lost dogs have as they run compulsively toward their elusive destination. I put my hand on one of the counters. The lights within made it feel warm and comforting.

"May I help you?" The young saleswoman wore a pink smock and looked as if she had carefully painted her face on by the numbers.

"What floor is couture on?" I asked.

Her eyes drifted over my pink and black tweed jacket. She was unimpressed. "Second floor."

"Thanks."

"Perhaps a little lipstick?" she offered, whipping out a silver tube from under the counter. "Wet Red?"

"No thanks. Which way are the escalators?"

"To your right."

I found the escalator and ascended into the aloof and detached world of fashion. Each designer had his own fiefdom. Clothes with names didn't mix. There was no lavishness or abundance of display. There was only a feeling of anal smugness in the few tiny-sized outfits that hung from hangers like colorful dead birds. There was also no sign of human life.

The mannequins, their bald heads not quite hidden underneath their synthetic wigs, watched me with dead, sexless eyes as I moved passed Chanel, Valentino, Ungaro. I checked a price tag on a pink wooly number. I blinked. Yes, they weren't kidding, it really cost three thousand and change. Clothes like this made me nervous. I mean, who wore them? It had to be women who never spilled, dribbled, or drooled. Women who never ate! That's it. Now I understood anorexia. But what about the bulimics? Maybe they shopped on another floor.

Hearing a female voice, I headed for a section where a thin blond woman sat at a desk talking on the phone. A customer, her hair dyed the color of a panther's fur, waved a bunch of what looked like receipts under the nose of a saleslady with more pearls draped around her neck than Marley's ghost had chains. Two men were dismantling a mannequin.

"First I was told to go to the accounting department. Then I was told to come back down here." The Panther Woman was frazzled.

"Excuse me," I said to the saleslady.

"If you'll just wait till Miss Platt gets off the phone," the saleslady replied to the Panther Woman.

Ignoring me, they both turned toward the blond Miss Platt.

"I'm sure you have the black Valentino skirt, Mrs. Rosenthal. Just look in your closet," Miss Platt spoke solicitously into the phone.

"Excuse me," I tried again.

"Why can't you help me?" It was Panther Woman. "For God's sake, I've spent thousands. And my husband. My husband . . ." Her voice quivered with anger. Or was it fear?

"You have to talk to Miss Platt or Mr. Golden," the saleslady snapped.

"You bought the Valentino when you were in here for your last fitting, remember, Mrs. Rosenthal? It goes with the white gabardine jacket with the black lace collar."

"I want to see the head of the department," Panther Woman demanded.

"I told you, Mr. Golden is at lunch."

"Excuse me." It was Maggie the Undaunted. "I was wondering . . ."

"I have better things to do than stand around and wait for her to talk on the phone," Panther Woman announced. "And for him to eat his lunch and for you to treat me like shit!"

"Shit?!" The saleslady went white. Her hands went for her pearls. "I will not be talked to that way!"

"What way?"

"Look in your closet, Mrs. Rosenthal."

The saleslady turned on me. "You heard her call me a shit."

"Well actually she didn't *call* you a shit."

"I would never use such language." Panther Woman turned on me. "Did I call her a shit?"

"Not exactly."

"It's black silk, Mrs. Rosenthal. It's too late for black velvet."

"This is kafkaesque," I said, pushing up the sleeves of my jacket.

"You think I care who designed your clothes?" Panther Woman growled.

This did not bode well for getting information. I walked over to the two men in the corner who now had the mannequin in more pieces than a Thanksgiving turkey.

"Excuse me," I said, displaying my manila envelope. "Mr. Golden wanted me to give this to him immediately. Do you know where he's having lunch?"

"In the café on five."

"Thank you."

I rode the escalator to the fifth and found the café by walking through a shoe department and something called Contemporary Sportswear.

The small restaurant was jammed into the back corner of the floor. Tables were shoved closely together. I honestly believe New Yorkers cannot digest their food if they are more than two feet apart from one another.

Frenzied female voices competed with the clatter of dishes and silverware. I asked the cashier to point out Golden to me. With a toss of long dark hair and the sway of a silver hoop earring, she cocked her head toward a man sitting alone. I made my way toward him.

Golden looked to be in his late thirties. He leaned forward sipping his soup, his tie thrown over his left shoulder so he wouldn't dribble on it. I don't think I could eat with a man who had to throw his tie over his shoulder every time he bit into a cracker.

"Excuse me, Mr. Golden. I'm Maggie Hill, assistant to Claire Conrad."

He stopped sipping and peered up at me, soup spoon in midair.

"Claire Conrad, the private detective," I explained.

That got him. He put the soup spoon down. "Detective?"

"She was wondering if you could identify a dress for her?"

"Identify?"

"If you could tell us who designed a dress? May I sit down?"

"How did you get my name?" he asked.

"Claire Conrad has handled certain cases, very discreetly, for some of your clients. In fact, I don't think it would be giving anything away if I said it was Mrs. Rosenthal who recommended that we talk to you."

"She's one of our best customers."

"She thinks highly of you."

I sat down and slipped the photograph of Jackie out of the envelope. He studied it with the concentration of a mathematician looking at an equation.

"Phillip St. Rome. From last year's fall collection. Who is this poor thing? She doesn't do the dress justice, does she?"

"Is St. Rome a European designer?"

"If a queen from Brooklyn is European, darling, he's a European."

"If I wanted to get hold of him, how would I do that?"

He reached into his coat pocket for a small, thin, black leather book. His long, manicured fingers flipped through blue pages edged with gold.

"St. Rome's sales representative is Blanchard Smith. Telephone number 555-5670."

I wrote it down in my stained and bulky Filofax.

"Thanks. Oh, by the way, Mrs. Rosenthal can't find her black Valentino skirt."

"Which one?"

"It goes with the white-and-black-lace jacket."

"We just sold it to her. She really should venture deeper into her closet," he said, breaking off a piece of bread. "It's not like it's Africa, you know?"

I almost made it through the cosmetics section but caught a glimpse of myself in a mirror and stopped. Pinched and angry, I was suddenly one of those women I had vowed at the age of eighteen never to become. My mother. The sales-lady, the one with her face painted by the numbers, appeared in front of me like a miracle. She took hold of my hand and turned it so the white underside of my wrist was exposed. Her hand was extraordinarily soft, as if it had been filleted.

"Wet Red," she said soothingly, drawing a red line with a tube of lipstick across my wrist right where a sad lonely woman might slash her vein.

It wasn't a bad shade. Oh, hell, lipstick was good for the soul.

Five

It was three o'clock when I got back to the hotel. Claire was having tea, surrounded by fashion magazines. I helped myself to a cup and a few crustless sandwiches, then sat at my desk. I told her what I had learned at Bergdorf's.

She put her cup down. "St. Rome? Look on page forty-two of the March issue of *Bonton.*"

I did. There was Sarah Grange wearing a white shirt and white jodhpurs, sitting on the whitest horse God ever made. Sitting behind her, in tight white jeans and no shirt, was the most handsome guy God ever made. Sarah and the bare-chested wonder looked like they had just experienced mutual orgasm, or at least an epiphany. On closer inspection, so did the horse. Below the picture were the words: THE ST. ROME WOMAN.

"There's the connection," I said. "St. Rome dress. St. Rome Woman."

"Yes, but what does the connection mean?" Claire asked peevishly.

"Remember when riding a horse was how girls said they lost their virginity?" I bit into a sliced cucumber sandwich.

"Miss Hill, I'm an accomplished horsewoman. I've been

riding since I was five. The only thing I ever lost was my hard hat."

"You didn't grow up in Versailles, Ohio. Where did you grow up?" I wondered.

"I was born in the city where you and I met. Pasadena. I was raised in London, Paris, Rome, and Berlin. I am a woman-of-the-world. Page twenty-two in the April edition of *Vogue*, Miss Hill." She popped a transparently thin slice of salmon laid out on a narrow piece of brown bread into her mouth.

This time Sarah Grange was in a white chiffon evening gown, her arms raised above her head, holding a bottle of St. Rome perfume. Kneeling at her feet was the guy in the tight white jeans. He still hadn't found his shirt. His broad hands clutched her narrow hips. His face burrowed into the layers of chiffon. The muscles on his back bulged with tension. Or was it passion? The caption identified her again as the St. Rome Woman.

"And I only bought a lipstick."

"I beg your pardon?"

"Nothing."

"Page eighty in the February issue of *Bonton*."

There were Cybella and Sarah: TWO GENERATIONS OF BEAUTY. Cybella was still beautiful. But time had softened her angular bones and made her lips thin and drawn instead of lush. The neck was long and elegant, but again, time had diminished her large dark eyes with wrinkled flesh.

"According to the insipid article," Claire said, "mother and daughter had not seen one another for some time. The writer, if you can call her that, seems to think it had something to do with each woman discovering that beauty comes from the inside, not the outside, and then she had a tizzy about drinking a lot of water. Once reunited, mother transformed daughter into a supermodel in order to carry on a short family tradition."

"That's nice. Then the daughter does a porno video."

"And the mother supposedly kills herself, and the other performer in the video is murdered." She reached for the anchovy paste sandwich, which I always let her have. "Call St. Rome's sales representative. Tell him I want to talk to the designer immediately."

I dialed the number and got Blanchard Smith's secretary on the phone. "This is Maggie Hill calling for Claire Conrad. She would like to speak with Mr. St. Rome."

"I'll tell Mr. Smith to inform him," she said, her voice thin with boredom.

As an ex-secretary, I knew I hadn't made it to the important-calls-to-return list.

"Listen," I said, "and listen carefully. We have a porno video of the St. Rome Woman, Sarah Grange. You tell him I'm ready to give it to the tabloids. Tell him inquiring minds are waiting to hear from him at the Parkfaire Hotel, Conrad Suite, in one hour."

"Is this some kind of joke?"

"Claire Conrad has no sense of humor and I lost mine this morning." I hung up.

Claire looked up from the pages of *Bonton*. Her hard intelligent eyes studied me.

"You've thought of something?" I asked. "A clue?"

"How did you lose your virginity, Miss Hill?"

"Bobby Polinsky. I was sixteen."

"Why?"

"I just wanted to get it over with. Virginity always seemed like a burden."

"You mean like having a hump on your back?"

"I mean like I would be freer. More equal and independent without it."

"Equal to whom and independent of what?"

"Equal to Polinsky and also independent of him."

"And were you?"

"No. Polinsky's mind was as flat as an Ohio field. I was far more intelligent, but everybody adored him. I was never adored. He strutted around the school and the girls whispered my name in the hallways."

"Poor women." She shook head and sipped her tea.

I wanted to ask her how she'd lost her virginity, but I couldn't. That would be like asking Queen Elizabeth if she'd lost it in the backseat of her Rolls. Maybe when she lost her hat, a stable boy had picked it up. They looked into each other's eyes.

"You've thought of something, Miss Hill?" she asked, gazing at me over the rim of her cup.

"No."

Boulton came into the room. "May I get you some more hot water, madam?" He checked the teapot.

"No thank you, Boulton. Take a look at those magazines."

He obliged. "So Sarah Grange is the St. Rome Woman."

"Miss Hill has learned that Jackie's red dress is a St. Rome design. And I learned that Miss Hill lost her virginity when she was sixteen with a young boy named Bobby Polinsky."

He smiled at me. "Regarding Mr. Polinsky, should I offer my congratulations or my condolences?"

I made a face. The phone rang.

"Conrad Suite, Maggie Hill speaking."

A female voice filled with self-importance announced, "This is Nora Brown, editor of *Bonton* magazine. I want to see Claire Conrad as soon as possible, here, at the magazine. We're at Forty-fifth and Madison."

"Any particular reason?"

"She threatened St. Rome, didn't she? In the fashion world that's like threatening the president of the United

States. And I suggest that Miss Conrad bring some proof to back up her outrageous accusations."

"Do you have a VCR?"

"Of course."

"Just a minute." I looked at Claire. "It seems my threats have upset St. Rome and a top dog at *Bonton*. She wants to see you."

"Tell her I'll be there."

"She'll be there," I said to Nora Brown.

She grunted and slammed down the phone.

Claire leaned back in her chair, stretched her long legs, and smiled. "It seems we have begun to move the rock. Bring the car around, Boulton."

I took off my jacket and examined the lumpy shoulder pads. I searched my desk drawer for scissors, in vain, then began to nibble at the threads.

"Must you gnaw on your clothes, Miss Hill?"

"I'm having a clothes attack. Big shoulder pads are out. We're going to *Bonton*. They know shoulder pads are out because they have deemed it so." I spit some thread into the wastebasket.

"When we first met you told me shoulder pads made you feel less melancholy."

"They do. Look, I know this isn't going to make any sense to you because you get up in the morning and put on your black pantsuit one day and your white pantsuit the next day, God knows why, and you have hundreds of black suits and white suits. But the rest of us poor jerks have to worry about color, pattern, style, and length."

"But why devour your clothes? It's like eating your young." She got up and left the room, returning with a Swiss pocketknife that did everything except ask you for a date. "I'd think," she said, "your need to feel less mournful would triumph over your need for fashion."

She expertly flipped open the knife. A silvery blade shone in her hand. I stared at it and wondered if Jackie had seen the shiny sharpness of the blade before it sliced into her belly. I took the pocketknife and cut the remaining threads, and the shoulder pads fell to the floor. They looked strangely indecent, like discarded parts of a body.

Six

Sitting in the Bentley was like being held in the palm of a giant gray kid glove. Claire and I sat in the backseat. The crystal bud vases in silver holders bloomed with wildflowers. It was Boulton's job to replace the flowers with fresh ones each morning. The small bouquets were a reminder of the mysterious death of Claire's parents. That's all I had been allowed to know. I wondered if Johnson had held anything back from Boswell. I reached in my purse and got out my mirror and applied Wet Red. Boulton's eyes watched me in the rearview mirror. The lipstick felt as smooth and as moist as a lover's tongue. I noticed how his hair almost touched his starched white collar. I wondered how many unloved women had felt the nape of his neck with their naked arms. I put the lipstick and mirror away.

"God gives you one face and you paint yourself another," Claire announced. "And yet you remove your shoulder pads."

"Confusing, isn't it?" I sighed.

At about five o'clock Boulton pulled into a NO PARKING space in front of the *Bonton* building. Claire asked him to wait.

We rode up to the twenty-second floor. Jackie's video

weighed heavily in my purse. My jacket hung limply on my shoulders, making me look like I was in a slump, but my lips glistened.

We stepped out into a narrow utilitarian foyer. A fatigued receptionist, her lipstick long talked off, sat behind a surgical-white table. A black leather banquette ran along one wall. Two thin men sat on it, legs crossed, hands folded on knees, purposely staring in opposite directions. Behind the receptionist, in big silver letters, gleamed the word *Bonton*. Below was a metal rack weighted with clothes. A green suit, about the size of a small box, was shoved against a purple crushed-velvet pantsuit. The purple number looked like it had been made for a demented poet. A yellow fake fur coat, cute as a teddy bear, cuddled against a limp floral print dress. The dress looked tired—like it had taken a couple of decades to drag itself in from Woodstock. The clothes had a silly childlike quality, as if they'd been designed for all those adult children of tasteless parents. I wished I'd left my shoulder pads in. Not only did I feel like I had tiny shoulders, now I felt like I had no spine.

"Claire Conrad to see Nora Brown," Claire announced.

"Just a minute." The receptionist pushed a button with a pencil, told someone that we were waiting, then took another call.

A slender woman with a stern tight mouth and hair and skin the color of cheap Chablis came out the door next to the clothes rack.

"Claire Conrad?" she demanded.

"Yes?"

"I'm Ms. Brown's secretary. This way, please." Turning sharply on flat heels, she spoke with all the warmth of a nurse ready to draw blood.

We followed her down a long corridor lined with more

clothes racks and windowed cubicles. Each cubicle contained one woman and a computer. The women, brows wrinkled with concentration, stared into their monitors, or over a cup of coffee, or through a curl of cigarette smoke. They looked as gray as the industrial carpeting and as dry as soot. In fact they looked like we used to think housewives looked: isolated and unhappy.

"We're preparing a layout," the secretary said in a clipped voice, gesturing toward the racks. "We mix and match the outfits to see what we want and what we don't want to use. It's an editing process."

Claire stopped and pulled out a yellow leather bustier from one of the racks. The empty cups of the bra arched stiffly outward in mocking imitation of the female breast. "Are the women in those offices trying to figure out how to sell *this* to other women?" she asked.

"Of course."

"No wonder they look tired," Claire observed dryly. The secretary marched us through a big square room.

Women's hats lined two long shelves. Feathers, nets, and silk flowers decorated brims and bands. Boxes overflowing with gold earrings, pearl necklaces, brooches, rhinestone chokers, and bracelets were piled on a large table. Another table held rows of large-size high-heel shoes. Chiffon scarves, silk scarves, and cashmere shawls were tossed in a pile.

"Our accessory room," the secretary announced.

It was the kind of room I had dreamed about when I was little and playing dress-up. But every time I opened my mother's closet door, there were only the limp rayon dresses, plastic belts, and safe, unsexy shoes with the squishy wedge soles. Picking up a pink suede high-heel shoe, I guessed it to be about a size eleven. "Did you ever play dress-up in your mother's clothes?" I asked Claire.

"I preferred the costumes of kings. Once I dressed up as Richard the Third and terrified the servants. Why do you ask?"

"Never mind."

"Models have large feet," the secretary informed me, taking the shoe from my hand and returning it. "Nora Brown is waiting."

We moved into another hallway where we encountered a closed door flanked by two desks. A red-haired woman sat at one, our guide took the other. They nodded and spoke in unison: "You may go in."

Nora Brown stood behind a massive desk carved from wood the color of blond hair. In her early fifties, she was small and lean. Her black hair, cut severely short, accentuated a wide, firm jaw, pale skin, and ruby red lips. Her white silk blouse was tucked tightly into a navy blue skirt. She was studying some kind of layout the way an admiral might scrutinize his invasion map. Instead of ships I imagined her strategically positioning tall, thin, big-footed models around the world. She looked up at us with quick furtive eyes the color of a basic black dress.

"Sit down." Nora gestured to two small, uncomfortable-looking steel chairs. My mother would've called them the going-home chairs: the kind you offered the guests when you didn't want them to linger.

Nora turned on Claire. "I've never talked to a private investigator before."

"Any clerk from the IRS can call himself an investigator. I prefer to be called a private detective," Claire replied, her eyes taking in the room.

"Blanchard Smith telephoned me. He was very upset by your threats."

"To be exact, Miss Hill threatened him. She has a certain aptitude for the profession."

Nora gave me a quick look, too quick for her to notice the charm of my smile.

"Where is Mr. St. Rome?" Claire asked.

"I thought it best to see if your accusations had any validity before disturbing him."

"I didn't know that an editor-in-chief of a fashion magazine fronted for the designers."

"I'm not fronting for anybody." Nora picked up a copy of her magazine. "I've been told by men that they find the women in *Bonton* sexier than the women in *Playboy*. The sexuality of the American woman is as important to us as what she wears. They go hand in hand. But there is a difference between sexiness and pornography," she elaborated, primly. "*Bonton* has taken a political stand. I even wrote an article on pornography."

"For or against?" I asked in my most innocent voice.

"Against, of course." Ruby lips curled in contempt. She brushed angrily at her skirt as if a little pornography had gotten on it. "Show me what proof you have."

"Miss Hill, the VCR is there," Claire pointed her walking stick toward some blond-colored shelves.

I got the video ready to go, grabbed the remote, and clicked it on. Again I stared at female flesh.

Nora sat stiff-shouldered in her chair, lips pursed. After a few minutes she pressed her fingers over the bridge of her nose as if trying to push a headache or the images on the monitor away. "Turn it off."

Claire nodded and I hit the button.

"Private investigation is a dirty little profession, isn't it?" Her black eyes challenged Claire.

"I'd say mine is a grim profession. The truth, and I always discover the truth, is usually very sad."

"Oh, please, spare me the platitudes. What do you intend to do with this video?"

"As Miss Hill suggested, there are always the tabloids, but for now I'd just like some answers."

"I have a magazine to run and I'd like to get on with it. So why don't you cut the crap and tell me how much money you want." She sounded like she was ordering another shipload of models.

"I never discuss money. Miss Hill handles my finances."

Nora studied me. I tried to adjust my expression to that of a blackmailing accountant.

"You need shoulder pads in that jacket," she snapped, then thrust her wide jaw in Claire's direction. "I don't know anything about this video. I don't know why Sarah did it or when she did it."

"The St. Rome evening gown dates the video," Claire said. "It's from last year's fall collection."

"The rag hanging on that creature is a St. Rome? There's no way you can prove that."

"The creature has a name. It's Jackie," I said.

Nora ignored me. "Videos are no longer an obvious source of reality." She slapped her hands down on a photograph of a beautiful young woman smiling as if she were the only beautiful young woman who had ever smiled. "That dress may look like a St. Rome, but it doesn't mean it is. You obviously don't know the fashion industry. We thrive on redundancy. That style of dress, with a little variation, has been done for years." She was better than a politician at putting spin on a story.

"How well did you know Cybella?" Claire asked casually.

Nora Brown's head jerked back in surprise, then she fell silent. The red lips pressed together. She almost looked human. She closed her eyes, then slowly opened them again. "I knew her very well. I discovered her. I made her the face of the sixties. I introduced her to a young unknown designer who called himself St. Rome and we created the St. Rome Woman. The rest, they say, is history. History. Makes me feel old. And alone. Why do you ask?"

"Why did she commit suicide?"

"I don't see what this has to do with your trying to extort money."

"Please, answer the question," Claire said patiently.

"Cybella, like all of us, made some wrong decisions when she was younger. She had trouble living with the consequences of those decisions when she was older. It's called depression."

"What were some of those decisions?"

"Giving up her daughter. Letting her parents raise Sarah. Other than that, I don't think Cybella's life is any of your business."

"According to the articles in your magazine, she was very happy to be reunited with her daughter. And she was making a comeback."

"Only because of Sarah. Because she was her mother. In fact the more successful Sarah became, the more Cybella seem to withdraw."

"Did you discover Sarah?"

"I knew the minute she walked into my office she had the looks and the hunger."

"Hunger?"

"The desire to endure as a model."

"Did Cybella bring her to see you?"

"No. She came here looking for Cybella. That was about eight months ago. She had been in the city for over a year working at some little lingerie shop near the porno . . ." She stopped.

"The porno district?" Claire offered.

"She had been trying to find her mother but couldn't. She

had saved some old letters that Cybella had written. I was mentioned. Sarah saw my name on the *Bonton* masthead and called me."

"Why couldn't she find her mother?" I asked.

"Cybella was in a sanitarium, Shadow Hills, being treated for depression. Sarah was desperate. She didn't have much money. She was working and trying to get modeling jobs on her own. The agents either rejected or ignored her. I'm sure that's why she did the video. Many women in similar circumstances turn to pornography."

Many women?" I echoed. "What are you talking about? A top model, earning hundreds of thousands of dollars doing a porno video?"

"She wasn't earning that kind of money then."

"How long had mother and daughter been separated?" Claire asked.

"Since she was a baby. She grew up in Buffalo. Cybella was a beautiful nomad flying from shoot to shoot, runway to runway. She was dedicated to her career. She got pregnant just as her career was ending. She was trying to be an actress. It was a difficult time for her. She thought it was best to let her parents raise the child."

"Where was Sarah's father?"

"Her father was a French skier. He was killed in an avalanche before the baby was born. They never married." She brushed at her shoulder as if snow had fallen on her. "I was with Cybella when Sarah was born. Now if you don't mind, I have work to do."

"The tape, Miss Hill," Claire reminded.

I snatched it from the jaws of the VCR.

"Oh, by the way, the young woman, Jackie, was murdered this morning." Claire peered at Nora over clasped hands.

"Murdered?" The skin tightened around her eyes.

"In front of my hotel."

"Are the police involved?" she asked quickly.

"Not yet. They think her death was a street crime of some kind."

"Maybe it was. Those girls are victims to such things." Hope shined in her black eyes.

"She told me she thought Cybella was murdered. And now she's dead. Quite a coincidence. She also thought Sarah Grange might know something about it. What do you think?" Claire stood.

Angrily, Nora got to her feet. "I told you what I think. You're in a dirty little business." She took a swipe at her sleeve, brushing off some of our dirt.

"I'll expect to hear from you and Sarah Grange," Claire warned. "Come along, Miss Hill."

Back in the Bentley I said, "Nora Brown is lying."

"People lie for other reasons than having committed murder," Claire observed. "The Parkfaire, Boulton."

"We did accomplish one thing. She thinks we're a pair of blackmailers. You know, blackmailers get shot."

"Boulton will protect us. Won't you?" Claire smiled.

"Yes, madam." His brown eyes appeared in the rearview mirror. I could tell by the fine lines forming around them that he was smiling. I wasn't.

It was that time of day that always depressed me. Twilight pushed me into a no-woman's land between light and darkness where familiar objects, such as buildings and trees, become shadows. And the lights that people switch on in their shops and apartments are ineffectual in holding back the night.

Seven

FEMALE LUST. XXXTASY. PORNO THRILL. BONDAGE. LAND OF THE DIRTY DANCE. UNDER NEW MANAGEMENT.

Neon words shimmied and flashed on every building along Forty-second Street between Sixth and Eighth avenues. It was eleven o'clock at night. Over dinner at the hotel, Claire had filled Boulton in on what we'd learned at *Bonton*. Now he and I were in a cab heading toward Peep Thrills. I had changed my jacket and was wearing my blue and brown check number. I almost felt secure under my shoulder pads as I peered out the car window.

SPANKING. LIVE DANCING MEN. FATHER AND SON SHOE STORE. LIVE GIRLS. FAMILY THEATER: BRING THE KIDS. U MUST BE 21. FLASH AND STEAK RESTAURANT. WRESTLING. SAFE AND COMFORTABLE.

You had to be fairly literate not to stumble into the wrong fantasy. Boulton removed his black tie, folded it neatly, and placed it in his jacket pocket. He unbuttoned the top two buttons of his shirt. The English butler was slowly disappearing.

The taxi pulled up in front of a shabby building with a sign that blinked and stuttered: PEEP PEEP PEEP THRILLS. Another sign steadily declared: PRIVATE FANTASY BOOTHS. There was a large, brightly lit picture of a big-breasted blonde with her fleshy legs spread open. Her nipples and pubic hair were blacked out, making her look like a masked bandit who didn't quite know how to wear her masks.

Men swarmed along the sidewalk, exuding almost palpable anger and hunger. A black man, wearing a black sweatshirt with the name FENDI stamped on it in big white letters, slouched against the building. A cop ran by, mumbling into a walkie-talkie. When he stumbled, it slipped from his hand. The man in the sweatshirt laughed as the cop bent over and picked it up. The cop and the men on the street all had the same haunted look in their eyes as the women at Bergdorf's: the look of the searching lost dog.

I felt Boulton's hand on the small of my back as he opened the door to Peep Thrills for me. I stopped and looked at him.

"Yes?" he asked.

"I just wanted to see if there was any irony intended in this gesture."

"Chivalry is dead, but why kick the corpse?"

We stood in a brightly lit hallway paneled with cheap woodlike veneer. The floor was covered in a sunshine yellow tile, the kind my mother used to have in her kitchen. A man the size of a cab sat at a gray metal desk.

"Four tokens for a dollar per person. Nonrefundable," he said.

Boulton put down two dollars. The man dealt out tokens the size of quarters as if he were counting chips in Vegas. All the time his eyes looked Boulton over.

"Only one in a booth at a time," he said to him. A smile displayed rotting teeth. He kept smiling, never looking at me. "Through the curtain at the end of the hall." His mouth snapped shut.

Boulton and I entered a large, well-lighted room that

smelled of sex and Lysol just as Claire had known it would. The floor and walls were cement and painted a bureaucratic green. To our left stretched a corridor of metal doors that resembled large lockers. A sign declared: PRIVATE VIDEO BOOTHS. There was an enormous round booth in the center of the room. Men lingered near it, peeking through open slots as if it were a construction site. No delight or release showed on their faces. Male sexual fantasy was a serious business.

A sign near a stairway declared: ONE-ON-ONE BOOTHS. An arrow pointed up. The second-floor room was partitioned by a wall of windows, separated on each side by a door. Women wearing panties and bras or skimpy slips sat on stools looking out from their glass display cases. Men wandered back and forth, trying to decide on the one who would best fit their needs.

One man in a warm-up suit and brown loafers gave a curt nod to a chubby redhead and opened the door next to her window. She slid off her stool and pulled down a drape. Now, she was only his.

Many of the men in the room looked to be in their twenties. Why weren't they on dates? Why weren't they taking a young girl to a movie and dinner? Why weren't they falling in love? What were they afraid of? Maybe this was the ultimate in safe sex. Safe desire. Safe xxxtasy.

Not one man had looked directly at me, and those who accidentally caught my eye looked quickly away. Claire was right. I could not be manipulated by their sexual needs. I was the intruder. The intruder in the male wet dream.

Boulton approached another giant of a man. He sat near the stairs at a cardboard table. You had to pay extra for one-on-one. The man's face was meaty, and beads of sweat, looking more like blisters, dotted the slope he used for a forehead. Three heavy gold rings, shaped like pyramids, decorated his left hand.

"For two," Boulton said.

"Only one in a booth," the man mumbled. The two slits from which he viewed the world studied me while his large flat hands counted out tokens, the size of silver dollars. I tried a smile. It didn't work. The figure of a naked woman was printed on the tokens. *In God We Trust* was missing. He handed them to Boulton.

Boulton moved me away from the bouncer and leaned close to me. I could feel his breath in my ear as he talked in a low voice.

"Remember, in order to communicate with the girl you have to use the telephone. That's an extra token." He stepped back, took my hand, and dumped some tokens in it the way a father might give his child some money to go to the movies.

"Wait a minute," I said. "We're going into the booths?"

He held up his hand. "Only one in a booth at a time." A smile played on his lips.

I looked around the room. Some of the women were mingling with the customers. "Why can't we talk to them outside the booths?"

He looked at the bouncer with the gold rings. "Discretion is the better part of valor. He'll know we're questioning them. Don't worry, Maggie, you'll be able to win them over. They'll identify with you, isn't that what you said?"

We stared at one another. He was the only man looking directly into my eyes in the whole damn place. Except his big brown eyes were fired with challenge, not sexual need.

"Don't test me, Boulton."

"I'll begin at that end of the partition. You start at the other."

He turned and sauntered toward a tall, long-legged, honey-colored woman draped in faded tiger skin. The English butler was gone from Boulton's walk. The woman's body grew alert as he moved closer. He nodded casually to her, closing the door behind him.

I stood alone, all eyes avoiding me. Except the guy with the two slits in his face and the Egyptian Wonders on his hand. I took a deep breath, which I always do when I don't know what I'm doing, and headed for the first open door. In an enclosed area about as big as a phone booth, I dropped my token into the proper receptacle. There was a creaking noise as the curtain on the glass in front of me slowly went up with all the professionalism of a child's puppet show.

A young Asian girl sat on a stool. Her long dark hair cascaded over her shoulders and down to her waist. Small breasts and dark nipples could be seen through a red lace bra. She didn't move. We peered at each other, then I put another token in and picked up the telephone.

"Hello, I'd like to ask you some questions." Why did I sound like I was trying to save the whales?

Tilted eyes stared.

"Do you know Jackie? Blonde. She worked here?" I struggled to get the photograph out of my purse.

"I like blondes named Jackie." Her voice was heavy with innuendo.

I could hear her clearly through the glass. What was the phone for? An instrument to communicate with your own fantasies? Another barrier between the man and the object of his desire? Or just a way to make more money? I'll never understand men; they never take the shortest distance.

She began to caress her breasts. "Blondes named Jackie turn me on." Her two front teeth were chipped.

"No, no. You don't have to do that, please," I said, slipping the photograph of Jackie out and holding it against the Plexiglas.

She stopped rubbing her breasts.

"Tell me about her."

"Jackie make me feel soooo good." She spread her thin black-and-blue-marked legs, her fingers played at her crotch. She managed a moan.

"No, no . . . please."

She stopped. Exasperation and hostility glistened in her eyes. My minute ticked away. The curtain dropped. Oh, hell.

When I stepped out of the booth a man waiting his turn stared through me. I did not exist. I found myself not looking at anyone else as I moved to the next available booth. I paid my token and the curtain began its noisy uneven ascent.

She was a fleshy, Rubenesque creature with pale rippled thighs and huge breasts pushed up by a black bra. The straps dug into her shoulders. A black bikini stretched across a round full stomach.

"Get out of my booth," she said, not bothering with the phone.

I was flustered. "It's my minute," I blurted.

"It's my booth. You want me to signal Goldie?"

"You mean the guy with the pyramids on his fingers?"

She nodded.

"Not particularly."

"Then say bye-bye to mama," she cooed, shaking her breasts at me. She hit a lever and the curtain made its noisy descent.

Wonderful. You'll be able to talk to them, Maggie. They'll identify with you.

I came out of the booth and looked around for Boulton. Goldie was now on his feet checking me out, and Goldie on his feet was something to behold. A man who looked like

Oswald went into the booth I had just come out of. Maybe assassins don't die. Maybe they just end up here. Goldie took a step toward me. Before the earth shook I ducked into the next booth and shut the door. I fumbled for a token. The curtain went up.

Black roots, like dirty fingers, seemed to clutch at her bleached hair. Lavender lace stretched over firm, high breasts. She had a small waist and long, nicely shaped legs. Her sculpted cheekbones were pockmarked. Lips that looked as if they could only form the words "fuck you" were painted baby pink.

"You're either a cop or a feminist," she said, her sharp eyes scrutinizing me.

"Neither. I need information." I pressed the picture of Jackie against the Plexiglas. "Do you know her? She worked here."

"A feminist is just like a cop. Both wanna tell me how to live my life."

"This is a family matter."

"You don't look related."

This time I decided to be blunt. "Jackie's dead. Murdered."

She sat, motionless, on the stool. A slight flush appeared on her cheeks. After a silence that took a chunk out of my minute, she spoke: "Men are bastards."

"Any man in particular?"

"Take your pick. It's your fantasy."

"This is reality. How well did you know her?"

She crossed her long legs and sat up straight, as if she were in a dress on a bar stool at the Plaza. "Your minute's almost up."

"Jackie said she was the special blonde here."

"Real special. Like all of us."

I stuffed Jackie's picture back in my purse and took out the photo of Sarah Grange. "What about her?"

She moved quickly off the stool, started toward me, then thought better of it and stopped. The sexual façade was gone. Her gray eyes took in the photograph.

I could hear the curtain begin to come down. I grabbed a twenty out of my pocket and held it so she could get a good look at it.

"Tell me what you know."

The curtain plunged down. Juggling the twenty and Sarah Grange's photo, I put in another token and waited as the curtain slowly cranked itself up. She was still there but she'd regained her pose of easy sex. She undulated toward me, picked up a folded piece of paper from the floor, and slipped it through the crack between the glass and the partition. "Just put your money inside the paper," she said.

"You haven't given me any information yet."

"Do you like women?" she asked.

"Being one, I'm rather fond of us, yes," I said.

"How much do you like women?"

Oh, hell. "Depends."

She pressed her body against the glass. "Do you like me?"

"What can you tell me about Sarah?"

"Do you like me?"

"What about Sarah? Do you know her?"

"I've seen her in *Vogue*, *Bonton*, and my dreams. Do you love me?" she asked, playing with her breasts. "Do you?" she demanded.

It was a sexual demand as threatening as if I were being held up.

"No." I put the twenty and the photograph back in my purse. I couldn't tell if she really knew anything or not. I just wanted out of the cheap titillation and the sexual tyranny. The door behind me was pulled open. I whirled around. Goldie filled the door frame. His face bore down on mine. Sweat gathered around the two slits. "You got a problem, lady?"

Yes, I did.

"She's asking me questions," the girl whined.

"What kinda questions?" He pressed toward me. The gold rings glimmered on his slab of a hand as he reached for my arm, which had never looked so fragile, so breakable.

"What kinda questions?" The slits widened and I could see blue emotionless eyes.

I twisted in his grip. Think, Maggie.

"Don't mess with me, lady. What are you doing here?" His grip tightened and I could no longer move my arm.

"This is degrading to women," I blurted. "No woman should be treated like this." Not bad, Maggie. Not bad.

A heavy sigh ended in a belch and filled the cubicle with a smell that made me want to stop breathing. "Not another one. What do you females want?"

"The question's already been asked by somebody a little brighter than you and he couldn't answer it, either."

I was yanked, as easily as a ribbon from a Christmas gift, out of the booth. "Well, I know what I want. I want you outta here."

"Women are not pawns of male sexual fantasy," I shouted at the top of my voice.

The men froze. All eyes on me. Finally.

"Pornography is a tool to keep women second-class citizens," I railed as Goldie jerked me toward the stairs. I had a hard time keeping my feet on the ground but I did manage to raise my fist in the air. "And to keep minority women slaves." I was on a roll. I wished Claire could see me. Maybe not.

"Shut the fuck up."

Some of the men tried to move and fade into the darker recesses of the room. The women watched me with knowing bored smiles. They'd heard these words before and they were still meaningless. Boulton stood by the entrance to the stairs looking at me with a strange grin.

"Get her out of here and don't come back." Goldie shoved me at him. But I turned and faced the room for my grand finale. "Pornography is oppression. Pornography is male tyranny. Pornography is male sickness." I raised both my fists in the air and gave the V for victory sign. Why did I feel more like Richard Nixon than Gloria Steinem? There was no applause.

"Let's not go over the top, Maggie," Boulton said in a low voice, half-pushing, half-guiding me down the stairs where the guy the size of the cab waited.

I was escorted out of Peep Thrills. Boulton followed, hands in his pockets, the smile still playing on his lips. The lights on the buildings blinked and beckoned in the cold night. A once-pretty woman swayed drunkenly on the arm of a man in a trenchcoat. Boulton looked at me. His smile grew broader and he began to laugh. I'd never heard his laughter; it had a nice warm genuine sound. I stood in the middle of the sidewalk, surrounded by usable women and men who looked like the walking dead, and watched Boulton laugh at me.

Now, this is where men and women have a big problem. Women laugh about men all the time, but we do it behind their backs. We do it as a form of comradeship with other women. We do it so we won't feel needy and dependent on men. We do it because we are also laughing at ourselves. We know how to laugh at men properly.

Men don't understand how to laugh at women. First of

all, they do it right in your face, which means they don't need another man to share it with. And it would never enter their minds that they might be laughing at themselves.

While Boulton continued to laugh I hailed a cab and left him standing on the curb. Now he could laugh at me properly—behind my back.

I stared in righteous anger out the window as the taxi plunged into potholes and swerved around corners. I hadn't learned one thing at Peep Thrills, except that the women didn't trust me and I don't like to be laughed at. Especially by Boulton. Wonderful.

The cab turned down Fifty-ninth Street. The park spread like a dark stain. A phalanx of hotels jutted up; hansom cabs lined the street. The horses, their big heavy heads hanging down in resignation, waited. The women at Peep Thrills, with their large heavy breasts, implanted breasts, small breasts, waited.

Waited.

I suddenly felt terribly depressed. Horses and women were very sad.

Oh, hell, so were men.

Eight

Claire was in her chair reading my notes on our first case together. A fire flickered in the fireplace, shadows of its flames dancing on the white sofas. The table lamps glowed warmly. She was wearing the black velvet robe that made her look like a flamboyant judge. Her initials were emblazoned in gold on her black velvet slippers. She took a sip of brandy and looked up, then peered around me.

"You seemed to have misplaced Boulton, Miss Hill."

"We took separate cabs."

"Not very economical."

I walked over to the drinks table and poured myself a brandy.

Did you find out anything?" she asked.

"Almost."

"Almost?"

"There was a girl who I thought might know something but she didn't. *Okay!* So they didn't identify with me."

"Did I say anything?"

"I know what you're thinking."

"I am a genius. It's impossible for you to know what I'm thinking."

I swallowed some brandy. "I know. Did Nora Brown call?"

"Yes. She and Sarah Grange will be here tomorrow at five."

"They should have their stories worked out by then."

"Probably." She put the pages on a table, then poked at them with her walking stick as if they were a dead rodent.

"You're so desperately modern."

"What?"

"It's as if all the women your age were born with mirrors in their hands so they can walk around looking at themselves, not to see how pretty they are, but to see where they are, who they are, and how they are doing."

"They're just notes, background, it's not even a rough draft."

"I'm sure there was a time when poor muddled Watson couldn't remember why he had sat down to write."

"Watson?"

"But it's difficult to imagine since the good doctor only wrote about Holmes, never his own personal life."

"But I was there."

"Reality is no excuse."

The front door closed. Boulton came into the living room with all the swiftness of a tackle coming off the line of scrimmage. He stopped short when he saw Claire.

"Ah, Boulton," she said. "We thought we had lost you."

"No, madam," he replied. "Just left in Miss Hill's dust, so to speak."

"That may be the fate of us all. Have a brandy and tell me what you've learned."

I moved away from the table and stood by the fireplace. Boulton shot me a look, then poured himself a drink.

"I discovered, madam, that Jackie lived at the Duke Hotel. She also had two, maybe three, regular customers."

"Well done, Boulton."

I thought she was going to get up and pat him on the head as if he were a retriever with a bird hanging out of his mouth. He bowed slightly, acknowledging her compliment. I couldn't stand it.

"I would have found out more if Miss Hill had not come along."

I slammed my drink down on the mantel. "But I did, and I don't like being laughed at. And your pride is wounded because I left you standing on the curb giggling like an idiot."

"My pride wounded?" He turned on me. "I think yours must feel a little bruised. You realize we won't be able to go back to Peep Thrills because of your grand exit?"

Claire stood. "I'm going to bed. As you both know, I do not like my meals or my sleep interrupted. Please, do not continue bickering as if we were some incestuous family on vacation. Miss Hill, tomorrow morning I want you to find out where the Duke Hotel is located. Good night."

"Good night, madam."

"Good night," I said.

As she strode out of the room, the hem of her robe lapped darkly around her feet. The gold initials glistened.

Boulton started putting out the lights. I grabbed my notes and put them in my desk. I wasn't exactly batting a hundred tonight. Or was it a thousand?

I noticed the sharpness of Boulton's profile as he leaned down against the silk shade of the lamp. "We're going to have to figure out how to work together," I finally said.

He switched the lamp off and turned toward me. Now only firelight flickered over our faces.

"No, Maggie, we're going to have to figure out how to live together," he said gently.

We stood. Not speaking. Both of us keeping our distance

for what seemed an eternity but was only a few moments. Then I placed my glass on the tray and picked up my purse. "Good night."

"Good night," he said.

Exhausted, I took a shower and crawled into bed. The sheets were as starched and as clean as a nun's veil against my naked body. I closed my eyes. I opened my eyes. Like hope, sleep on its feathered feet was nowhere to be seen. I turned on the light by my bed. I stared at my room. Hotel furniture was like a dowdy woman struggling to look chic. No matter how much money she spent, her skirt wasn't going to hang evenly. No matter how expensive the room, hotel furniture looked used.

I could hear Boulton moving around next door. Grabbing the TV remote control off the nightstand, I aimlessly clicked from channel to channel. All I saw were women. We were everywhere, like locusts. Women selling cars, jeans, perfume, douches, Ajax, lipsticks.

Click.

Women on the porno channel selling themselves without the car, without the jeans, without the Ajax.

Click.

Women on the music channels shaking their tits to rock and roll. Who were all these women shaking their tits for? Did they know? Did it matter anymore? Was it only for the money and the camera? At least at Peep Thrills there was a connection between the act and the fantasy. I mean who were these women shaking themselves silly for? Twelve-year-old boys? Five-year-old girls? Circus performers? Waitresses? Lawyers? Crooks? Lonely old men? Lonely old women? Anybody. Anybody who tuned in. The universe. The black hole. The Bermuda triangle. Me.

Click.

More women acting pouty, carnal, officious, aloof, dopey. Sexy preadolescent girls looking like a child molester's delight.

Click.

The image of a plump plain woman with short brown hair appeared. She had on a simple blue sleeveless blouse that tied at the neck and tucked into a plain white pleated skirt. She was writing a sentence on the blackboard: *Hello, I would like you to meet my uncle Bob.*

Instead of her breasts, the flesh on her upper arm shook as she exuberantly diagrammed the sentence. Her eyes shone with an honest love for taking the English language apart. Her round face glowed as she drew arrows pointing at subject and predicate. Okay, so she was one of those women who made a simple declarative sentence look like a physics equation. At least she wasn't depressed because she didn't have a man, or because her hair was mousey brown, or because her waist pushed at the seams of her dated skirt. She didn't care that the fat on her upper arm shook when she wrote on the blackboard, revealing her a vulnerable fleshy human being. The woman cared about something. She had a passion for understanding how to write and speak, *Hello, I would like you to meet my uncle Bob.* I'd never seen her kind on television. I found her comforting.

I closed my eyes, listening to her breathless, teacher voice. There must be a sleepless Peruvian somewhere in a tiny room in the city repeating: "Hello, I would like . . ." Or maybe a Russian . . . Chinese . . . all the sleepless Americans watching some young woman shake her tits. Hello, my name—

The phone rang. My body jerked awake. I grabbed for the receiver while checking the clock. It was 1:00 A.M. I'd been asleep fifteen minutes.

"Miss Hill." It was Desanto. "This is not acceptable."

"Don't you ever sleep, Desanto? Or do you just hang suspended like a bat from the lobby ceiling?"

"There is a woman in the bar who will not leave until she sees you."

"What's her name?"

"I don't know her name. But I do know we don't want *her kind* in our bar."

"What kind is that, Desanto?"

"And we did not have *her kind* in this hotel until you started working for . . ."

I hung up on him, threw on a pair of beige slacks and a beige sweater, put my key in my pocket, and made my way down to the bar.

The city must have taken its well-publicized nightlife someplace else, because it wasn't happening in the Parkfaire Bar. There was an older man, wearing a toupee that looked like a dead cat wrapped around his head, sitting in a corner booth. He was with a woman, probably my age, who was trying to look like she was in her twenties. She stared at her drink. He stared at her. At the bar, three men, ties pulled loose, tried to concentrate on their conversation and their beers, but their eyes kept searching out the lone woman sitting a few spaces away from them.

Perched on the bar stool, smoking a cigarette and drinking an espresso, the young woman exuded easy sex just as she had at Peep Thrills. The candlelight glow softened but couldn't hide her pockmarked cheeks. Her dark roots were still doing battle with the blond tips of her hair. A tight black dress defined every curve of her body. I took the stool next to her.

"The hotel manager is a real pisser," she said.

The eyes of the men drifted toward me, then quickly back to her.

"You made quite an exit from Peep Thrills." She blew smoke and laughed. "Very entertaining."

"So I've been told. What's your name?" I asked.

"Linda Hansen."

She was only in her early twenties but every move was weighted with experience.

The bartender sauntered over. "Brandy," I told him.

"Another espresso," she said. "Why don't we go to the table near the window?" Her smoke gray eyes came to rest on the three men. Her hard mouth carved out a smile. "I look at them and keep counting the money I could be earning. Very distracting."

She slid off the stool and swayed to a small table facing the street. Her long black-stockinged legs looked as if their only purpose in life were to wrap around a naked man. My legs suddenly felt short and utilitarian. They carried me along as if they'd never felt a man's body. The group at the bar fell silent watching her. The Toup in the corner even took his eyes off his date. We settled at the table.

"What do you want?" I asked.

"No bullshit. Right to the point."

"I've had a bad day. Jackie had even a worse one."

She smiled again. Her face softened, and for a fleeting moment she was almost beautiful. "Hope Goldie didn't hurt your arm. He doesn't know his own strength."

The bartender brought us our drinks. I took a sip of the brandy. Linda fell silent. I waited, looking out the window. The drivers leaned against their limousines the way torch singers lean against their pianos. A black BMW convertible as small as a child's coffin was parked between the limos. The churches' genteel lighting was lost in the garish yellow glare of the street lamps and the endless streak of headlights. I turned back to the table. Five thousand dollars was spread in front of me.

"What's this for?"

"Information." She ran her long platinum-colored fingernail across the money. "The coin of the realm. Sexy, isn't it?" Insinuation turned her voice low and husky.

"I'm wondering how many male fantasies you have to act out to earn this kind of money," I said.

"I could make an easy two thousand right over there." She gestured toward the men at the bar. "I've never understood how women could put out for nothing."

"I know it's un-American, but some of us just lack the entrepreneurial spirit. Look, I work for Claire Conrad. Five thousand dollars won't make a dent in her household expenses." I began to stack the money neatly.

"This is for you. Claire Conrad doesn't have to know."

I fingered the money.

"What's the matter? Not enough? What if I offered you the money and me?" The professional seductive look was back, masking her face. She leaned toward me, secure in her money, secure in her sexiness. "Would you like that? You're not afraid of sex with me, are you?"

"I don't like it when men try to intimidate me sexually. And I don't like it any better when a woman tries it."

I was tired. I was tired of women. I was tired of men. I was tired of sex. I took a chance and stood up.

Startled, she looked up at me. "Where are you going?"

"Back to bed."

She grabbed my wrist. Her long fingers were ice-cold. "You can't."

I jerked my arm away and headed toward the lounge. She was right behind me. The men at the bar watched.

"Please, don't go," she said. Something in her voice had changed. I turned. The hard lips trembled. Tears glistened in her eyes.

"Please." Her hand moved up to cover her now vulnerable mouth.

"Please, don't go," one of the men mimicked. "Please, please." His friends snickered.

She turned on them. "Why don't you shut the fuck up?"

Eyes that had once desired her now shone with belligerence, even hatred. Defiantly, she stared back at them. One teardrop broke loose and ran down her pockmarked cheek. The man who had mimicked her moved threateningly toward us. She just stood there, almost welcoming the violence. I pulled my only weapon. I smiled. Sweetly. Warmly. Obsequiously.

"It's all right. She's just upset. You know how it is with women: PMS. Ms. BS." All the time smiling, I guided her back to the table.

His buddies pulled the man back toward the bar. We sat down. Linda's eyes were bright with tears and excitement. My smile disappeared. "Put your money away," I said angrily.

She stuffed it back into her purse. "Did you see how quickly they turned on me? Men do that, you know?" She stared out the window. The excitement drained from her voice, replaced by a deep melancholy. "We all hate what we desperately need."

I sensed that if I asked her what she needed, she'd turn street on me, defenses back in place. So I went for a more general tone. "Why do you think we do that?" I asked.

"Because we need to be loved at face value." Her fingers touched her scarred cheeks and discovered the tear. She quickly brushed it away. "Of course we never are. If I didn't have this body nobody would love me." Bitterness edged her voice.

She lit another cigarette, cupping her hand over the match

just as Jackie had. The cold wind of the streets was never far away.

" 'Only God could love you for yourself alone and not your yellow hair?' " I quoted.

"And I'm not too sure about him." Her lips carved out a smile. "That's why I like Peep Thrills. The men need me."

"Until the curtain goes down."

She shrugged. "If it's not that curtain, it's another one. Or a door that closes. Or a hand that reaches out for another girl instead of me."

"So what kind of trouble are you in?"

"Who said I'm in trouble?"

"Your tears."

"I wasn't crying." She stared right into my eyes as if she had never seen water, let alone a tear.

"Look, I'm tired of making dramatic exits, but I'm ready to walk if you don't talk to me."

She blew smoke. "How did Jackie die?"

"She was stabbed this morning, or, I should say, yesterday morning around eleven—across the street from the hotel."

Linda paused, running her finger along her lower lip. "Goldie loved her, at least she had that. Do you know who killed her?"

"You tell me. Does Goldie use a knife?"

There was only a slight movement of her lips as she pressed them together. I was suddenly aware of the shape of her head. Her skull. It was as if I could see that voluptuous curve of white bone beneath her thin, tight skin. I felt a chill.

"He uses his fists. What does her death matter? Who's going to miss her besides him?"

"You're not going to win the Humanitarian Award with that kind of an attitude."

She threw her head back and laughed. The men automatically turned, eyes following the curve of her body and neck. She stopped laughing and leaned forward, her eyes the color of cold cigarette ash.

"Jackie was naïve. You may think that's impossible for someone like her, but it's true. She believed what anybody told her. She also believed her own lies. Her own dreams."

"Like what?"

"That somebody was going to rescue her. One day she'd turn around and there would be the perfect father, the perfect mother, the perfect lover. The perfect family. I mean she called herself Jackie Kennedy Onassis Murphy, for God's sake, and never saw the irony. Look, just take whatever she said with a grain of salt. That's all I'm trying to say."

"With a grain of salt and five thousand dollars. You talk like you've been to two years' worth of college."

"One."

"What happened?"

"I needed money. I started working at Peeps for extra cash. It was more lucrative than studying English lit. What did Jackie tell you?"

"She wondered why Sarah Grange would do a porno. You know Sarah, don't you?"

"She used to work at a little shop where some of us bought our outfits, if you can call 'em that. We became friends."

"Did she ever do porno videos for extra money?"

"You'll have to ask her. Was Jackie beat up?"

"When she came to see Claire Conrad, she had a bruise on her cheek. You're frightened, aren't you?"

Shrugging off my question, she asked, "Is Claire Conrad good?"

"Yes."

"What does it matter to her who killed Jackie?"

"It's what she does. It's her profession."

She gestured toward the BMW. "That's mine. Nice, isn't it?"

"Very expensive. How can you afford it?"

"I know where Sarah lives," she said, not answering my question. "I'll take you. But first I have to call and see if she's awake." She stubbed out her cigarette and stood.

"They can bring a phone to the table."

"I want to talk to her in private. Wait here." She moved through the room as if her body belonged to everyone else except herself. Even the guy at the bar who wanted to beat her up.

I quickly crossed to the in-house phone on the bar and dialed the suite. Boulton answered.

"It's Maggie," I said. "I'm in the bar with one of the girls from Peep Thrills. A Linda Hansen. I think she's going to take me to meet Sarah Grange."

"Where does Sarah live?"

"I don't know."

"Do you have your gun?"

"Yes," I lied. He had given me his mother's gun in L.A. and he was partial to it.

"Then Miss Conrad and I look forward to hearing what you have to tell us over breakfast," he said stiffly. There was a pause. When he spoke again the English butler was gone. "Well done, Maggie."

"Thank you."

I asked the bartender for the bill and sat back down. The black BMW was still there. I was suddenly aware of the Toup's date chattering behind me.

"I've always wanted to open this restaurant. In Baltimore. Between the racetracks. Food and jazz. It would clean up."

"I can just see you standing in the doorway in a low-cut black dress." Toup's voice.

"Is this a sexual fantasy or are we talking business?" The Date's voice was edged with hurt.

The bartender put down the bill. I wrote the tip and Conrad Suite on it. My hand shook. Fear?

"Did you see *Tom Jones?*" It was the Toup.

"No."

"That movie had one of the sexiest eating scenes in it."

"What made you think of that?" the Date whined.

"Your idea for a restaurant."

These two had really developed the art of conversation. What was taking Linda so long? Maybe she bolted. Maybe the BMW wasn't hers.

"Did you see *Flashdance?*" It was the Date.

"No."

"That had one of the sexiest eating scenes. You should've seen it when she bit into that lobster."

"But *Tom Jones* was the greatest," the Toup countered.

"*Flashdance* was the greatest of 1983."

"*Tom Jones* was the first." A competitive edge had crept into the Toup's voice.

Where was the hope for men and women? I wondered.

"He's never turned me on," the Date announced.

"Who?"

"Tom Jones. I can't stand his voice."

"No, *Tom Jones* is the name of a classic novel. It was made into a movie."

I turned and looked at them. They were miserable. I hoped she got her restaurant. I hoped he got his orgasm. What did he do with his toupee? Leave it on the nightstand? Put it in a glass of water like false teeth? How could she? For that matter, how could he?

"I've always loved *Romeo and Juliet*." Oh, God, the Date. She was relentless.

The men at the bar were looking at me. No, they were looking past me. I turned and saw Linda leaning against the BMW. She cocked her finger, beckoning me. The guys let out a few groans. My fear came back.

As I left the bar, one of the guys commented loudly, "Now that's what I call safe sex."

"Can we join you?" another asked derisively, then the three of them tittered like schoolgirls.

I headed through the lobby and the revolving doors wondering when sex had ever been safe for a woman. Passionate, yes. Boring, yes. Fulfilling, yes. Unfulfilling, yes. But safe?

I wished I had my gun.

Nine

Linda wove in and out of traffic. The top was down, the heater blasting. The cold wind slapped at our faces and tugged at our hair. When she slammed to a halt at a stop light, I turned and studied her. Her mood had shifted. She was sullen and remote. The streetlights cast a waxen sheen on her pitted skin and turned her blond streaks a greenish color.

"Did you ever do a porno with Jackie?" I asked.

"A few."

"With Sarah?"

"No."

"What happens when you do a video like that? I mean, who holds the camera?"

"Sometimes the client. Some guys like to look at us through a camera. They even like to direct. I don't know which excites them more, us or that they think they're Oliver Stone."

"Is it always the client?"

"Look, I don't know who shot Sarah's video. Why don't you save the questions for her?"

She threw the car in gear, cutting off one taxi and tailgating another. In Manhattan people gained or lost by inches.

"Did you know that Sarah had a famous mother?" I talked over the wind, brushing my hair back from my face.

"God, you don't give up, do you?"

"Did Sarah talk about her mother?"

"Sarah and I'd go out drinking. She'd get drunk and babble about how her mother was once a famous model, how she was going to find her, and when she did she'd be famous and rich. She sounded just like Jackie, dreaming there was somebody out there to rescue her, love her, take her out of her shitty life."

I wondered if the candle I'd lit for Jackie was still flickering in the cold chapel of the church. "So you didn't believe Sarah."

"Why should I? One night I'm over at her place. She pulls this cardboard box out of her closet and shows me all these fashion magazines from the sixties with Cybella on the cover. She told me her grandmother had collected them and given them to her so she'd always have a memory of her mother." She shook her head at the sad image of a young woman saving a box of magazines. "She said they were her only connection to her mother."

I could see the Met Life building that used to be the PanAm building squatting over the street like a giant weight-lifter pressing tons of cement and steel.

"One day," Linda continued, "Sarah comes to me and says she met a woman who knew Cybella. Then I don't see her around anymore. Couple of months go by and I open a magazine and there she fucking is. And there is a picture of her mother. I was impressed. I mean, my mother is a drunk. God knows where she is now, probably with a bottle somewhere on the Coast. Where's yours?"

"With a rosary in Versailles, Ohio."

Swerving left, she tossed her head back and laughed. I pressed my hands against the dashboard. We sped down one of those side streets that suddenly turns the city quaint, even at night. The East River lay at the end of it. I could feel its dark damp presence the way you can feel a dark basement at the bottom of the stairs. And again I felt fear. I decided a gun is very much like a rosary. Clutching one in your hand, even if you didn't believe in it, gave you a sense of security.

She made a quick right and jerked to a stop in front of a large old building. The wind suddenly stopped. My hair felt like it didn't belong to me. I looked at the address. One Bedford Place.

"Posh, very posh," I said.

Linda's face was a shadow. Only her lips, glistening a garish blue-pink, were defined in the dim lights. "Yeah, some people have all the luck. It's her mother's apartment." She opened the car door and swiveled her long legs around.

A doorman let us in. Linda told him Sarah Grange was expecting us. He checked this out on the telephone, then nodded toward the elevator. But I was looking at a stairway that curved down into the middle of the gracious lobby. The steps were marble and the banister was mahogany. Prim stiff-backed chairs were grouped near the stairs like nuns waiting in silent judgment. I walked over to the stairwell and looked up. The stairs spiraled toward the dome-shaped ceiling. The banister twisted past each floor like a highly polished serpent.

"What are you doing?" Linda asked.

"This must be where Cybella jumped."

She hesitated.

"You do know Cybella killed herself?" I asked.

"So? This is a society that doesn't like to see a lot of aging women. We turn into jokes, fag hags, or just get lost."

"Sometimes I think men like us better than we like ourselves."

"That's real radical. But I think we like men better than we like ourselves. I know it for a fact." Her face hardened with memory.

We took the elevator to the tenth floor. Linda knocked on apartment 10C and Sarah Grange, in tight jeans and a white silk shirt, opened the door. Her left hand clutched a blue dress. Her right hand rested on her slim hip. She had long dark hair and no split ends. Her skin was flawless, legs long and graceful. Eyes, nose, high cheekbones, and chin were all perfectly balanced. She was the kind of woman that with looks alone could stop a conversation, a train, a wedding, a heart. When you looked at her, it didn't matter that beauty was only skin-deep. She was about twenty-two and I immediately disliked her.

"Shut the door," she commanded, flipping a few thick strands of her lush dark hair back over her shoulder. She moved into the living room with an elegant disdain for having to make a physical effort.

It was a large, wide room with a picture window framing the blackness that was the East River. It was decorated with the benign taste that only a lot of money and a decorator can buy. Yellow silk love seats faced one another near a fireplace. Striped chairs mingled with ones covered in a flowered chintz. Crystal lamps wore saucy silk shades. A small round table draped in fringed brocade held a collection of crystal paperweights. Its mate displayed a collection of hand-painted porcelain boxes. Other objets d'art were scattered around the room. It was like being in a gift shop. Over the white-painted mantel was a black-and-white blowup of the *Bonton* photograph of Cybella and Sarah.

Through an opened door near the fireplace I could see an unmade bed. On top of the bed was a suitcase.

"Leaving town?" I asked.

"Nora Brown's furious with me. She wants me to move in with her tomorrow so she can keep an eye on me."

"What does she think you're going to do?" Linda asked.

"Obviously another porno video," Sarah said sarcastically.

"Sorry about your mother," I offered.

"Thank you." The coffee-colored eyes, not as deep or as haunting as Cybella's, peered at me suspiciously. Her face showed no sign of grieving but there was a tightness around her eyes and mouth. She tossed the dress into the bedroom, where it landed on the floor, then sat on one of the love seats. Uninvited, I sat in one of the yellow and white striped chairs. The silk fabric felt as cold as a marble slab.

Still standing, Linda looked awkward, as if the furniture were not for her use. She leaned against the picture window. In her black dress, framed by the black sky and river, she merged more with the cold darkness than with the lamplit radiance of the room.

"It must be tough to leave a place like this." Linda lit a cigarette, again cupping her hand around the flame. She blew a long curve of smoke.

"I hate it here. None of it's mine. Everything's Cybella's. You don't need to stay, Linda. I can handle it." Sarah waved a hand against the cigarette smoke, then turned to me. "What was your name again?"

"Maggie Hill."

"Maggie can get a cab back to her hotel," Sarah said to Linda.

Linda shrugged. "See you around, Maggie."

"Wait a minute. Where were you yesterday morning around eleven?" I asked, sounding like a real detective.

Another hard smile formed. "At home. In bed. Alone. I work late. Why don't you ask Sarah where she was?"

"I was here. Alone. Why?" Sarah demanded.

"That's when Jackie was murdered. You forgot to tell me about that, Sarah," Linda observed dryly.

"Well, I had a lot on my mind. Nora screaming at me about the video, telling me my career was on the line, that what I had done could ruin her in the business. I mean, God, you'd think I robbed a bank. And it's not like I knew Jackie. We did a porno together, we didn't become best of friends. I told you to leave," she said to Linda.

It was hard to read these two women. Each seemed to be hiding—one behind her street sexuality and the other behind her passive beauty. As Linda left, Sarah pulled her knees up and put her arms around them, giving herself a good hug.

"You know, when I was trying to find work as a model, the people who were the nicest to me were the secretaries and the assistants."

"Is that why I'm here—because I'm Claire Conrad's assistant?"

"Nora doesn't want me to speak to Claire Conrad without her being there."

"Is she afraid you're going to say something you shouldn't?"

The dark eyes grew defensive. "No, but I thought maybe you and I could have a talk, see where things really stand."

"Okay." I leaned back in my chair and waited for our talk. Sarah hugged herself a little tighter.

"See, I'm still having trouble figuring out why this is such a big deal."

"You mean, besides the fact that Jackie was murdered?"

"Let's be practical. Sometimes terrible things happen to girls like her. I'm always warning Linda to be careful." She curved her long legs into a lotus position. "Now a lot of models, if they're honest, did a porno when they were scuffling." She rested her hands, palms upward in the curve of her legs, and began to sway her head from side to side stretching her long neck. "God, this is all making me so tense."

I have no tolerance for women who just can't sit with their feet on the ground like the rest of us. I'm always waiting for these adored creatures to wrap a leg around their necks and strangle themselves. "So you think you're a politically correct slut." That stopped her from swaying her head back and forth.

Sarah started to say something but thought better of it. Instead, she smiled as if she'd just won a beauty contest. "I was hoping that you could somehow convince Claire Conrad not to show the video to St. Rome."

"If it's no big deal, why worry about him?"

"It's no big deal to me. But he may think differently, especially if it were made public."

"Because of the red dress?"

"Red dress?"

"The one that Jackie was wearing."

"That was some cheap thing she brought with her. St. Rome's already heard about the video because you called Blanchard Smith. But he hasn't seen it. We're doing a shoot tomorrow and I'm going to have to face him." She uncurled her legs, gave me an exasperated look. "He's going to be furious. But Nora will get him under control. I helped bring the guy back. Nobody was wearing his stuff until Nora put me in one of his outfits. Still, it would be easier for me tomorrow if he hasn't seen the video."

"When did you shoot it?" I asked her.

"Over a year ago in some cheap motel." She stopped caressing herself long enough to think. "It was the Royal Motel."

"Where's that?"

"It was near JFK. It's been torn down," Sarah said.

"Convenient. Who was involved?"

"Just me and Jackie and this guy with a camera."

"Does the guy have a name?"

"I didn't ask. He was some creep. I just did what he wanted, took the money, and left." She nibbled at her lower lip—not out of nervousness, it was more like little love bites. When she finished she said, "All I'm asking is that you don't show St. Rome the video. I don't think that's a lot to ask."

"You don't seem too broken up about your mother."

Her coffee-brown eyes gave me a slow steady stare as if I were a camera. "I don't cry."

"Not good for the complexion?"

Her fingers played with the ends of her hair. "Tears are such a contrast to the way I look. I feel removed from them. You know, like they don't mean anything. So I just don't cry."

"What about shock? Surprise? Sadness?"

"At what?"

"At your mother jumping down a stairwell."

"My mother was very depressed. I tried to make her happy but God knows I wasn't her reason for living, otherwise she wouldn't have left me with my grandparents. She only took me in because I was beautiful." Her voice broke. Anger flushed her cheeks. "She'd just sit here, drinking, watching me. It was like being in prison. Like . . . oh, what does it matter." She ran her slim fingers through her hair.

"Jackie thought Cybella was murdered," I said.

She scrambled to her feet. "Jackie didn't even know Cybella. And she only met me once and that was when we did the video." She put her hands on her hips. "Look, all I'm asking is that you don't show St. Rome the tape. Is it a deal?"

"Jackie never mentioned the fact that she knew you before you became a big-time model."

"So?"

"So I think she would have told us unless of course you were a big-time model when you did the video."

"You weren't very popular in school, were you?" She flipped some more gorgeous hair back from her face. "You hated girls like me. It still shows."

She was right. Girls like her always traveled in twos and threes and stood around in their tight little groups reeking of drugstore perfume and lipstick and exclusion.

"You know why I don't like you? You have the power of all that beauty and you use it with all the grace of a sledgehammer."

"I guess that means you're going to show St. Rome the video. Well, fuck you. I've gotta get some sleep. I have to go be beautiful tomorrow. Show yourself out." She stomped into her room and slammed the door.

Oh, hell.

I got up and walked into the foyer. Next to the dining room was another door. It opened into a bedroom carefully decorated in the same deep yellow as the living room. Crossing to the front door, I opened and closed it loudly.

I walked back to the bedroom, stepped inside, and quietly shut the door. Stillness had settled on the room like the weight of a lover's body. As I moved through the hush, I caught a glimpse of myself in the mirrored closet doors. I looked like a fugitive from the female sex trying to avoid one more mirror. I turned away from my image and studied the room. The bed, draped in a gold-colored damask, displayed a collection of antique linen pillows. A crystal lamp graced the nightstand. A silver-framed photograph showed Cybella smiling at Sarah and Sarah smiling at the camera. Another photograph showed Cybella arm-in-arm with a handsome gray-haired man. They looked like a happy middle-aged couple who had invested their money wisely. What was I doing here? I crossed to a small bookcase filled with leatherbound books. I took one from the shelf and opened it. It was *The Golden Notebook* by Doris Lessing, inscribed, *To Cybella, with love only a woman can understand, Nora. 1973.* The bindings were stiff, the pages untouched. The book had never been read. I took down another one. *Madame Bovary.* My favorite. This time Nora had written: *For Cybella, my love, my life. 1968.* Flaubert was unread too. Which woman in this relationship was really Madame Bovary?

Inside the mirrored closet doors, clear plastic zippered bags hung in a straight line. The clothes in the bags looked like shadowy corpses. When I unzipped one, a deep, rich perfume drifted into the room. For the first time I had a sense of Cybella alive. Five suits hung on padded hangers, all Chanel. I zipped up the bag and opened another one. Again her perfume summoned a presence so strong, it was as if she were standing next to me. I stared at evening dresses. The empty bodices of the gowns seemed to be waiting for breasts to fill them, to give the gowns their reason for being. Among the chiffon, the sequined, and the basic black was a slip of red silk gown. I took it off the hanger. It looked like the dress Jackie had worn in the video. The label was St. Rome's. When I hung it back up, the others swayed tipsily on their hangers like slightly drunken ladies. I closed the closet doors. Why were they all lying about this dress?

I moved to an art deco vanity and went through the drawers. Exquisite lingerie, the sort I could only dream of wearing, was folded with a loving neatness. Lipsticks, makeup, brushes, silvery cases of eye shadow filled the center drawer. Two keys shimmered next to a box of loose powder. I reached for them, knocking the box. Puffs of pink powder floated up into the air and curled away like a spirit. I looked at the keys. One was a Baldwin, like the lock on the front door? I assumed the other was to the lobby door. I slipped them in my pocket, closed the drawer, and slowly crossed the room. The smell of Cybella's perfume embraced me as I silently let myself out of the apartment.

I had disturbed the dead.

Ten

Something rattled. The bones of dead women rattle. Their teeth rattle when they smile. Old women. Young women. Spreading brittle legs. Offering lifeless breasts. Rattle, rattle.

"Throw cold water on her."

"She's only asleep, madam."

Water? Cold?

I sat up, peering through strands of tousled hair at Boulton and Claire, who stood at the end of my bed. Claire, all in white, leaned on her ivory walking stick like an angel in exile. Boulton held a tray loaded with a china coffeepot, cup and saucer, pot of marmalade, and a small pitcher of cream. Toast was lined up like envelopes in a silver holder. Something was wrong.

"Did you sleep well?" Claire asked, tossing me my bathrobe.

She had a strange expression, maybe an attempt to look motherly. I blinked. Yes, she was definitely trying for a sort of domesticated warmth and kindness. But on her it looked as if she had just bit into the wrong piece of candy in the box.

"I'm not sure. What's all this? What time is it?" I struggled into my robe while Boulton, the good butler, stared at the wall just over my head.

"Time for us to talk," she said, settling into a chair that had been pulled up beside my bed. "I can't let you sleep the afternoon away." Another sickening smile. This one didn't work either. For a horrified moment I thought she might even start knitting.

"It's afternoon?" I felt dazed. Boulton placed the tray on my lap and poured my coffee. His arm brushed against my shoulder. I could smell soap. The tips of his hair looked wet.

"Is it raining out?" I took a sip of coffee.

"There now," Claire said. "Head all clear?"

I drank some more and nodded.

"Then please, begin." She leaned back and closed her eyes. Her large pale hand rested on her ivory stick. The lapis shimmered.

Two pieces of toast, with marmalade, and three cups of coffee later I recounted the night's events, omitting only my feminist diatribe at Peep Thrills. Some things should remain personal. She opened her eyes and almost looked at me.

"Sarah kept the magazines in a box in her closet," she repeated.

"That's what Linda said."

"And Cybella owned the red dress."

"It's in her closet and it's definitely a St. Rome." I spread marmalade on another piece of toast.

"So Sarah Grange does a porno video letting Jackie wear her mother's dress," Boulton said. "It doesn't make sense."

"It does if you consider the tape as not just pornography but also as a tool for blackmail." Claire's eyes came to rest on the toast in my hand.

"How do you force somebody like her to do that?" I asked.

"The blackmailer says, 'If you don't do this video, then I will tell what I know and destroy your career.' The St. Rome dress is used to show that the video was taped as recently as six months ago. Not one year ago."

"So Sarah has something to hide," I said, licking some marmalade off my finger.

"Are you going to eat that toast or not!" Claire snapped.

"What's wrong with you?"

"You're sitting there holding it as if it were an award."

"What happened to that phony motherly smile?"

"It gave me a headache."

I bit into my toast.

"Then why is Jackie wearing the dress and not Sarah Grange?" Boulton asked.

"I don't know," Claire said, tapping her fingers on the head of her walking stick and still eyeing my toast. "This Linda Hansen definitely knows more than she is saying. Aren't BMWs expensive?"

"Not if you drive a Bentley," I said.

Gerta stuck her head into the room. "Your breakfast is ready, Miss Conrad."

"Thank God."

"Breakfast?" I said.

"I'm starving." Claire stood and stretched. "Listening to you eat your toast made it very difficult for me to concentrate. But my disciplined mind was able to overcome such a minor annoyance."

"Breakfast? Wait a minute! You said afternoon. 'Sleep the afternoon away,' that's what you said. What time is it?" I looked at my nightstand. My clock was gone.

"Seven in the morning," Boulton said.

"You mean I've only been asleep for two hours?"

"So it would seem," Boulton said.

"Seem?!"

"You can go back to bed if you wish," Claire said.

"I've had three cups of coffee."

"Well, you know best just how much sleep you need. When you decide to get up, I want you to call St. Rome's sales representative. I want to see St. Rome here as soon as possible," she said, walking out of the room. "And don't forget to locate the Duke Hotel."

"Where is my clock?"

"She put it in the drawer of your nightstand." I caught a glimpse of my small, two-and-a-half-inch-barrel Navy Colt as Boulton opened the drawer and placed the clock on the table next to me.

"She couldn't have waited a couple more hours?"

"You know she does her best thinking in the morning."

"No, I didn't."

"Would you like me to draw your bath? Scrub your back?"

"No, I would not."

He moved to the side of the bed. His expression turned serious. "Maggie, you didn't have your gun with you last night."

"I didn't need to shoot anybody last night, Boulton."

"That's not the point. You told me you had it."

"I didn't want to lose Linda. I called you and told you what I was doing. Those are the rules and I followed them."

"You lied to me, Maggie. My job is to protect. You understand that."

"To protect her, not me. I don't need a bodyguard."

"The fact that I am not in your hire doesn't mean you don't need watching. Especially when you act as stupidly as you have." His eyes were hard.

"Boulton, I carried a gun in L.A. and I didn't like the consequences."

"You mean the fact that we're all still alive? I want you to carry it."

"I do not need you to watch over me. And you have no right to prowl around in my room while I'm not here."

"A butler never prowls, he insinuates himself." The brittle English veneer was firmly in place.

"Why is it that, whenever we talk, you end up hiding behind that butler image of yours?"

"I am in service, Maggie. And why is it that, whenever we talk, you make it clear you don't need a man?"

Again we were reduced to staring at one another. He took the tray and turned crisply on his heels.

Oh, hell.

Well, sleep was definitely out of the question. Forty minutes later I was showered and dressed and surveying my reflection in the dresser mirror. I had on my pink and black jacket and black skirt. My brown hair, which just curved under my chin, was brushed back from my face. It would remain that way until I moved my head. My lips shined Wet Red. They looked kissable, but I didn't feel like being kissed. A paradox. Or was it just hypocrisy? Maybe that's why women always feel a little surreptitious. We never look how we feel and we never feel how we look. Of course I could go without makeup, but I've never trusted women who walk around barefaced. I always feel like they're hiding something.

Claire, having eaten, was back to her normal self. Enthroned. Boulton was plumping the pillows on the sofa. Deep in thought, Claire held her walking stick up and peered down it as if it were the barrel of a rifle. I dialed Blanchard Smith.

"This is Maggie Hill. Do you remember me from yesterday?" I asked Blanchard's secretary.

"What do you want?" By the tone of her voice I could tell the memory wasn't a fond one.

"Claire Conrad would like to see St. Rome in her suite at the Parkfaire this morning. It's very important."

"Just a minute." She put me on hold. I was suddenly listening to Johnny Mathis singing "Misty." I sang along.

"Must you, Miss Hill?" Now Claire tapped the tip of her right foot with the stick.

"One of my favorite songs."

"What about unrequited love?" Boulton asked, smacking a pillow.

"I don't know that tune."

"I suppose if you're a poet or a songwriter, unrequited love is profitable," Claire observed. "Other than that, I see no reason for it."

"I was thinking of the inscriptions Nora Brown wrote to Cybella," Boulton replied.

"Oh, as a motive for murder, that is something quite different. But if Miss Brown killed Cybella for that reason, then why all this business about the video and the red dress?"

The secretary replaced Mathis. "I reached him at home. He can be at the hotel in a half hour."

I hung up. "Half hour." Then I called information and got the number and the address of the Duke Hotel. Claire slouched down in her chair and leaned her head back. A slight smile played on her lips. "So you believe pornography is male tyranny, Miss Hill?"

"And men wonder why women get angry," I observed, watching Boulton. He was inscrutable.

"It's his job, as it is yours, to tell me exactly what takes place," she said.

"If I hadn't gone to Peep Thrills, no Linda Hansen would've led me to Sarah Grange and Cybella's closet."

"Nobody is questioning your competence. Boulton and I are concerned that your flair for the dramatic lacks discretion."

"Discretion? I've got a three-hundred-pound guy wearing gold rings the size of my ears who wants to jerk me inside out, and you're asking for discretion?"

"Only as a goal, Miss Hill."

Boulton smacked another pillow.

Twenty minutes later the doorbell rang. Boulton showed St. Rome into the room. The designer was in his fifties and had wavy dyed black hair with a touch of real gray at the temples. He was short and lean, with the quick precise movements of a ballet instructor. He had on gray flannel pin stripes and a pink turtleneck. A rose foulard silk square gushed from his breast pocket.

"Under other circumstances I might have enjoyed your man searching me," he announced to Claire.

"Please, sit down," she replied. "This is my assistant, Maggie Hill."

He nodded and sat on the sofa as if he had designed it. Boulton took his place behind him.

"I assumed you've talked to Nora Brown?" Claire asked.

"She's in an absolute snit. I'm not sure I blame her. Blackmail is so unattractive."

"So is murder, Mr. St. Rome. When you look at this tape, I want you to pay close attention to the red gown." Claire pointed her walking stick at the VCR, I hit the remote, and there were Jackie and Sarah.

St. Rome stood, peered closely at the dress, then returned to the sofa. "You can turn it off. I have never had one sexual thought about a woman in my entire life. It would be a great irony if I were ruined by something like this."

"Mr. St. Rome, do you recognize the gown?"

"Darling, how can one tell? It looks like a red bag on that poor creature."

"You will admit that your couture fall collection of last year had a red evening gown in it?"

"Of course. But it's not the dress in that video."

"How many of those gowns did you make?"

"I'm not sure." He tilted his head to one side.

"But you would know who you sold the gowns to?"

"We have records, of course."

"Then your records would show that Cybella owned one of the gowns."

"Cybella? It certainly would not show that."

"And how do you know?"

"Because I looked up our billing . . ." He stopped. He licked his lips.

"Why did you bother to do that?" Claire studied him.

He fell silent.

"Mr. St. Rome, one of your gowns is hanging in Cybella's closet. Would you like the police to look at your records?" Claire pressed.

"Cybella did not buy the dress." He paused, moving uneasily. "Look, you must believe me, I know nothing about this video. And I'm not admitting that the dress worn by that sad creature is from my fall collection."

"How did Cybella acquire the dress?" Exasperation filled her voice.

"You have to understand. My company is spending over twenty million dollars in ad campaigns featuring Sarah Grange. We are shooting this week. You've got to understand the position I'm in."

"I am noted for my discretion," Claire assured him.

"And it's not just the campaign. I also must protect my

clients. I'm like a psychiatrist; I can't afford to divulge their secrets."

"I'm waiting for an answer."

"What about them?" He flipped his hand toward me and gazed up at Boulton.

"Boulton is absolutely trustworthy and Miss Hill is one of the most tactful women I know." This was said with a perfectly straight face.

"I can't. I just can't . . ."

"Boulton." Claire spoke his name in a bored flat voice. He drew his gun and pressed the barrel against the back of St. Rome's neck.

St. Rome went white. "You call this discretion?!"

"No. Intimidation."

"Sheridan Reynolds bought the dress for Cybella."

"And who is Sheridan Reynolds?" she asked patiently.

"Tell him to put the gun away." His fingers trembled against his chest. "This is cashmere. I don't want it ruined."

"Thank you, Boulton."

"I've never seen a man lose his charm so quickly," St. Rome observed testily as Boulton returned the gun to his holster. "I don't know why I shouldn't tell you. The whole city knows. Cybella was Sheridan Reynolds's mistress. To be honest, I tried to talk him out of buying her the dress. Much too youthful for her. Heterosexual men have no sense of what is appropriate. They fall in love with these women when they're young and beautiful and keep buying for them as if they stayed that way."

"Mr. Reynolds is married?" she asked.

"Aren't they all, darling? Married to a ton of money. When she isn't having nervous breakdowns, Elizabeth Reynolds also buys from me. I'd appreciate it if you wouldn't mention the dress to her."

"How long had Cybella been his mistress?"

"Forever. But it wasn't till she was older that she had settled for the life of a mistress. You know, waiting for Reynolds to see her. Alone on the holidays. I think that was part of her depression. I'll never understand women." He sighed and crossed his legs in imitation of those he did not understand. "Women are masochists."

"All of us?" I asked.

"Oh, yes." He looked at me with eyes that would never desire, only assess. I felt as if he could see through me into my past, see all the men I had dated, gone to bed with, including Bobby Polinsky, and the one I had married and divorced. I felt as if he could name all the men that had hurt me.

"I dress women, darling. I give them their façade, the image they want to hide behind. They are all masochists. And the more beautiful the woman the more masochistic."

"And what about Nora Brown's relationship with Cybella?" Claire asked.

"My, you have been busy little bees. She, too, loved Cybella. It was a toss-up as to who Cybella would choose. She settled for being Sheridan's mistress. Women are such masochists." He made a helpless gesture with his hands. "They think heterosexuality is safer when it's really just a bore. I think Cybella killed herself out of boredom."

"Where does Sheridan Reynolds live?" Claire asked.

"Please, can't you find that out yourselves?"

"Where does he live?" Boulton demanded.

"That outré building, The Avenue 8000."

"The discovery of Sarah Grange seems to have brought new life to your career," Claire said.

"Not just mine, darling. *Bonton* was losing readers like rats from a sinking ship. Nora was on the verge of being beheaded or dethroned or whatever it is they do to these editors. And up she pops with Cybella's daughter. She starts running articles about Cybella and Sarah. She uses her on the cover and convinces me to use her as the St. Rome Woman. Nora is back in power, the new Diana Vreeland." He paused, eyeing Claire. "Nora has assured me that Sarah has done nothing wrong. I'm gambling my reputation on that being true."

"Did Sarah tell you how the red dress got into the video?" she asked.

"I haven't talked to her yet. Nora assures me the video was shot before Sarah even found her mother, and that the sad creature was the one who had the dress. That is all I care to know."

"Thank you for your help, Mr. St. Rome."

He uncrossed his legs and stood. The gossipy voice turned steely. "If you annoy my clients or damage my reputation in any way, you will hear from my lawyers. Do we understand one another?"

"Show Mr. St. Rome out, Boulton. Miss Hill, call the Avenue 8000. I want to talk to Sheridan Reynolds."

I got the number from information.

"Avenue 8000," a man proclaimed.

"Sheridan Reynolds, please."

"Who shall I say is calling?" He dribbled his vowels in my ear as if he'd been trained at the Sorbonne.

"Claire Conrad."

"Just a minute."

"Sheridan Reynolds's residence." Another man's voice, trained but not French.

"Claire Conrad would like to speak with Mr. Reynolds."

"He's not available at the moment."

"When will he be available?"

"I'm Paul Quentin, Mr. Reynolds's assistant. May I ask what this is regarding?"

"Just a minute." I put my hand over the receiver. "The assistant wants to know what this is regarding?"

"The death of Cybella."

"Straightforward." I removed my hand from the receiver. "The death of Cybella." Long silence. "I wonder if you could have him call Miss Conrad at the Parkfaire Hotel. ASAP."

"I'll give him the message." Paul Quentin never regained his full voice.

Eleven

The Bentley rolled down Forty-second Street. The morning light had drained the blood and life out of the area, leaving a dirty gray skeleton. Some homeless people, who had stuffed themselves in large boxes for the night, were still sleeping. Shopkeepers washed down the sidewalk in front of their stores. The naked women in the giant photographs plastering the theaters and the buildings looked like a man's worst dream. The nighttime had softened, even bewitched, the images of their flagrantly exposed bodies, rendering these women as soft and as pliable as pillows. But daylight showed the ravages of weather and time. The large breasts and thighs were chipped and peeling. The hot sultry eyes and opened mouths were streaked with black as if tears had mixed with mascara. Pink skin had faded to a sickly bluish white. These were the images of women that men ran away from, promising never to return. Until the next time.

"No wonder Nero Wolfe never left his brownstone," Claire said sadly, peering out the car window.

Boulton found a garage a couple of blocks away from the Duke Hotel. We made an odd group. Claire, an imposing erect figure all in white, striking the pavement with her ivory walking stick as she strode down the sidewalk. I, hurrying next to her, now and then catching my bewildered reflection in the discount store windows. Not an unusual expression for me. And Boulton walking behind us looking as if he were going to colonize Manhattan. New Yorkers, who never turn their heads to look at anything for fear it might chip another piece off their soul, craned their necks and stared.

The sign over the glass-and-wood door vapidly blinked DUK HOT, giving the hotel an Oriental flair. We made our way into the lobby. The floor was bumpy under my feet. The edges of purple and black linoleum tiles curled. A woman screamed from somewhere deep in the building. The hotel clerk, unmoved, sat behind a Formica counter. He wore a gray sweatshirt with the hood up. The curved peak on the hood made him look like a drab elf. He sipped his morning coffee from a Styrofoam cup and watched us with rabbity red eyes over the top of his newspaper. The woman screamed again. The man gave his paper a good shake, yawned, and took another sip. A handsome boy slept it off on an old purple velvet settee. An old woman, hair as white as paper, got up from her chair and teetered toward us. Expectation flickered in a face wrinkled with disappointment.

"Sit down, Violet. You don't know these people," the clerk said.

Violet slowly obeyed and continued her waiting. I thought of the Bovine Lady at the Parkfaire. I thought of my mother waiting with a rosary in her hand.

"A young woman named Jackie lives here. We'd like the key to her room," Claire said.

The clerk bit into a chocolate doughnut and tried to look thoughtful. "Can't do that."

Boulton took a twenty from his pocket and laid it on the

counter. "The key is just a courtesy. I can enter any room in this place without a key, and I will until we find her room."

The man set his coffee cup on the bill. "I want no trouble and no damage. Room's on the second floor. Number 2. Stairs are down the corridor in the back." He handed Boulton the key.

Again the woman screamed.

"Don't you want to see what's wrong with her?" I asked him.

"I know what's wrong," he said, licking a chocolate crumb from his thin pink lip. He gave his paper another shake.

We crossed the square patch of lobby and moved down the long narrow hallway. One greasy bulb shed a feeble light. I could hear people behind their closed doors, coughing, moaning, slamming drawers, trying to prepare for the day. A lone male figure leaned against the wall. He stepped in front of Boulton. His face was sweaty with fear and need.

"Sammy?" he whispered, his body shaking.

"No," Boulton said, pushing him away. He shrank back.

We took the stairs. The woman's scream echoed closer. At the top of the landing a door banged opened. A half-naked woman clutched a few shreds of clothes. Her pendulous breasts hung down on a bloated stomach.

"I'm being raped," she said in a voice thinned by her constant cries. "Help me, help me."

Claire stopped. Her body grew rigid as her eyes fixed on the woman and the room behind her.

"Help me." The woman whimpered, moving back to her bed and pulling a dirty sheet around her.

The look in Claire's eyes grew distant, as if she were seeing beyond the woman into another place, another room.

"I couldn't," Claire said.

"Help me, help me."

"I couldn't."

Boulton moved toward Claire. "Madam," he said firmly.

"Help me, help me," the woman moaned.

"There wasn't time." Claire's voice was frighteningly hollow.

"Close the door, Maggie," Boulton said quickly.

I reached in and pulled the door shut. The woman sobbed quietly. He put his arm around Claire, steadying her.

"There wasn't time, there wasn't time," she repeated over and over to the closed door.

"Boulton, what is it? What's wrong with her?" I asked.

"She'll be herself in a moment."

"There wasn't time." Claire's voice grew tired. Slowly she looked from the door to Boulton, then said: "Either you've had a passionate desire to throw your arms around me or I've had one of my spells."

"Sometimes, madam, I cannot control myself."

A wry smile formed on her quivering lips. "Thank you, Boulton." She moved away from him and fixed her gaze, now sharp again, on me. "Close your mouth, Miss Hill."

I closed my dry mouth.

"I see no reason to discuss this any further," she said.

I looked at Boulton. His butler face covered any emotion, any answer. I had never seen Boulton or Claire touch, let alone comfort one another. I knew I wouldn't find out what had happened to her unless she chose to reveal it. But I found his ability to comfort her touching. I found myself responding to that ability. We proceeded down the hall to Jackie's room as if nothing had happened. Boulton unlocked the door.

Gray light filtered through a narrow window over an unmade bed scattered with fresh pink carnations. A pair of lavender high heels leaned into each other on the floor. A white bra dangled over the back of a small wooden chair.

Next to the chair was a half-empty bottle of Wild Turkey. A mirror hanging above a dresser held the image of a half-open door, still moving. I turned and Claire stepped to one side. In one swift movement Boulton had his gun in his hand.

"Come out, slowly," he commanded.

The door swung wide. Goldie stood in the bathroom, his large hand clutching a bunch of carnations. The gold pyramids on his fingers shimmered. His narrow eyes were red and swollen. Tears gathered in the fleshy crevices of his large face. His lips were slack from too much Wild Turkey.

He squinted. "What are you people doing in my Jackie's room? Get out."

"Goldie," I informed Claire. "Bouncer at Peep Thrills."

"Get out!" he yelled.

"Move over to the bed and sit down," Boulton said.

Goldie stood, head thrust forward, staring at Boulton, like a bull wanting to charge but unable to move his limbs.

"Go on," Boulton said.

Goldie's dazed eyes came to life. He lurched, then rushed Boulton full force, shoving him back against the dresser. It was like two trains colliding in the small room. Carnations exploded from Goldie's hand, fluttering down on us. He grabbed for Boulton's gun. I backed into the corner between the dresser and the door. Claire pressed against the wall. I fumbled in my purse for my gun. Claire's stick came to rest on my wrist.

"Trust Boulton, Miss Hill."

Trust?

Boulton shoved Goldie, who staggered back toward the window. His feet crunched the lavender shoes, snapping off a heel. Goldie grabbed a chair. Boulton ducked and the chair sailed right at me. I ducked. It hit the wall, came down on my head, bounced onto the floor. The white bra was now draped at my feet. Ineffectual. Out of place. As Goldie spun to his right, reaching for the bottle of Wild Turkey, Boulton smashed his gun into the side of his head. Goldie went down hard on the bed and the carnations. The bed screamed out from the force of his weight. He dropped the bottle. The smell of booze mixed with a sickeningly sweet smell of flowers. Boulton raised the gun again.

"That's enough," Claire said. "I want to be able to talk to him."

"Quite." Boulton stepped back. He turned and looked at her. "Are you all right, madam?"

"Fine," Claire said, picking up the chair and placing it next to Goldie. Acting as if nothing unusual had happened, she tested the little wooden chair with her stick, then enthroned herself. I rubbed my head.

Just a moment of violence. And it was over. But I felt unnerved, more so than when I had looked at Jackie. Death was final. But violence was incomplete, always waiting to erupt. I watched Boulton, who stood, gun in hand, ready for the next eruption. That's what I didn't like, what I didn't want to get close to. It was in him, it always would be. I had trouble reconciling this with the man who had just put his arms around Claire Conrad.

"All right, Maggie?" he asked.

"Yes."

"Go through her things, Miss Hill," Claire said.

I opened the top dresser drawer. Once again I was searching through a dead woman's intimate apparel. Only this time it wasn't ecru silk and lace. Jackie's neon-colored bras and panties were cheap, designed with a need to titillate so desperate that they looked tired and joyless in their little wooden box of a drawer. I closed it.

"I'm a private detective," Claire said. "Jackie saw my picture in the newspaper and came to me for help."

"She needed help, she came to me," Goldie mumbled.

The second drawer contained a few T-shirts with CHANEL stamped across the front. There was no label. Some Jamaican street vendor selling fakes was the closest Jackie'd ever gotten to an original. I ran my hand under the T-shirts, felt something, came out holding a dead cockroach.

"Nothing," I said.

Goldie watched me with eyes stunned by loss and booze. "Whadda ya looking for?" Blood trickled down the side of his head mixing with sweat.

Ignoring his question, Claire asked, "How did you find out about Jackie's death?"

"Linda."

"When did she tell you?" Claire asked.

"After I threw these two outta Peeps. Then I went down to the morgue and saw Jackie." He groaned. "I saw her." The groan ended in a howl. He rocked back and forth. His big flat hands clasped his huge thighs.

It's always been difficult for me to watch a man cry, maybe because it takes such a physical effort for them to turn their pain into tears. Claire picked up the bottle of Wild Turkey and handed over what was left of it. He took a long swallow.

I opened the closet door and stared at a fake leopard coat, three skimpy dresses, and a pair of black boots run down at the heels. I thought of the cuddly fake fur at *Bonton*. It was a joke created for rich women who could afford the real thing, but knew the times were against them. Slipping my hand in the pockets of Jackie's coat, I knew she wanted people to think hers was real, a gift from a very important man. There was nothing except a button and some shreds of tobacco. I ran my hand inside the boots. Nothing.

"What are you looking for?" Goldie rubbed his face.

"Tell me about the porno videos you make." Claire said.

He took a quick swallow from the bottle. "I'm jush a bouncer." His words slurred.

"I find that hard to believe." Claire's voice was patient. "Don't you, Boulton?"

"Very hard to believe." His voice was devoid of emotion.

Goldie raised his large head and tried to focus on Boulton. "Go to hell."

Boulton grabbed him by his shirt and pulled him to his feet. He was almost deadweight. "Make it easy on yourself. Tell her what she wants to know." He shoved him back down. The bed moaned.

"I make some extra on the side. So do the girls. Our cush . . . customers like to buy the videos. Good for everybody. So what?"

"Tell me about the one you made with Jackie and the model."

"They all think they're models."

"This young woman *is* a model. Successful. Famous."

"I don't know what you're talking about."

"You were blackmailing her, weren't you?"

"Leave me alone."

"Did you make her bring the red dress?"

"You're crazy."

"What did you know about her?"

"Nothing, nothing. She jush like doing porno."

Claire leaned forward. "Jackie had a bruise on her cheek. Why did you strike her?"

"She wouldn't shut up."

"Why wouldn't she shut up?"

"She kept on about someone following her. I didn't believe her."

"Maybe you were following her. Maybe you killed Jackie."

He stared down at the broken lavender shoes. "No, no. Not Jackie."

She leaned closer. "Don't you want to find out who did?"

A sloppy triumphant grin spread across his face. "I don't need to." His eyes became like two slivers of glass; then, like a large, downed animal, he rolled over on his side, crushing the pink carnations, and passed out. The bed cried.

Twelve

"'I don't need to,'" Claire repeated. "Does that mean Goldie knows who killed Jackie or that he killed her or that he's simply not interested? I do wish people could be more precise with the English language." We were on our way back to the Parkfaire.

"Goldie didn't kill Jackie," I stated astutely.

"How do you know?"

"Because he loved Jackie. He was honestly grieving."

"I have seen men and women cry with the utmost honesty over the loss of the very people they have murdered, Miss Hill."

"If he was involved in blackmailing Sarah Grange," Boulton said, "he might've had a very good reason for killing Jackie."

"Okay, so much for heartfelt grieving." I sighed.

The car phone rang. It was Gerta. She informed me that Paul Quentin would like Claire Conrad to call him as soon as possible at the Reynolds residence. I dialed the number.

"I'm glad I reached you, Ms. Hill," he said. "Elizabeth Reynolds would like to speak with Claire Conrad. I'm afraid that means a drive out to Shadow Hills Sanitarium. It's near Greenwich, Connecticut."

"Hold on." I relayed the message to Claire.

"After the Duke Hotel, I think a breath of fresh air is needed."

"She's looking forward to the fresh air," I told Quentin.

"Fresh air? Oh yes, of course. Would you mind coming to Avenue 8000 first? Her daughter, Alison, would like to drive out with you."

"We're on our way." I turned to Claire. "Elizabeth Reynolds's daughter wants a lift. Didn't Cybella also stay at Shadow Hills?"

"It seems we have turned over another rock." Excitement shone in her eyes.

"If we keep on, we could have an avalanche."

"Allow yourself the thrill of the hunt, Miss Hill." She almost beamed.

The Reynoldses' building was on Eighty-fifth and Park. A modern tower of black tinted glass, its circular drive was more reminiscent of Century City than Manhattan. A greening bronze statue of a woman the size of a midget stood in the curve of the drive. Windswept and homeless, she looked like she needed a tin cup in her hand. She did have perky little breasts but they seem to have been applied by a plastic surgeon after the sculptor had given up and gone home.

Boulton stayed with the car. The lobby was done in black granite and black leather furniture. It had all the warmth of a savings and loan. The reception desk was a massive curve of black stone with a row of built-in monitors that flickered a deathly blue-gray. A sign on the counter warned: ALL VIS-ITORS MUST BE ANNOUNCED. A man, wearing a brown uniform with the panache of an SS sergeant, sat behind this barricade.

"Claire Conrad to see Paul Quentin," I told him.

"Just a minute, please." He announced her name into a

speaker, then said, "You may go up. The penthouse elevator is to your right."

We were swept skyward in an elevator designed to make the passenger feel like cheap jewelry in an expensive box. We stepped into the foyer of the Reynoldses' penthouse. The walls were lined in a burgundy and black striped fabric. A chair, too old and too expensive to sit in, was displayed under a gilt-framed painting of ballet dancers by Degas. For a moment I forgot where I was. That's the power of art and the power of the money that owns the art.

"It's the best of his ballet series." A man, about my age, sauntered toward us. He extended his hand. "I'm Paul Quentin, Mr. Reynolds's assistant." His straight ash-blond hair was trimmed short. The blue eyes were unassuming, even slightly apologetic. So was his charming smile. He wore his expensive sports jacket and jeans with a confident ease.

We exchanged greetings and entered the living room. A vast expanse of limestone floor was scattered with the silkiest Oriental rugs. Neoclassical columns were placed strategically around the enormous room but they didn't appear to be holding anything up. Fat black velvet sofas heavy with gold fringe were grouped into conversation areas. A Bonnard and a Renoir shimmered and fought for space on the walls with the slashing boldness of contemporary art. Claire peered at a large painting of wavy grotesque people, their huge mouths wide open.

"This is a Beirborn, isn't it?" she asked.

"One of his best," Paul proclaimed.

"You know he was an obese man with a slight palsy. Alas, in his case, art didn't triumph over affliction."

"Contemporary art is an acquired taste," Quentin replied coolly, then flashed another charming smile.

He had the kind of easy smile women adored, the kind

of smile they could interpret any way they pleased. And if the crooked slide of his lips made them feel uneasy, they could always change it with kisses. I know, I'm one of those women who has tried to change a man with kisses. Why do we think we have such power? Avoiding the smile, I decided to take a look out the window. We were so high up that the cabs were as small as slices of Kraft cheese. People shouldn't live this high in the air. It makes them feel too close to the angels and not close enough to their fellowman.

"Please, sit down," Quentin offered.

We settled into the black chairs. It was like sitting in the velvet lap of a plump widow.

"Alison will be out in moment." He crossed his legs and leaned back in his chair. I was waiting for *Town and Country* to rush in and take his picture.

"I hope that Mrs. Reynolds's request to see you doesn't seem odd. She was concerned that at this delicate time there should be no publicity . . . any unnecessary focusing on . . . the situation. Well . . . you can understand."

"Situation?" Claire repeated.

"The tragic death . . . suicide."

"Oh, *that* situation. Mrs. Reynolds is allowed to have visitors?" she asked.

"Yes. She's always been emotionally fragile. Shadow Hills has become like a retreat for her. I must say, after you left your message, I did some research and found that you're highly respected. Mrs. Reynolds thought it best to talk with you herself. If you were just any private detective she wouldn't be seeing you."

"I'm flattered. And where is Mr. Reynolds?"

"He's staying at his club. The Horizon Club," he added, with the same pompous inflection he used for the Degas and the Beirborn.

"I had dinner there with Graham Sitwell," Claire said.

"I believe they allow women to dine on certain evenings." He smiled, but there was disdain in his voice.

Claire peered at me with a wicked glint in her eye. "Did you say something, Miss Hill?"

"No."

"I could've sworn I heard you say something about men and women."

"No." I was working on my discretion.

"Mr. Reynolds needs to be alone right now," Quentin explained. "Her suicide was very difficult for him. I thought it best he shouldn't be disturbed. I'm sure you can understand. Of course, it's an awkward situation for the entire family."

Without mentioning her name, Quentin talked softly, as if Cybella were lying in her coffin right next to him. *She* was the situation. Maybe that's what all mistresses become, a situation to be dealt with.

A young woman with long auburn hair curling around her small delicate face came into the room. She wore a gray sweater and matching slacks. "Claire Conrad? I'm Alison Reynolds." She extended her hand.

"How do you do? This is my assistant, Maggie Hill," Claire said.

Alison gave me a firm handshake. Her manner was straightforward, hazel eyes steady and bright, but it was her left hand that got my attention. A diamond engagement ring, as big as the one the hustler had tried to sell me yesterday morning, flashed on her finger. The only difference was that this ring was real; and it didn't cost any twenty bucks.

"I'll come right to the point. I tried to talk Mother out of seeing you. She's not well and I don't want her upset," she said to Claire. "I know about Cybella." The name was finally spoken. None of the paintings fell off the walls. "What is it about her suicide you want to know?"

"May I speak freely in front of Mr. Quentin?" Claire asked.

"Of course." Alison sat on the arm of his chair and put her hand in his. His fingers stroked the diamond. So the ring was Quentin's. One of us was making the wrong salary.

"Miss Hill, show them the photographs."

I displayed the pictures. They both decided that they recognized Sarah but not Jackie.

Without going into detail, Claire gave a general description of Jackie's visit and murder. Paul listened with his lips slightly parted, as if he were trying to find the proper moment to offer us one of his smiles. Alison's pointed chin jutted forward. Her eyes watched Claire with all the anxious intensity of a student being quizzed for an exam by her professor. When Claire finished, it was Quentin who spoke first.

"What does the death of this Jackie have to do with the Reynolds family or Cybella?"

"That's what I would like to find out. It's possible that Cybella knew why Sarah Grange was being blackmailed. That knowledge might have led to her being murdered. And Jackie might have had the same knowledge—which also might've led to her death."

"Cybella murdered?" Alison looked at Quentin.

"Why don't you talk to Sarah?" he asked Claire.

"How well do you both know her?" Claire asked.

"We don't know her, I mean, personally," Alison said.

"When do you think I could speak with your father?"

"That's impossible right now." There was a protective tone in her voice. "My father is grieving. He loved Cybella deeply." She spoke without rancor. "Paul, would you call down and have my car brought around?"

"That won't be necessary. My driver is waiting for us," Claire said.

"It's no problem. Our Greenwich home is near the sanitarium. I'm used to the drive."

Claire became agitated. The thought of driving in a car other than her own Bentley, or a leased one, put her in a state of anxiety. I know, having driven her in my Honda. "You don't drive a Bentley by any chance, do you?" I asked.

"A Range Rover."

"Miss Conrad can only ride in a Bentley," I explained, trying not to sound like a lunatic.

They stared at her as if she'd just stepped off another planet. "How nice for you," Quentin mumbled.

"I'll just get my coat and purse." Alison hurried out of the room.

"Well, shall we go? I'm looking forward to a day in the country." Oblivious to her own peculiarities, Claire tapped her stick on the limestone floor, then strode into the foyer ready to ride to the hounds, or chase a fox, or go to the devil, or whatever it is they do in Connecticut.

The Degas had so commanded my attention that I hadn't noticed the rest of the foyer. A wall next to the elevator was painted burgundy and held an arrangement of black-and-white photographs. There were pictures of a Victorian brass pull on a weathered door, a black lantern burdened with years of paint, the wheel of a hansom cab, and the curve of a deco stairwell. The bits and pieces of the city were drenched in the glamorous lighting usually saved for beautiful women.

"Alison did those. She's rather good, isn't she?" Paul observed. "Sheridan built her a dark room. I think that's where she's most happy."

I realized that Alison's vision of the city was how one should view it—in a blink of the eye, in a snap of the lens. Out of the camera's range a drunk might be pissing on one of the steps of the deco stairwell but it didn't matter. The gliding curve of the wrought-iron railing endured.

"New York should only be observed in fragments. Otherwise it can be overwhelming," Paul explained.

"It's the same with solving a murder," Claire replied.

He put his hands in his pocket and jingled some change. Alison came into the foyer, a camel's-hair jacket thrown over her shoulders, carrying a canvas tote bag filled with a camera and attachments.

"We're discussing your work," Claire informed her. "You're quite talented."

"Thank you." She spoke too quickly, dismissing the compliment.

"You really are," I said.

"It's just a hobby." She turned to Paul. "I've decided to stay at the house tonight and take the afternoon train in. I have a fitting at Bergdorf's at two tomorrow afternoon." She blushed. "Modern Bride." She tilted her face up to his and kissed him. He gave her another wonderful, self-deprecating smile. It was as if he knew he was worth the girl and her money but, God, he just couldn't believe his good luck. As the elevator doors closed, he was still jingling his change and smiling.

Thirteen

In less than two hours the Bentley was turboing quietly down a narrow country road. Expensive homes squatted like monuments behind rows of piled rocks. These houses shared a kind of colonial nobility—as if they'd all been designed with the *Mayflower*, the American Revolution, the Constitution of the United States of America, and the Federal Reserve Bank in mind.

I sat in the front seat. Alison was in the back with Claire. When we left the city Alison had begun chatting nervously about her love of photography, which she persisted in calling a hobby, and her upcoming wedding. Then her voice had turned somber and she had said: "I was obsessed with Cybella when I was about twelve years old."

"You knew she was your father's mistress at that age?" I'd asked.

"I think I've always known. When parents fight they forget their children are listening. Besides, Mother would talk to me about her. She had to talk to someone. I'd sneak off to the library, look at old copies of *Vogue* and *Bonton*, study Cybella's pictures. I wanted to see what my father saw in her, but I discovered something I wasn't looking for."

"And what was that?" Claire had asked.

"Instead of understanding Cybella or my father, I began to understand photography. There was something mysterious happening between Cybella and the camera, something creative." She paused, brushing some unruly strands of hair back from her face. The diamond ring gleamed.

"Mother would've been furious if she ever found out." Then she had looked nervously at Claire. "You won't tell her?"

"Tell her what? That when studying Cybella's photographs for some clue to your parents' unhappiness, you discovered the unexpected—the artist in yourself? Your mother should already know that about you."

"I mean that I was sneaking off to look at Cybella's pictures in the library. It would hurt her. She'd feel betrayed," she had said.

Now we drove in silence, I stared at the houses. The sun danced in and out of the trees, scattering its light on the road and the hood of the car. I turned in my seat. Alison's fingers played with her ring.

"That's some diamond," I said.

She smiled. "It's kind of embarrassing."

"Only if you think the guy who gave it to you is embarrassing."

Instead of defending Paul Quentin, she laughed. I liked that.

"Lemmings," Claire muttered. "Laughing all the way to the altar."

"Claire doesn't share the dark humor women have about men," I said.

"Nor do men," Boulton said under his breath.

"I want my marriage to work more than anything," Alison said simply.

I wanted to ask her, Why? At what cost? But I was thirty-five and divorced. She was young and beginning her life.

There was no cost, only Paul Quentin's easy ingratiating smile. Boulton swerved the car. A deer lay dead in the road. Its long graceful legs crumpled under its body. Its dark melancholy eyes stared straight up into the spring sky. I put on my sunglasses.

"They're dumb animals. They run right out of the woods into the cars," Alison said. "There's the sanitarium. Turn right."

A modest wood sign declared we had entered Shadow Hills. The car's tires crunched the gravel as it followed the driveway to an old portly home covered in layers of white paint so thick it looked like icing. Beyond the home, newer structures and cottages were scattered over the vast grounds. These buildings were perfectly square and made out of wood as gray as a bureaucrat's imagination.

Two women jogged past me as I got out of the car. Their bodies were lean and aerobicized but their faces were gaunt with tension and their eyes nervous with memory.

Boulton stayed with the Bentley. The three of us walked up the steps of a sweeping verandah. Once, corseted and bustled ladies had sat stiffly in wicker chairs along this porch waiting for their husbands to come up from the city. Now emaciated women, mouths drawn tight across their bloodless faces, sat on plastic chairs. They no longer needed corsets to force their bodies into a shape they were never meant to be.

"You've come a long way, baby," I said.

"You're not going to give a speech are you, Miss Hill?"

"I'll try to restrain myself."

"Some women have empty lives," Alison stated earnestly. The hall of the sanitarium had a frayed majesty. Mahogany walls were graced with intricate moldings. Two large stained-glass windows, faded with dust, mirrored their pallid colors on the brittle parquet floor. Gray industrial runners laced across the floor like footpaths to the modern dysfunctional world. Near the stout mahogany staircase a woman, stiff as her starched white uniform, sat behind a metal desk. Attendants, nurses, and doctors walked with brisk purpose through the hall.

"Hi, Jane," Alison greeted the nurse.

"She's on the patio, dear."

The nurse turned to a young man sporting a ponytail and an array of fresh pimples. "Roger, take Alison and her guests out to Mrs. Reynolds."

We followed Roger out of the hall into a glassed-in garden room. The room should have been filled with lush indoor palms, mysterious velvety flowers, and ladies and gentlemen lingering on chaise lounges. But there was only a starved teenaged girl with long blond hair, sitting alone at a cardboard table. She stared at a glass of thick pink liquid. Her body was as flat as an eight-year-old's. She had managed to stop the curve of breast, of hip, of stomach. She had stopped herself from becoming a woman.

"Drink all of that down," Roger reminded her cheerfully.

She made a face at him and played with the straw. Nearby a man in a blue blazer with a gold crest on the breast pocket paced back and forth.

"You're supposed to be in group, Mr. Collins," Roger scolded warmly.

"What? Oh, yes, yes," the man said, as if he were too important to be interrupted.

We stepped out onto a flagstone balcony. A woman wrapped in a mink coat sat alone. Graying auburn hair was twisted into a messy knot. The hem of her flannel nightgown was frayed and dirty. With bitter watery eyes she surveyed the people on the grounds below her: attendants hurrying along the footpaths, patients sitting, running, wandering. Alison rushed to her. Roger, his finger feeling for a new pimple, retreated.

Embracing her daughter, Elizabeth Reynolds burst into tears.

"It's all right, Mother. It's all right." Alison stroked her hair, her cheek, her shoulder. "It's all right. Please don't cry."

The tears didn't stop. She buried her face into the curve of Alison's neck and sobbed with abandon. Claire watched her intently, then abruptly looked away over the grounds.

"Mother, Claire Conrad is here. You wanted to speak to her, remember?"

Slowly the weeping subsided and Elizabeth separated herself from Alison. Spite had carved deep lines around her mouth. Betrayal glistened in her eyes. "Get some chairs, Alison. There are never any chairs for guests. I pay a lot of money for the privilege of being depressed. You'd think they could at least have chairs."

As I helped Alison drag over some plastic ones, I had the repellent feeling that there was nothing left of Elizabeth Reynolds except decay. I could almost smell it. Her easy tears were like pouring water on rotting wood. When we sat down, she pointed toward two women who had stopped jogging and were now leaning against a tree talking. They acted as if they were at a spa resort.

"They have children. What is happening to their children while they run and talk about themselves? Where are their children?" she demanded accusingly. "I should've divorced Sheridan years ago but I wanted to make him suffer." Her voice was laced with resentment. A new set of tears formed as she looked at her daughter. "Instead, I made you suffer." The tears reappeared, but they weren't for Alison.

"Please, don't do this to yourself. I'm having the final

fitting on my dress tomorrow." Alison reached for her hand. Her mother's diamond ring was not quite as big as her own.

"Don't let them leave the hem too long. Brides always wear their gowns dragging on the ground, as if they don't want to admit they have feet."

"You wished to see me, Mrs. Reynolds?" Claire reminded her.

"Yes, I did." She didn't bother to dry her tears. Like tiny medals, they were to be displayed proudly. "Alison, be a darling and leave us alone for a moment."

"I'm not a child, Mother. Why can't we talk openly?"

"Alison, please, do as I say."

"Yes, Mother." Alison obediently left.

"You have a lovely daughter," Claire said.

"She is, isn't she?"

"She's very creative," I offered.

"That's because she was left alone so much of her life. If only I had spent more time with her," Mrs. Reynolds said, as if creativity could be remedied by a mother's attention. She fixed her watery eyes on Claire.

"I'll get right to the point. Paul Quentin called me after you left our penthouse and told me the reason you're looking into Cybella's death."

"I was under the impression that Mr. Quentin worked for your husband. Was I mistaken?" Claire asked.

"He does not work for me. But Paul understands what I expect in a son-in-law. There is no way I can prevent your investigation?"

"No."

"Then you force me to do something I detest."

"What is that?"

"Tell the truth. And I am only telling it to you because you'll eventually dig up our dirty little secret. I don't want Alison hurt. Promise me that she'll never know."

"If there's no professional reason to tell her, then I won't. That's all I can promise." Claire stretched out her long legs. Her finger tapped on the head of her walking stick. Elizabeth Reynolds scrutinized her.

"I'm waiting, Mrs. Reynolds," Claire said in a bored voice.

"Waiting? You don't know what waiting is. I do. Waiting for Sheridan day after day, year after year." She licked her lips as if she could taste her own venom, then blurted, "Sarah Grange is my husband's daughter. Alison's half sister. He got Cybella pregnant a year after Alison was born. How could he do such a thing?" she demanded, as if it had all happened yesterday instead of twenty years ago. A new set of tears formed. After they subsided, she said:

"Do you know what my psychiatrist wants me to do? Give up my tears." Her small hand curled into a fist. "They're all I have left."

"I'm not interested in your tears, Mrs. Reynolds." Claire stood and leaned against the balustrade. "Self-pity bores me."

"How dare you!"

"Are you the reason Cybella gave up her child?"

For the first time Elizabeth Reynolds smiled, displaying small yellowed teeth. "I threatened to divorce Sheridan if he didn't make Cybella get rid of her baby."

"I can't believe that was the only time you threatened to divorce him," Claire observed.

"It was the only time I meant it. And he knew it. There is one thing Sheridan loves more than Cybella. My money. It's a curse to be born into family wealth. I've learned that I feel insecure because I've done nothing to earn all my money."

"In other words, you're so wealthy you're worthless," I said.

"That's not exactly the way my doctor put it."

"Why was it so important that Cybella give up her child?" Claire asked.

"I wasn't going to have my Alison living in the shadow of Sarah Grange as I've lived in the shadow of Cybella."

"Don't you think it would be better if you told Alison?" I asked.

"So she could find out that her father thought so little of her that he had another daughter with his whore? I'm not surprised Sarah is involved in something sordid. Trash is trash."

"And this is what you wanted to tell me?"

"There is something else. A little over a year ago Cybella and I were here at the same time. Most men put only one woman into a sanitarium, my husband has driven two into seclusion and depression." Self-pity pulled the corners of her lips down. "One night she came to my cabin wanting absolution. They're big on forgiveness in this place. Instead, I told her what I knew would destroy her, that it was I who had determined the rules of her love affair. I explained to her that she had not given her daughter up for the love of her man or even her so-called career, but that she had given her up because I had demanded it. That's why she eventually killed herself."

"Has Sarah Grange ever contacted you or your husband?" Claire asked.

"No. Don't you think that's odd? I mean with all my money. She must want something." The watery eyes narrowed. Claire stood directly in front of her.

"Why are you really in here, Mrs. Reynolds?"

"Because all of us in Shadow Hills defy the American dream. We can't be fixed. There are no solutions for us. That young girl, who can eat whenever and whatever she wants at the most expensive restaurants, is going to die of starvation. Those women and men running around that track as if they were preparing for the Olympics will never be able to run fast enough. And I cannot be depressed enough." Tears lined her face.

Claire placed one hand on the arm of Elizabeth Reynolds's chair and leaned in, close to her face. "You avoided answering my question. Why so many tears?"

"I thought my tears bored you."

"They do. But their source is beginning to intrigue me."

"I'm through talking with you. Get out! Get out!" Elizabeth Reynolds pulled the collar of her coat up around her face. "I want my daughter. Where is my daughter?"

"Come along, Miss Hill."

We left her sobbing. A little more wood rotted.

We walked back through the garden room. The starved young girl was gone. The glass, still full of pink liquid, remained on the table. The straw was bent and twisted.

We stepped out onto the porch. Boulton leaned against the Bentley. Alison peered through her camera at an empty rocking chair. Her auburn hair, the color of a brownish red autumn leaf, glistened in the sun. She looked up from the camera and smiled.

"The light is so beautiful here. Are you finished?"

"Yes," I said. "Your mother wants you."

Holding her camera in her hands, she rested her arms on the back of the chair. "I think now that Cybella is finally out of her life, Mother doesn't know what to do, who to hate. All she can do is cry. I thought it would be different."

"In what way?" Claire asked.

"I don't know. When I heard about her death, I felt a kind of loss, but I also felt an enormous relief. I thought Mother would finally be free, but she's not. Well, I better go to her."

"Would you like us to wait for you? Drive you to your house?" Claire asked.

"I can walk. It's just through the woods. Thank you."
Alison tilted her head, studying me, then brought the camera
up to her eyes. "Don't move, Maggie." It buzzed like a me-
chanical insect. The flash smeared a bright light across my
vision. I smiled. Always too late.

Fourteen

"I'm feeling peckish," Claire announced in the Bentley.

"Did you notice, madam, that there were no walls around the sanitarium?" Boulton guided the car down the winding road. "I wonder what keeps the patients from wandering away?"

"Their need to get better," I said.

Claire grimaced. "And if they have no need to get better, Miss Hill?"

"You mean like Elizabeth Reynolds?"

"Can the patients wander off and then wander back whenever they wish? You know, Boulton, our Sarah Grange is the daughter of Sheridan Reynolds."

"Really, madam."

"I always thought a dead Frenchman was a convenient excuse."

"I've used it many times myself, madam. What was your impression of Alison Reynolds?"

"She's in secret collaboration with her mother. Like many mothers and daughters, they're protecting one another."

"From what?" he asked.

I peered out the window. *No, Maggie, your father's not*

going to die. Don't ever use that word. I'll take care of you,
Mother. You'll never be alone. Never.

"They're protecting each other from the truth," I said.

We had lunch in a quaint old inn that was really brand-new
but decorated to look old by a New York designer. The
menu proudly displayed a spa cuisine. Heart-shaped sym-
bols heralded the entrées that were guaranteed by the chief
not to kill you. Our waiter explained that he was not our
waiter but our server, and that his name was Gerald. This
dining experience left Claire with the belief that there was
no hope for humanity. On the trip back to the city she fell
into a gloomy silence sporadically broken by sudden excla-
mations of: "Spa cuisine?! Server? Gerald!"

I called Gerta to see if there were any messages. There was
one. Nora Brown and Sarah Grange would be unable to
meet with Claire Conrad at five o'clock.

"Still trying to get their story together," I said to her.

"I believe the expression is stonewalling. Take us to the
Horizon Club, Boulton. I think it's time we visit the grieving
Mr. Reynolds."

We hit the city at about five o'clock and crawled our way
toward midtown. Boulton stopped the car in front of an
aged nondescript brownstone. A small, highly polished brass
sign discreetly stated that this was the residence of the Horizon Club.

"Bring the photographs of Sarah Grange and Jackie with
you, Miss Hill."

Boulton helped Claire out of the car. I managed it on
my own.

She and I entered through a heavy oak door into the
dried-out dreams of rich old men. An ancient plank floor
creaked under our feet. The reception room was dimly lit
by brass lanterns. Next to the door a black porter, wearing

a gray uniform, sat in a chair designed with all the daring of a Presbyterian pew. He immediately stood when he saw us.

"May I help you?" There was a soft southern flow to his words.

"Claire Conrad to see Mr. Sheridan Reynolds."

"I'm sorry, ma'am. He left instructions that he was not to be disturbed," he said, moving with us like a sheepdog circling two strays.

"This is an emergency." She took a card from her pocket and the photographs from me. "Give this to Mr. Reynolds. I'm sure he'll see me."

"I'm sorry, ma'am, but you can't be in this club unescorted." His dark eyes were undecipherable. It was a learned look. Nobody could ever question his expression.

"But I do have an escort." She inclined her head toward me. "Miss Hill."

I had to restrain myself from making certain adjustments like baseball players do.

"I meant you cannot be here unless you are escorted by a member."

"I'm not in a very good mood. I was just forced to eat spa cuisine, an oxymoron that consists of fava beans, cilantro, and fried sage leaves. You have a public room, take us there and order me a brandy."

"Follow me, please," he said stiffly.

He ushered us down a dark oak-lined hall. The smell and the burnt-brown color of the walls made me feel like I was inside my grandfather's pipe. The porter left us in a large room with a great stone fireplace. Oriental rugs were carelessly scattered on the oak planks like towels on a locker-room floor. Portraits of men dating from Revolutionary times to the present filled the walls. Men in white powdered wigs, white jackets, and white stockings. Men in long beards and long dark jackets. Men with narrow mustaches in narrow tweed jackets. Gray-haired men in paisley ties and gray business suits.

Men.

A live one sat in a brown leather chair examining us, a look of sad resignation on his aged pink face. I smiled at him. He blinked as if trying to make the vision disappear.

"Fine day, isn't it?" I said in my most hearty voice.

In response he stared down at his hands.

"Don't try, Miss Hill, it's embarrassing." Claire stood by the fireplace.

"I can't help myself." I sat on the sofa. We waited.

The man in the leather chair got up and walked stiff-jointed from the room. He creaked like an old boat tied up to a dock. The smell of cold ashes drifted from the fireplace. A clock on the mantel ticked ploddingly. Claire poked her walking stick at the ashes. She looked like she belonged in this place.

"What do you think Reynolds's connection is?" I asked.

"So far, only that he was Cybella's lover and Sarah's father."

"*And* Alison's father," I said, thinking of the young woman with the camera in her hands, excitement and creativity shining in her eyes. And a big heavy diamond on her finger.

We fell silent. The clock ticked. The porter came in with her brandy and informed us that Mr. Reynolds would be down shortly.

It was a toss-up as to whether Peep Thrills or the Horizon Club depressed me more. Peep Thrills offered only one view of women: the object of the male sexual fantasy. But the Horizon Club was devoid of any image of women. We did not exist within these oak-lined halls.

"We don't exist," I said, breaking the silence.

"Is that an existential observation?" she asked.

"In this place. It's as if women never existed."

"Refreshing, isn't it?"

"You are so reactionary."

"I see nothing wrong with the sexes uncoupling for a few moments and retreating to their prospective camps."

"But one camp has more power than the other."

"Which one?"

"You know damn well there is no equality."

Restraining a smile she sipped her brandy.

"Speaking of no equality, why do you think Alison is marrying Paul Quentin?" I asked.

"Why shouldn't she? She has to go off the cliff and marry somebody."

"At her age women mistake great sex for great love. Maybe that's it."

She placed her glass on the mantel. "That reminds me, Miss Hill. What does your capacity for sex have to do with my capacity for ratiocination?"

"I beg your pardon?"

"Most everyone, Miss Hill, has had sex. Only writers and teenagers find it an astonishing experience. But not everyone has solved a murder." She jabbed her walking stick at the ashes. "Watson would roll over in his grave if he read what you've written."

"The reason I wrote about going to bed with my ex-husband was to explain my emotional state when I met you. Do you remember when you asked me to write about you?"

"I rue the day."

"You told me how men write boldly and bravely about one another, but women crawl off by themselves and write these desperate, personal diaries. Well, there are two of us now, and you would help if you told me more about yourself, such as what happened to you when you saw that woman at the Duke Hotel."

"The art of detection is to allow for the discovery. I assume it's the same for writing."

"You enjoy being impossible, don't you?"

"It's the fava beans," she said contritely.

"Mrs. Conrad?" A man stood in the doorway, holding the manila envelope in his hand. He was tall and trim and wore an expensive gray suit. He was the same man smiling with Cybella in the photograph.

"*Miss* Conrad better describes my philosophy of life. This is my assistant, Maggie Hill."

He gave me a quick nod. "I'm Sheridan Reynolds." His wavy gray hair was just long enough to brush over the collar of his blue striped shirt, giving him the look of a careful wealthy rebel. On a better day he was the kind of man that women would like to be seen with. But right now he looked as if he were just barely holding it all together. His eyes, the color of razor blades, were weighted with dark circles. The downward corners of his mouth turned his wide handsome face grim. He quickly scanned the room, making sure there were no other men hiding in the deep leather chairs.

"Just who are you?" he demanded, approaching Claire.

"You haven't heard of me?" His ignorance seemed more irritating than offensive.

"No, and I'm a little perplexed by these photographs." He tapped a well-manicured finger on the manila envelope.

"The only redeeming quality of pornography is its absolute clarity. What is there to perplex you?"

"Your reason for wanting me to see these pictures."

"I thought you might recognize one or both of the women."

"Well, I don't. The porter will show you out." He threw

the envelope on the coffee table and headed toward the door.

"I'm surprised you didn't recognize Sarah Grange," Claire said.

That stopped him.

"And by the way," she continued, "I visited with Alison and your wife at Shadow Hills this morning."

"You did what?"

"I guess Paul Quentin didn't tell you." She leaned against the mantel. Her hand rested on her walking stick. The hard intelligent eyes never left his.

"What was your purpose in seeing my wife and daughter?" he asked, reluctantly sitting down across from me.

"First tell me about the photographs."

He decided to smile. It was a little tired and forced, but it had the same self-deprecating charm as Quentin's. "I recognize Sarah, but I have no idea why she's posing like that. Was the picture taken some time ago?"

"That's what people would like us to believe. Did you recognize the other woman?" Claire asked.

"I've never seen her."

"And the dress?"

"Dress? I didn't notice."

She handed him the picture of Jackie. He studied it, then carefully returned it in the envelope and placed that on the table. His hand rested on the envelope. He patted it the way you might stroke the lid of a coffin in farewell to a loved one. "It's difficult to tell but the dress looks similar to a gown I bought for . . . someone."

"Cybella?"

"Yes." His voice cracked.

"When did you purchase the gown?"

"I don't know. Six months ago. It was the last thing I bought for her before she . . . she died." He rubbed his face with his hand. "What's this all about?"

"Why did Cybella commit suicide?"

He leaned back in his chair. "I'll be very honest with you. I have managed in my lifetime to make the two women I love very unhappy. I'm the reason my wife is back in Shadow Hills, and my mistress committed suicide."

He looked too comfortable in his chair, too comfortable being the reason. I stood up and moved restlessly around the sofa. He watched me. "Have you ever been in love?" he asked.

I was taken aback by the question. "Of course." My voice sounded like a parrot's, repeating words it didn't understand.

"Of course." He echoed the hollowness of my voice. "I loved Cybella, with all my heart. But I didn't love her with my guts. I didn't love her with commitment."

"And yet you were with her for a very long time," Claire observed.

"Was I really? I never left my wife." His eyes clouded with memory and the lines around his mouth deepened. "In the beginning, when we were young, that didn't matter. Cybella didn't want marriage. I would fly to Paris, to Rome to be with her. It was perfect. God, she was so beautiful then." Again he rubbed his face with his hand as if trying to force himself back into the present. "The day before Cybella jumped, she told me she felt like an outsider looking in on her daughter's life, looking in on my life. She felt that freedom was just another word for isolation." He closed his eyes for a moment, then opened them.

"The next day I got a call from the doorman at Bedford Place telling me to hurry over. That a terrible accident had happened."

"Accident?"

"He wasn't going to use the word *suicide*, was he? Now why are you bothering my wife and daughter?"

"Why didn't Cybella tell Sarah Grange that you're her father?"

He stiffened. "Because I'm not. We had an argument, she hooked up with some French skier . . ."

"Your wife told us, Mr. Reynolds."

"I see." He studied his manicured hands. He didn't look at us when he spoke. "Cybella was proud. She wanted Sarah to succeed on her own. And she has."

"Why haven't you told her?"

"Elizabeth can be irrational, cause scenes. I see no reason to upset my wife."

"How do you convince a woman to give up her child?" I asked him.

He looked up from his hands, his troubled gaze came to rest on me. "Cybella was in her thirties when she got pregnant," he said, as if he had nothing to do with it. "Her modeling career was over. The phone had stopped ringing. She was no longer Cybella, she was just a pregnant mistress. She went away to France, I thought to get rid of the baby, but she didn't." He paused. The razor gray eyes moved from me to the ashes in the fireplace.

"I have never generated a dime on my own. I'd grown accustomed to certain things." An elegant shrug. "When she came back with the baby, I had to leave her. Now Cybella was an ex-mistress with a child. She needed money, so she gave the baby to her parents and tried acting. The still camera loved her, the moving camera didn't. It made her look awkward and stiff. Her voice sounded empty. She was devastated. She went to Europe and tried acting there and failed. Five, six years later she came back. I put her up in Bedford Place."

"For old time's sake," I said.

"You might say that. Her parents didn't want her to see Sarah; they had never liked Cybella's way of life. And Cybella couldn't face the child. She became my mistress again, accompanying me certain places, always there waiting for me."

"Why? Because you could offer her Bedford Place? Clothes? Money?" I asked.

"No, because I still made her feel beautiful." He stood.

"So beautiful she killed herself," Claire said.

"I've answered your questions."

"Just one more, Mr. Reynolds. Why are you staying at your club and not at your home?"

"I thought it inappropriate to grieve for my mistress in front of my daughter. I'll get the porter to show you out." He left us. The clock ticked. Claire poked the ashes.

"A father's love, nothing like it," I finally said.

Fifteen

That night Gerta cooked us a sumptuous dinner. Claire went to bed early. There were no phone calls. Nobody was murdered. Trying not to forget why Watson had sat down to write, I did a little work myself, then went to bed.

I dreamed I was standing in front of my mother's closet. It was filled with red evening gowns and, of course, a nun. Her heavy black skirts and drifting dark veils tangled around me like long dark hair. My mother prayed for my return.

The next day Claire took to her Queen Anne. She sat in meditative silence. I asked her if she wanted me to do anything but she just shook her head. I knew she was thinking, sifting through the information we had gathered so far. I tried some sifting on my own and decided everyone we had talked to was the murderer—or maybe not. We were just sitting down to lunch when the phone rang. I got up from the table and answered it. A muffled woman's voice told me to get over to the Duke immediately. I told Claire.

"Did you recognize the voice?"

"Could be Linda Hansen."

She stared despondently at her plate of untouched shrimp risotto. "Bring the car around, Boulton."

Violet waited in her chair. The young drunk had slept it off and was long gone. The hotel clerk watched a talk show on a portable TV. Today he had on a hoodless green sweatshirt. Long, thin strands of white hair tried to protect a tender pink scalp. The rabbity eyes followed us. We made our way down the dim corridor and up the stairs. Claire walked by the closed door of the whimpering woman as if she didn't exist, as if only Boulton and I knew she was in there.

Jackie's door stood slightly open. When Boulton pushed, it swung wide. The gray light from the window sifted down onto the bed and the crushed flowers. Goldie was on the floor, his head propped up against the side of the bed. His chin rested on his chest. One leg was bent, the other extended. Arms flopped at his side, palms facing up. A dark stain spread over his belly.

"This is very inconvenient," Claire said indignantly. "Close the door, Miss Hill."

"It seems to me, Goldie's the one who should be upset," I replied, closing the door.

"Turn a light on, Boulton."

They knelt beside the body. I stared at Goldie. He stared at the blood on his belly as if he were still trying to figure out how it got there.

"Knife wounds," Boulton said.

"Yes. I don't hear you breathing, Miss Hill. Breathe."

I breathed in the smell of wilted carnations and booze and death. I was better off not breathing.

She took in the room. "Something's not right, Boulton."

He looked around. "What is it? What's troubling you?" he asked.

"Something . . ." She cocked her head.

All three of us gave the room a quick look, avoiding what I thought was obviously wrong, the body on the floor.

"I can't quite grasp it. Never mind." She put on her black

gloves and carefully began to go through Goldie's pockets. She came out with a telephone number written on the back of a Peep Thrills card. "Do you recognize the number, Miss Hill?"

"*Bonton.*"

She slipped the card into her pocket.

"I think it's safe to assume that he knew who killed Jackie," Boulton said.

"Could a woman easily kill a man that size?" I asked.

"He'd been drinking and there is always the element of surprise," Claire answered.

"Men are doomed to be surprised by women," Boulton observed sadly.

"Unless of course Goldie was surprised by a man," I replied.

"I suppose we can't avoid calling the police," Claire said.

"The hotel clerk saw us come up here," Boulton said.

"Get him."

"Right." He left the room.

"Don't you ever long for a normal, happy life?" I asked forlornly.

"I have always avoided the normal, happy life, Miss Hill." She leaned on her walking stick and stared down at the corpse as if he were personally annoying her. "Goldie identified Jackie's body. The police will eventually make the connection between Jackie and me at the hotel. They're not going to like the fact that I lied about not knowing her."

"What about client privilege?" I said.

"I don't think that will impress them since my client was dead before she became my client. Just out of pique they'll probably take us in for questioning." She glared at Goldie, the bane of her existence, then looked at me as if I were next on her list of annoyances. "After we talk to the clerk I want you to leave here."

"Leave the scene of a crime? Isn't that against the law?"

"Miss Hill, this is no time to collapse into a morass of middle-class morality."

"Morass of what?! You're not leaving the scene of the crime, I am. What happens when the clerk tells the police that I was with you and Boulton?"

"I'll take care of everything. I want you to go to a pay phone and call New York Insurance. Talk to Graham Sitwell. See if he can put in a good word for me with the NYPD. I can't avoid them but maybe I can shorten the ordeal."

"What else?" I was resigned to being a fugitive.

"I want you to get Nora Brown and Sarah Grange, keep them at the Parkfaire until I get there."

The door opened. The clerk poked his head in. He blew air through his thin pink lips. "Oh my God, oh my God."

Boulton pushed him into the room.

The clerk peered at the body. "It's Goldie." He ran his hand through his hair, leaving the white strands in disarray.

"Who came up here in the last hour?" Claire asked.

"You people."

"Before we arrived. Think. Was it a woman?" she persisted. "A slender, middle-aged woman with dark short hair?"

"Yeah, but I don't know if she came up here. But you people did." He looked at us as if he were staring at three serial killers. "I'm calling the police."

"In a minute. Do you know Linda Hansen? She works at Peep Thrills."

"I seen her come in but I don't see her go out."

"Is there another way into this hotel?"

"Why are you asking me questions?"

"Answer her," Boulton said.

"The only other entrance is a door to the alley but it's kept locked."

"Show us."

"I'm calling the police."

"Show us," Boulton said, shoving him toward the door.

On the first floor under the stairs, was a door. Above it was an unlit exit sign.

"See?" He pushed on it. The door opened. Light the color of dishwater filled the alcove. "Jesus Christ, it's supposed to be locked."

Claire stepped outside, looked around the alley, then came back in. "Nora Brown came through the lobby. Someone else could have entered through this door and gone up to the room without being seen. And that someone would have to know about this door being unlocked."

"It's supposed to be locked," the clerk repeated, angrily. "I probably got people staying here that haven't paid."

"Did you and Goldie talk?" Claire kept the door slightly open so she could see the clerk's face. The light cast a dirty shadow over all of us.

"Yeah. Hello. Good-bye."

"He never talked about himself?"

"Lady, Goldie wasn't exactly introspective." But a memory flickered in the clerk's eyes.

"He did say something. What was it?" Claire prodded.

The clerk turned, trying to run down the hallway, but Boulton blocked his way.

"Hey, what's going on here?" the clerk protested. "I gotta call the police."

"Answer her," Boulton ordered.

He looked at Claire. "Goldie came in here with some video equipment. And I told him he better not leave that stuff around, that it would get ripped off. That's all."

"Miss Hill?" Claire said, looking at my purse.

I reached in, took my gun out, and pointed it at the clerk.

His eyes widened. Lips parted. His hands shot up in the air. White strands of hair fluttered.

"No, no, Miss Hill," Claire said with all the patience of a dog trainer. "Not the gun. The money. I think our friend here would like some money."

"Sorry, just a little fragmented."

I put the gun back and rummaged around for my wallet. The clerk's eyes darted nervously from Claire to Boulton to me. His hands stayed in the air. His fingers trembled. I came out with a twenty.

"Now," Claire said to him, "what was Goldie doing with the video equipment? You may put your hands down."

"Porno."

"When was this?"

"On and off."

"But you're thinking of a particular time, aren't you?"

"About four, five months ago."

"Did you see any of the people who performed in the video?"

"I see this one girl, long dark hair, big sunglasses, beautiful. I showed her up to the room."

"Did she have a garment bag with her?"

"More like a dry-cleaning bag with a red dress in it. I kept thinking she wasn't going to need it." He leered, looked nervously at me, then reached out and took my twenty.

"I'm calling the police now," he spoke carefully, backing away from Boulton. "And none of you better leave." He shook a bony finger at us.

He turned and beat it down the hall, stopped, threw his head back, and yelled toward the upper floors. "And I'm locking the back door, you bastards. You bunch of loonies!"

"Get those two silly women to the Parkfaire, Miss Hill, and don't let them out of your sight. What time is it, Boulton?"

"A little after two o'clock."

"Alison Reynolds is having her fitting at Bergdorf's," Clair continued. Find out what she knows about Sarah Grange, including Sarah's parentage. It's time to break the protective bond between mother and daughter."

There was the sound of sirens converging on the hotel.

"Quickly, Miss Hill."

I ran down the alley as if I had committed murder. I came out on the side street where trucks were lined up making their deliveries. A man with a cigar hanging out of his mouth carried a tray full of raw meat down the steps of a restaurant. Flies circled above the tray, like the dark angel's halo. I followed him into a long, narrow empty restaurant. The only light came through the front windows. The delivery man walked straight to the back. An Asian in a loud sport shirt sat at a table smoking. He waved his hand at me as if I were one of the flies following the raw meat.

"No open. No open. Tonight."

"I need to use your telephone."

"No open."

"Telephone."

He took a drag on his cigarette and stared into space. I took a five out of my purse and placed it front of him. He shrugged, took it, and told me the pay telephone was in the back. You can get anything in this town if you know how.

The phone was behind a red curtain. I made it through to Sitwell's secretaries, then his assistant, and then was put on hold. The kitchen door swung open and the guy munching on the end of his cigar, now carrying an empty tray, walked out. Before the door swung back, I glimpsed a sinewy young man. A scarf printed with the rising sun was wrapped around his forehead. He held a knife above the pile of meat. The door closed.

"Graham Sitwell speaking."

"This is Maggie Hill."

"Maggie? I thought you and Claire had already left for Los Angeles."

I told him in general what had taken place.

"Dead client? She has no business sense. I've asked her repeatedly to come on board here. She'd be set for life."

"Yes, well, I think she wants to stay based in L.A. In fact I think she wishes she were there right now. Look, can you put in a word to somebody with influence on the NYPD? Maybe the commissioner? Even the mayor?"

"Don't worry. It'll be done."

I thanked him and dialed *Bonton*. Nora Brown was not available. I left a threatening message, making sure she understood it was in her best interest to get Sarah Grange over to the hotel to see Claire Conrad. The Chablis-colored secretary informed me Nora couldn't possibly be anywhere before five. I informed her that if she and Sarah weren't at the hotel by five-fifteen, I was calling the tabloids and the cops. Then I got Gerta and told her we were expecting two visitors and I would be there as soon as possible.

I made my way out of the restaurant. I started walking, keeping an eye out for a cab. I could still hear sirens, but that was nothing special. It was the Muzak of the city. The sun was out, but that didn't seem to mean anything either. I don't trust a city where the sun comes out and you don't need to put on your dark glasses. Okay, so they've got seasons back here. But at least in Los Angeles we can tell the difference between night and day. I waved down a cab and got in. "Bergdorf Goodman."

"What?" A red knit cap was pulled down just to the top of the cabbie's bushy black eyebrows.

"Bergdorf's on Fifth near the Plaza Hotel."

He pulled out into the traffic.

"You're not from here, are you?" Liquid black eyes studied me in the rearview mirror.

Oh hell, he was going to talk to me. I leaned my head back against the seat, closed my eyes, and thought of Goldie and Jackie and carnations. The cab smelled of some kind of strange sharp herb. I rolled the window down a bit. The cool air, mixed with exhaust, rushed in over my face.

"I can tell you're not from here," the cabbie continued. "It's the way you walk."

Walk? Don't say anything, Maggie. Walk?

"New York women got this funny little walk. I think it's their short legs."

Don't speak, Maggie. New York women can take care of themselves.

"And their short arms. They all got short arms and short legs and funny hair."

"Short?" Shit. "Short? All New York women have short arms, short legs, and funny hair? All of them? Is that what you're saying?!"

"Yeah. They walk just like Mickey Mouse."

"I'm surprised you didn't say Minnie."

"Minnie who?" He craned his neck around and looked at me.

"Mouse. And watch where you're going." Oh God, why was I in this conversation?

He looked back at the street. "No, Mickey. They walk like Mickey."

"I don't want to hear how they walk." I leaned forward, holding on to the strap. "I don't want to hear if women have short arms or long arms. I don't want to hear if we look like Mickey or Minnie. I'm tired of what men think about women. I'm tired of what women think about women.

And I especially don't want to know what you think about women. I just want to go to Bergdorf's."

"I'm taking you there. Don't get so excited. I love women."

"I'm sure you do." I leaned back and closed my eyes while he explained to me why he loved women.

Sixteen

The bridal department was on the sixth floor. Three puffy
white gowns that looked like they could've made it down
the aisle without the brides hung on a rack next to a dainty
sofa. A saleslady sat behind a knockoff of a Louis Quinze
desk. Its gold-leaf corners were chipped. She searched
through a box filled with white lace garters. Brown age spots
smudged her hands. Her dulled diamond ring and wedding
band needed cleaning. I looked in the box. Tiny blue silk
rosebuds decorated the lacy garters.

I thought of all those awful coy photographs of brides
holding up the hems of their gowns to show off their legs
and garter. I hadn't worn one when I got married. Of course
when I got married I hadn't worn a bridal gown either.
Something about all that virginal white in a Las Vegas
chapel.

"Is Alison Reynolds here?" I asked.

"She's in the last fitting room through the curtains."

"Thanks."

I went through the curtains and knocked on the last door.

"Come in."

Alison stood alone, wearing a wedding gown of white brocade. Rows of baby seed pearls lined the bodice and hem. A

veil of Chantilly lace draped softly over her curly auburn hair, cascaded down her back, and trailed onto the floor. More baby seed pearls glistened like frozen teardrops in the lace. She was beautiful in a cultivated, old-fashioned kind of way—like the subject of a Sargent painting. Her eyes shone with promise. Surprised, she blushed like a bride when she saw me.

"Maggie, what are you doing here?"

"I need to ask you some questions."

"Sit down. I'm waiting for the seamstress. The hem's too long. I have to remember I have feet." She laughed.

I took her tote bag and purse off a chair and sat down, trying not to look at myself in the mirror. But I did. Yes, I looked like somebody who had just seen a dead man. Perhaps a little lipstick?

"I look a little silly," she said.

"No you don't. You look lovely."

"Why do we still wear white?" she asked. "It's such a lie and yet nobody seems to mind."

"Wear it with a wink. With a sense of irony," I suggested.

"I can't. If you think of white as a commitment, then it does have meaning. I'm going to make it mean something." She stopped, fidgeted with her veil, then turned to the mirror. "Not like my parents. What did you want to ask me? Is it about Cybella?"

"Yes."

"When you visited my mother, did she tell you that Sarah is my half sister?"

"Now I don't have to ask the question. Your mother thinks you don't know."

"It's easier for Mother to believe I don't know certain things."

"And your father?"

"For him too. It's not as if I was told not to ask questions about Cybella. I just knew I couldn't. Mother was always so fragile. I never wanted to upset her. And Father was my father. I was afraid I'd lose him if I mentioned it. I always lived with the fear that he'd leave us and go off with her." She smoothed her dress.

"Did he tell you that?"

"Mother did."

"So you're going to make a better marriage than your parents." My voice lacked confidence.

She heard it and stared defiantly at my reflection in the three-way mirror. "Yes. Isn't that what all parents want for their children? To do better than they did?"

"Do you have to marry to prove that?"

"That's the battleground, Maggie. That's the ground I have to win on." Her fingers stroked a row of baby seed pearls.

"Who told you about Sarah?" I asked.

"You have to promise me you won't tell Mother."

I decided to quote Claire. "If there's no professional reason to tell her, then I won't."

"Cybella."

"When?"

"I went to see her a couple of weeks before she died."

"Why?"

"I don't know if I can explain it. I think because I'm getting married, because my life is changing. I wanted to somehow come to terms with her."

"And meet your muse face-to-face?"

The hazel eyes questioned me. "Are you making fun of me?"

"Not at all. I've just begun to realize that I'm an assistant to my muse."

"Claire Conrad's a detective. I have to remember that. I don't have many friends, Maggie, anyone I can confide in.

It's easy to talk to you. I have to keep reminding myself that you could hurt me, my family."

"How?"

"I don't know."

I didn't want to hurt her. I wanted to leave her here. Perfect. Still untouched by her choices, by her decisions, by Paul Quentin with his self-deprecating, self-serving smile. But I didn't. I asked her another question. "What did Cybella say to you about Sarah?"

"She told me there were two things she regretted about loving my father: the hurt she had caused Sarah and the hurt she had caused me. She never mentioned Mother."

"Did Cybella strike you as depressed?"

"More confused."

"About what?"

"Sarah. She said that her own daughter made her feel uncomfortable. Cybella blamed herself. But she thought Sarah was afraid of her, afraid to reach out to her. She wondered if she might even be in some kind of trouble."

"How did it make you feel to find out you had a half sister?"

"I wasn't shocked. It was as if I already knew. And maybe I did in some vague way. As I said, my parents argued all the time, especially when I was a child. I'm sure it was in one of those arguments I heard Father had another daughter."

"Did you tell Cybella about going to the library and studying her pictures?"

"No. I couldn't."

"That would be a betrayal of your mother."

"Yes."

Before I could ask her how that was a betrayal, the door opened. A wide-hipped, heavyset woman, with pieces of white thread clinging to her black skirt, came in and knelt before Alison as if she were the Virgin Mary. Instead of praying she took a box of pins from her pocket and began to pin the hem.

"Not too long," Alison ordered.

The seamstress nodded. Glistening pins jutted between her colorless lips. Her thick legs were covered in beige knit stockings. Black shoes shaped her bunioned feet. Her nimble fingers moved expertly along the hem of the gown as if they had a happy life of their own.

Alison glanced in the mirror and quickly adjusted something that didn't need adjusting. "I have your picture with me, Maggie. It's in my bag."

"Picture?"

"The photograph I took of you yesterday. I was going to drop it by your hotel later."

"May I look at it?"

"It's in the white envelope."

I found the envelope slipped in next to her camera. I pulled out the photograph. The curve of my lips was much too arrogant and my eyes far too sad. It was a brutally honest picture.

"What is it? Timing?" I asked.

"What do you mean?"

The seamstress moved slowly around Alison. I could hear the sound of her thick legs rubbing together.

"How do you manage to capture the right expression?"

"You take a lot of pictures and hope."

"You're too good just to snap and hope."

"Have you ever been married?" she asked, changing the subject.

"Yes."

"Were you happy and excited about it?"

"Yes."

"Did you think it would last?"

"Yes."

"Are you still married?"

"No."

"Did you love him?"

"Yes."

"And now?"

"No. How long have you known Paul?"

"Ever since he came to work for my father. About three years."

"Was it love at first sight?"

"I've only experienced love at first sight through the lens of my camera."

"You mean only in your art?"

"I don't consider what I do art."

"Why are you afraid to give it value?"

"You thought you were in love and then you weren't. You can't give anything value, Maggie. It might be taken away."

The only sound was the rustle of the white wedding gown and the heavy movements of the seamstress.

"You said white was for commitment," I reminded her. "That's a value."

"It's the only value I have left." Her small, pale lips pressed together. The delicate chin thrust forward.

The seamstress got painfully to her feet. She lowered the veil over Alison's face.

We were all going to make it work, I thought. All young brides looked through a veil whether they wore one or not. Each believed *she* would be the bride who could reach back to the time when marriage meant something. When men and women knew how to love one another. When we each knew our proper place in love. They would make it work, better than their mothers had. The seamstress pinned the veil. Her fingers danced their way down the train. A simple plain wedding band shined.

"Okay?" she asked Alison.

Alison turned, her image reflected over and over in the three-way mirror as if she were not one bride but a thousand.

"Perfect." She was a shadow behind the veil.

The seamstress made some notes on a card and left. The saleswoman swept in and started to help Alison get out of the dress.

I waited outside. Alison appeared, all breathless.

"I'm meeting Paul at the Plaza for tea."

I looked at my watch. I had time before meeting Sarah and Nora at the hotel. "I could use a cup of tea," I said. But what I really wanted was to take another look at the man behind the smile.

She stared at me, unsure. "You don't like Paul, do you?"

"Why do you say that?"

"I can tell."

"He's a lucky man to have won the heart of such a talented artist."

"Maggie, I'm not an artist." She sounded like a schoolgirl saying, "I'm not pretty," when she knew she really was.

We took the escalator down. The mannequins with their bald heads and sexless eyes watched me. They knew I should have left her wearing her wedding gown, standing alone in that dressing room.

Seventeen

The Palm Court is in the lobby of the Plaza Hotel. A red floral carpet is scattered with small round tables draped in pink linen. White marble columns are surrounded by enormous potted palms. A violinist was playing music that could soothe a migraine, or cause one, depending on your taste. He dipped and swooped around the tables. Like a mortician guarding the dead, a maître d' stood at the entrance to the court. Crystal chandeliers dazzled. A line of people waited to gain access, their faces strained with feigned patience. They looked like a wealthy bread-line.

Alison walked straight up to the maître d' and announced her name.

"Right this way." He tucked some menus under his arm. We followed him to a table in the corner. A palm in a large ceramic cachepot held out its leafy arms, brushing the back of my head and neck as I sat down in a red velvet chair. Alison ordered tea for three. When he left she leaned forward with an impish look on her face. "Was your ex a good lover?"

"To me and to every woman he met."

We laughed.

"What did he do?" She brushed her unruly hair back from her face.

"He's with the LAPD. Is Paul a good lover?"

She continued smiling but something happened to her eyes. The brightness faded.

"The best," she said.

We fell silent. Okay, so it wasn't lust and passion that was driving her to marry Paul Quentin. I looked around the room. Chic women—so sharp-edged and thin you might get a paper cut if you touched them—leaned toward one another over their teacups. I knew they were confessing, minutely going over every inch of their lives. They say confession is good for the soul, but I think women never get out of that dark confessional box. They're always peering through the grille, waiting for the next priest in the form of a friend to go over it with them all again. There is no redemption for these women; there is only the hope of another lunch, another tea.

The violinist did a low dip toward a table where a man and a woman sat in habitual silence. The leaves of the palms fluttered ever so slightly, as if stirred by the music, the voices, and the clattering of china.

The waiter placed our tea on the table with all the grace of a well-trained prizefighter. I watched Alison pour with the studied skill of a well-trained debutante. I liked her. What was I doing in her life? It was no different from being in Peep Thrills or the Horizon Club. I didn't belong here either. We smiled at each other over our teacups. The violinist sawed through a waltz.

"I wish I'd met you under different circumstances, Maggie."

"Just because I work for Claire Conrad doesn't mean we can't be friends. Why are you so nervous about me? Who are you protecting?"

"No one. Why do you keep asking me so many questions?" Her eyes moved from mine; I could feel the presence of another person.

"Paul!" she said. "You remember Maggie Hill."

He moved from behind me, his smile in place, his hand extended. I took it. "Of course, how are you?" Then he took Alison's hand and kissed it. "How was the fitting?"

"The dress is so beautiful. Wait till you see me floating down the aisle into your arms," she said dramatically, her eyes fixed on him as if she were never going to let him out of her sight. He, however, was looking the room over.

"I didn't know you were going to be meeting Maggie," he said, still trying to see if he knew anybody else. "You don't mind if I call you Maggie?" He settled into a chair.

"Not at all."

"She found me at Bergdorf's." Alison poured him tea.

"Just like a good bloodhound." His smile broadened but it didn't make his blue eyes any warmer.

"I was following Claire Conrad's orders just like a good assistant. You know what that is."

He adjusted another one of his great-looking sports jackets. This one was gray and maroon checked. You didn't have to feel it to know it was cashmere.

"What was so urgent that you had to track my fiancée down at her bridal fitting?"

"She just wanted to know more about Cybella and Sarah," Alison answered.

He studied her for a moment, the way a lepidopterist might study a butterfly pinned to a piece of cardboard. "You don't have to answer her questions, Alison."

"I know." Her voice was tense.

"I thought your father made that clear."

"He's come out of his club? He's through mourning?" I asked.

"That's not funny, Maggie," Alison snapped.

There was an awkward silence. He took a bite of a watercress sandwich, swallowed, thought a moment, and said politely: "I understand Claire Conrad is L.A.-based."

I nodded.

"I was out there once."

I waited for more. But that was it. He seemed to enjoy the tension, as if it somehow gave him control over Alison. She somberly watched the violinist who was dipping and swooping around the tables. "Mother used to love to come here. It made her happy. Not much else in her life did."

"You're not her protector," I blurted.

Alison looked as if I'd slapped her. "She needs me, Maggie. She always has."

"You entered Alison's life by leaving a threatening message and now you act like her therapist. What exactly do you want from her?" Paul demanded.

I didn't have an answer.

"You don't have to put up with this," he told her. "I think I should take you home."

She stood and gathered her two bags. "I wish I'd met you earlier, Maggie." She walked out toward the lobby.

Paul grabbed some money out of his pocket. "Don't bother her again." He tossed it on the table. A couple of coins rolled around the teapot. He reached for them but I was quicker. I opened my hand and looked at a quarter and a large token with the silhouette of a naked girl stamped on it. It was the kind of token that got you into a private one-on-one booth at Peep Thrills. I looked up at him. His nice handsome jaw twitched.

"Make any excuse you have to, but put her in a cab and come back here. If you don't, you may not be walking down the aisle as soon as you think."

He turned and walked stiffly out of the place. I drank my

tea and bit into a chocolate éclair the size of a big toe. Finally, a solid clue. I could hold it in my hand. Why didn't I feel better about it? Oh, hell, at least Alison's diamond was big enough to throw back in his face. The violinist swooped up to the table playing some ditty that sounded like a cross between Leibestraum and "Stranger in Paradise." He swayed back and forth in a studied rapture. Without missing a beat, because he'd never found one, he glided to a table of tourists. Cameras hung around their necks like albatrosses, reminders of all they had seen or missed. They listened politely, nodding their heads. I poured another cup of tea and ate the rest of the éclair. Paul returned.

We stared at each other across the plates of thinly sliced sandwiches and miniature desserts. Very civilized. I leaned back in my chair. The leaves of the palm gently brushed at my hair and touched the back of my neck. It was a ghostly touch—as if the long delicate fingers of a dead woman were tapping on my shoulder.

"You know," he said, pouring himself a cup, "peep shows are Victorian in their concept."

"Look, I don't care what your hang-ups are."

"It's Victorian in nature because it compartmentalizes. The Victorians loved to put everything in its proper place. They loved little boxes, desks, and dressers with hidden drawers. They liked to tuck things away." He took a sip of tea.

"Fascinating."

"In a sense, I'm Victorian. I have to keep my sexual needs in a special area. I don't want to get involved with the women. I don't want to touch them or be touched by them. I just like to unlock the hidden drawer and there they are." He studied me, and decided a smile might help.

"What about Jackie?"

"I liked to watch Jackie among others, yes."

"And now she's dead."

"It happens to them sometime."

"You denied knowing her."

"Not an unusual response under the circumstances."

"Did you ever see her outside of Peep Thrills?"

"No." He took another sip of tea and pressed his napkin against his lips.

"I don't believe you."

The violinist swirled over. He sawed away, trying for something that sounded like "Some Enchanted Evening." Sweat beaded on the musician's upper lip and dampened his dyed black hair at the temples. Playing the violin was hard labor. Paul never took his eyes off me. The fiddle player did his dippy-do, then rushed another table.

"Many men go to peep shows. I'm not unusual, Maggie."

"Unless you're a murderer."

A woman sitting next to us swiveled her head in our direction. She munched a tiny torte. He shot her a disarming smile, then looked back at me. "Would you like to take a walk?" he asked, carefully folding his napkin.

We made our way out of the hotel and down the stairs.

I stared across at Grand Army Plaza. The tourists, the homeless, and the hustlers sat on the steps leading up to the fountain. Water tiered down into the basin, creating a white foam. I put on my sunglasses.

"I stayed in a big pink hotel when I was in Los Angeles," he said, as if my sunglasses reminded him of the visit.

We headed toward the park. Waiters gazed out of the long windows of the hotel dining room. On Central Park South the horses and drivers still waited. Horse piss mixed with the smell of car exhaust.

"Jackie thought she was being followed," I said. "Where were you Tuesday around eleven in the morning?"

"At the Reynolds residence. Alison will verify it."

"Tell me about the video," I said.

"I don't know anything about a video."

"Some men like to direct the girls in these porno videos."

"Anything is possible."

We stayed on Fifth. Paul moved with the physical ease of an athlete, his weight pitched slightly forward onto the balls of his feet, as if he were ready to make a run for it.

"Did you like to watch Sarah Grange?"

"She's not my type."

"You know, Goldie thought he knew who killed Jackie."

"Goldie?"

"The bouncer at Peep Thrills. Big guy. Hard to miss."

"Oh, yes, with the gold rings."

"He's dead. That makes two people you knew from Peep Thrills who have been murdered." I caught him between grins. His lips were a weak line.

"Next you'll be saying I killed Cybella."

"Does the Reynolds family know about your Victorian tendencies?"

"No. But Sheridan is a man who has loved another woman and lived off his wife's money. I think he'll be tolerant of my one vice."

"What about Mrs. Reynolds?"

"I think she knows what's best for her daughter."

"And you're it?"

"Alison is a woman who sees the world through a lens. I on the other hand like to see a certain part of life through a smeared Plexiglas partition. We have more in common than you think."

"How old is Alison? Twenty-one?"

"Twenty-two."

"Hardly a woman. Don't you think you're a little old for her?"

"I need somebody young. Less intimidating. Or so I

thought." He tilted his head toward mine. "She's very jealous of me—but then, jealousy runs in her family."

"Of course her money helps."

"Yes, it does. But I'll treat her very well."

"Like you treated Jackie?"

He stopped and looked at me. "Jackie was going to die sooner or later. She's safe now."

"You mean she's where she belongs. In her proper place. You never asked me how she died."

"How did she die?" The wind ruffled his hair. He quickly smoothed it.

"She was stabbed to death."

"That's a little too intimate for me. I have an appointment. Good-bye, Maggie." He extended his hand. I didn't take it.

"You think I'm going to touch you? I don't like to touch a man I think might be a murderer." My voice was coldly exact. "I don't like to touch a man that I think is marrying a young woman for her money and will probably end up destroying her life. I want to see you put in your proper place."

He reached quickly around me, pulled me to him, and pressed his open mouth against mine. Just as quickly he released me, smiled, and sauntered up Fifth.

I could feel my anger all the way down to my fingertips. I had acted like any other dumb woman who had let her guard down because she thought she was in control. I wiped the taste of Paul Quentin off my lips with the back of my hand.

I waited for the light to change and headed toward Madison.

I needed a moment to myself. I stopped and gazed at the black-and-white spectator pumps.

Eighteen

Gerta let me into the suite and told me we had visitors. Sarah Grange sat in the Queen Anne, draping her long legs over one arm of the chair. She wore a tight yellow sweater and a short skirt. Nora Brown, wearing a red suit with a lot of pockets and gold buttons, sat on the sofa balancing a crocodile handbag on her lap. She looked as shiny and as hard as a new sports car.

"You can sit in any other chair in the room except the one you're in," I informed Sarah.

She gazed up at me from under her long lashes.

"That's Claire Conrad's chair. You can't sit in it." I sat down at my desk.

"Isn't that a little childish?" she asked, not moving.

"Where is Claire Conrad?" Nora demanded. "We've been waiting for twenty minutes."

"I guess she's still with the police. Why don't you sit on the sofa?"

"Police?" Sarah's eyes widened.

"She went to the police?" Nora asked.

"No. They came to her. We were at the Duke Hotel. You remember the Duke, don't you?" I asked Sarah.

She was too busy surveying the skin on her well-manicured hands to respond. And she still hadn't moved from the Queen Anne.

"We found a dead body in Jackie's room," I continued. Nora never blinked.

"Linda?" Sarah asked carefully. Now she was scrutinizing the ends of her thick lustrous dark hair.

"No, a man named Goldie. Ever hear of him?"

"No." Her fingers stroked her neck. It was like watching a beautiful monkey absorbed with picking itself clean.

"He shot the video you were in."

"That doesn't mean I know him."

"Why'd you think it was Linda?"

"She doesn't answer the phone."

She pulled her hair back from her sculpted face, twisted it up, then let it fall. She kept doing this. She was something, all right, a party of one.

"What's Linda's number and address?"

She gave them to me. I got the machine and left a message asking her to call. Then I reached into my purse, pulled out my gun, and aimed right for Sarah's forehead.

"Get out of Claire Conrad's chair."

Nora leaped to her feet, dropping her purse on the floor. "Have you gone crazy?!"

Sarah let her hair slip from between her fingers. She stared at the gun as if it were a camera. She smiled. Another heavenly smile. I was tired of people smiling at me. I released the safety catch.

"For God's sake! That gun could go off by accident," Nora said.

"No accident," I said.

"Sarah's worth millions. Please, put it away."

Still smiling, Sarah said, "How sweet that you care so much about me, Nora."

How do people talk and smile at the same time? Maybe that's why they earn the big bucks.

Sarah swung her long legs around in one graceful bored movement and stood.

"I'm worth millions. Do you mind if I fix myself a drink?" she asked.

"Not at all," I said.

She moved to the drinks table and poured herself some bottled water. We were in the decade of sobriety but it didn't seem to be improving anybody's manners or decreasing their inclination to murder. I put on the safety catch and placed the gun in my desk drawer. Nora grabbed her purse off the floor, as if it were going to crawl away, and sat back down.

"Do you know what it's like to be beautiful and worth millions, Maggie?" Sarah asked, holding the glass of water in her hand as if it were a double martini and she were the life of the party.

"Let me take a wild guess." I leaned back in my chair and stretched my arms. "It's no fun to be worth millions. Everybody uses you. Nobody cares about you. They just love you for your beauty and not your inner self. I'm glad you got that off your chest. Feel better?"

"You don't know what it's like. You never will. A man will leave a beautiful woman quicker than he'll leave a plain woman. They like to conquer a beautiful woman, show her off for a while. But they really don't like all the attention she gets. In the long run it's a big bother to them. But if you have money, nothing is a bother. For the first time in my life, nothing is a bother."

"Not even your mother's death?" I asked, opening my desk drawer and taking out a yellow legal pad and a pen.

"Be quiet, Sarah," Nora said, brushing something off her skirt. Maybe the crocodile did a nasty in her lap. "We're here to speak with Claire Conrad." Her tone let me know she wasn't here to speak with me.

She looked at her watch, took a portable phone the size of a graham cracker out of the crocodile, and began making calls. Sarah grabbed a large leather bag from next to the Queen Anne and plopped down on the sofa. She placed the bag between her feet and began rummaging through it. She came out with a brush, a hand mirror, and some small zippered bags. She unzipped the bags and dumped their contents onto the coffee table. There was an array of makeup, vitamin pills, perfume, lotion, and a toothbrush.

"Where's your diaphragm?" I asked.

"Who needs sex?" she countered.

"I forgot. You're worth millions."

While she revised herself and Nora made important decisions on the phone, I wrote a thorough report on my meeting with Alison and Paul Quentin for Claire. I got some Scotch tape from the drawer and taped the Peep Thrills token to the paper. Twenty minutes later Sarah had redone her face, taken her vitamins, worked the toothbrush around her gums, sloshed and swallowed, and was now putting all her makeup away. Nora was still on the phone. I was just finishing up my notes when I heard the key in the front door and Claire's voice.

"Idiots!"

"Quite, madam," Boulton replied.

She strode into the room holding her walking stick in front of her as if it were a machete. Boulton followed behind her.

"It's only a quirk of fate that those so-called detectives are policemen and not out stealing cars," she announced, then stopped and glared at our visitors, giving Sarah a closer inspection. "Behind your youthful petulance, there is a resemblance to Cybella."

Sarah couldn't have cared less. All her attention was directed at Boulton. Her every movement was now in response to his presence. I don't like women who only wake up when a man comes into the room. I bet she was never without her diaphragm. Nora folded her portable phone back into the shape of a cracker and put it in her purse. Claire sat in her chair. I handed her my notes.

"Tea, Boulton," she commanded.

He withdrew. Sarah was disappointed. She went back to staring at her skin, hair, nails.

"Did you show the police the video?" Nora asked Claire.

"I saw no reason to."

"Then you've kept Sarah's name out of it so far?"

"So far."

"Good."

"But I expect something in return," Claire said.

"Such as?" The basic black eyes narrowed.

"Truth. Candor. Veracity. Are either one of you even familiar with these words?"

"How dare you be so condescending!"

"Three people have been murdered, Miss Brown, one of whom you knew quite well."

"Cybella killed herself," Nora said flatly.

"Yes, yes, I know." A faint smile formed on Claire's lips. "Middle-age depression. I'm surprised that all the stairwells in Manhattan aren't filled with the bodies of aging, depressed women." Her eyes settled on Sarah. "There is a red St. Rome evening gown hanging in your mother's closet. It was bought for her by Sheridan Reynolds six months ago. It was carried by you into the Duke Hotel four months ago. It was worn by Jackie in the video, a video shot four months ago at the Duke Hotel. The hotel clerk will identify you if need be."

"Tell Miss Conrad what you told me," Nora prompted, awkwardly patting Sarah's hand.

"When I was sixteen I used to steal makeup from Mr. Feller. He ran the drugstore." Sarah moved her hand away from Nora's.

Claire began to read my notes.

"I was in there one day by myself," Sarah continued in a faltering voice. "And he came up to me and said I could have any lipstick I wanted." She turned to Nora. "She's not listening to me."

Claire, still perusing my chicken scratches, said, "I'm quite capable of concentrating on more than one subject at the same time."

"It's difficult to talk to somebody who's not looking at me." Her voice trailed off into a whine.

"Mr. Feller was offering you a lipstick. Continue." Claire did not look up from my report.

"A lipstick if I'd just be nice to him. I told him I wanted thirty-five dollars." She tossed her hair back and giggled like a naughty girl. "I was nice to him and I got thirty-five dollars. Now I'm worth millions, and I haven't had to be nice to anybody." She looked at Nora.

"Go on," Nora directed.

"I did know Jackie. From the lingerie shop. A few months ago I ran into her on the street. We got to talking. She was really impressed with my success. I brought her up to Bedford Place to show her around. We did a little coke and hung out."

"Jackie never mentioned she'd been to Bedford Place." Claire turned to the next page of my notes.

"I'm mentioning it." Sarah's voice was nasty. "She told me she was doing some pornos. She made it sound kind of exciting." She ran her long fingers through her long hair and crossed her long legs. "She kept at me, asking me if I'd like to be in one. I agreed. I don't know why, but it just seemed a kind of out-of-it thing to do. You know, fun."

"You did it for a lark? Or in memory of Mr. Feller the pharmacologist?" Claire asked, finally focusing her penetrating eyes on Sarah.

Unsure, Sarah decided to study some strands of her hair. Nora gave her handbag a quick jerk as if it were disobeying and said, "Mr. Feller is an example of Sarah being forced into using her sexuality, which is all she felt she had, to gain some kind of identity. Sarah is not that different from Jackie. And Jackie sensed that. Used it."

"How did Jackie acquire the evening gown?" Claire asked in a bored voice, extending her long legs and leaning back in her chair. Only the finger with the lapis gave an impatient tap.

"She said she wanted to wear something pretty," Sarah said. "I showed her Cybella's clothes and she picked the red evening gown. I didn't look at the label. I didn't know it was a St. Rome."

"Did Jackie?"

"If she did, she didn't say anything. I was discussing all this with Nora and I discovered that I was really angry at Cybella."

"Because she had abandoned her," Nora added.

"I always felt it was something I did. Something about me that made Mother leave me with my grandparents." She was trying for some kind of introspection, but her eyes looked like they were searching for a mirror. "I thought if I could be like her, then she would love me. But no matter how hard I tried to be her daughter, she didn't want me."

"Sarah's need to do this video was because of the emotional tug-of-war between a mother and a daughter," Nora said. "Sarah understands it now." She gave the crocodile a pat.

Sarah nodded in agreement. Both of them watched Claire, who was now concentrating on the ceiling. Boulton wheeled in the tea.

"Well, they finally got their story worked out," I said to nobody in particular.

"Weren't you worried that a pornographic video could be used against you in some way?" Claire asked Sarah.

"I just didn't think." Sarah's eyes followed Boulton.

"That is the first example of veracity we've had."

"Are you calling her a liar?" Nora demanded.

Claire didn't respond. Boulton served tea. I took a pass. Sarah made a big deal about her weight, then took the fattest scone on the plate. Her eyes still on Boulton, she bit into the scone as if it were her lover's face. Claire sipped her tea. I watched Sarah seduce some more of her scone. I watched Boulton watch Sarah.

"What did Cybella say when you showed her the video?" Claire asked.

It took a lot of strength but she forced her eyes from Boulton back to Claire. "I didn't show it to her."

"What's the good of retaliation if nobody knows you've retaliated?"

"I was kinda embarrassed about it. And . . ."

"And she didn't want anybody to know. We do silly things out of pain and anger. She was suddenly afraid that Cybella would show the video to me, that I would be upset with her." Nora stroked Sarah's hair. It was a tentative gesture, like stroking a lion.

Sarah smiled seductively at Boulton. He still had his butler face on, but just barely.

"We've tried to help you the best we can." Nora set her teacup on the table.

Sarah was now caressing her lips with her napkin.

"That was very good," she said to Boulton, as if they'd experienced mutual orgasm.

"It's déclassé to speak to the butler," I said.

"This is America." She stood up, giving him a good look at what was available in the United States, undulated around the drinks table, and poured herself some more water.

"Teatime is over," I said to Boulton. He didn't flinch but his right hand curled into a fist.

Claire turned and peered at me. She said nothing but I knew I had stepped out of bounds. Discretion was still a distant goal. She nodded to Boulton, who wheeled the table out of the room. I was going to hear from both of them later, but right now I felt fine. I had committed Sarah interruptus.

"Let's go, Sarah." Nora stood, giving her skirt a good brushing with her hand.

"Sit down," Claire commanded.

They remained standing.

"The front door is locked. Unless Boulton or Miss Hill unlock it, you will not be able to leave. If you prefer to remain standing, do so."

They sat on the sofa.

"This is ridiculous." Tugging at her skirt, Nora crossed her legs.

Claire leaned forward, fixing Nora with her dark blue eyes. "I do not believe one word you and Sarah have said to me. Miss Brown, you have all the psychological and intellectual depth of your capricious and inane magazine."

Nora moved angrily on the sofa. Her mouth opened to speak.

"Do not say one more word," Claire warned.

Nora closed her mouth with such force, I thought we would have to pry it back open.

"Jackie was never in Bedford Place. Nor was she in Cybella's bedroom picking out a St. Rome dress to wear in a porno video because you were annoyed with your mother." Her eyes came to rest on Sarah. "I detest stupidity." She struck the floor with her walking stick.

"The truth is not always to our liking." Nora had her lips working again. "And sometimes it falls short of our so-called high standards. But it is still the truth."

"Jackie never mentioned Bedford Place to me," Claire said. "If she had been there, she would have gladly told me about it in every detail. Nor did she ever mention knowing Sarah before the video was shot."

"Because she failed to tell you about these things does not mean they didn't happen."

"I think Sarah was forced to do that video because of something she knows or did. Something neither one of you want discovered."

Sarah's coffee-colored eyes turned opaque. Claire leaned back in her chair and watched Nora. "I think that's why you went to see Goldie this morning. The same Duke Hotel clerk who saw Sarah also saw you."

Nora didn't move. I could almost feel her weighing her options. "I didn't kill him," she finally said. "He was dead when I got there."

"I asked her to go see Goldie," Sarah confessed. "He wanted so much money. He kept asking for more and more. I just didn't have it."

"I thought you were worth millions," I said.

"Only if she has staying power," Nora said. "I was hoping to reason with the man. He wanted four hundred thousand dollars as a final payoff."

"Where does Linda Hansen fit in?" Claire asked Sarah.

"I paid the money to her. She gave it to Goldie."

"Why was he really blackmailing you?"

"We told you," Nora said. "Because she did the video."

"Cybella meant a great deal to you, didn't she, Miss Brown?" Claire asked gently.

"I don't know what you mean."

"Miss Hill was in Cybella's bedroom. She's an avid reader—Miss Hill, that is, not Cybella—so of course she looked at the books you gave her."

"She didn't love the books I gave her. She didn't love me." She looked evenly at Claire. "Yes, I loved Cybella. Are you shocked?"

"People fall in and out of love every day. The only shock is that they continue to do so."

"May we go now?"

"One final question." She turned to Sarah. "Who is your father?"

"I never met my father. He was French. He died when I was very young."

"Is that true?" She asked Nora.

She nodded.

"Show them out, Miss Hill," Claire said, leaning back in her chair and closing her eyes.

I unlocked the front door. Nora swept past me into the hallway. Sarah showed me her perfect teeth. "It must be fun to have a butler all your own. Too bad you can't talk to him."

I closed the door on her ever so gently. After pointing a gun at her forehead and taking away her tea, I didn't want to appear inhospitable.

Back in the living room I sat down at my desk. "They're lying," I said. "Even about who her father is."

"Sarah believes the dead Frenchman is her father, Miss Hill, because that is what she has been told."

Claire stood and prowled near the window. "So Paul Quentin admits to knowing Jackie." I could tell by her stance she was looking for pigeons. "His involvement changes the entire case."

"He killed her."

"Why?"

"Maybe Jackie was going to tell the Reynolds family that he was her customer. There's a ton of money to be made by marrying Alison."

"And yet when you threatened to tell the Reynolds family about Jackie, he wasn't upset. In fact he was very confident of their support. And how did he know to be waiting outside our hotel for her?"

"He was following Jackie."

"We are back to the same problem. If he was following Jackie with the intent to murder, why didn't he do it before she got to the Parkfaire?" Claire slowly raised her walking stick. "Why did he let her stand out there while you were up here eating your breakfast? Why didn't he kill her then?" She swung at the window. A pane of glass shattered. The pigeon remained on the sill scrutinizing her.

"Call somebody, Miss Hill," she said through clenched teeth.

I reached for the phone, got hold of those-who-pick-up-after-us and told them we'd be needing a new pane for our window. Claire paced in front of my desk, waiting for me to hang up.

"One more thing, Miss Hill: you interrupted my tea. Until you start paying for Boulton's salary, please leave his instructions to me."

"It won't happen again."

"You embarrassed him."

"Boulton? Impossible."

"I want you to apologize to him. I know he's sulking. I can't stand it when he sulks, it disrupts the household."

"Apologize?!"

"Yes, Miss Hill, apologize. Oh, I almost forgot. The police are also very upset with you," she said accusingly.

"About what?"

She thought for a moment, then waved her hand vaguely in the air. "Something about your leaving the scene of a crime."

"You told me to leave. You told me you'd take care of it."

"I'm sure you'll be able to calm them. Just don't give them any pertinent information."

"Calm them?"

"They should be here any minute. A Detective Alvarez and a Detective McGuire. Why do they always travel in pairs like lovebirds? I'll be in my room. I need to think. There's no reason to call me." She strode out.

Oh, hell.

Nineteen

I poked my head in the kitchen. Gerta was washing the tea things. Her arms and legs were as white as flour against her solid black dress and her sturdy black shoes. Boulton wasn't there. She shook her head at me. "He's in his room, Maggie."

"This is ridiculous."

"He is very sensitive, Maggie." She rinsed a teacup.

"About as sensitive as a bullet."

She wagged her head again. "How can you call yourself a woman and not know how to handle a man?"

"They call themselves men and they don't have a clue about women."

"That's because we cannot be handled. They can."

"Really?"

She nodded sagely.

"What do you suggest besides giving him chicken soup?"

"You think I'm a silly old peasant woman."

"No I don't. What do you suggest?"

"Maggie, I know what went on in there." She wiped her hands on her apron, then took my hand. I remembered my mother's wet hands and her polka-dot apron.

"I listened. You acted out of jealousy."

"I just couldn't stand watching Sarah throw herself around. Women give women a bad name."

She shrugged. "Then you give yourself a bad name."

"Talking with you is like talking to my mother. The conversation loses all sense of reality and we end up talking about bad names. And I don't even know what that means."

She looked at me, shaking her head in disappointment. I was a hopeless case. "If you feel a pang of jealousy, then you must feel something for him. That's all I'm saying. I've done my best. You don't listen."

She turned back to the sink and the dishes she didn't have to do. There was room service but not for Gerta.

All right, I had felt something—not jealousy, something deeper and more defensive. The distance I kept between Boulton and me allowed any woman to step in except me. I went down the hall and knocked on his door.

"Come in."

I opened the door. He sat on the edge of his bed cleaning a derringer that he sometimes tucked into his vest pocket. The vest and jacket hung on a chair. The sleeves of his white shirt were rolled up and his tie was loose. His great-great-grandfather's comb-and-brush set were on the dresser. He is the only man I know whose great-great-grandfather was killed by Zulu warriors. He checked the gun, then looked up. "What is it, Maggie?"

"I've come to apologize. It seems I have embarrassed you, and believe me, Boulton, I would never intentionally want to do that to you. I know you take orders only from Claire and I was out of line."

He leaned forward, resting his arms on his knees, gun in hand. "Which is it you despise the most?" His watchful brown eyes studied me. "The bodyguard or the butler?"

"I don't know what you mean."

"When you think of me—and you do think of me—am

I the servant who polishes the silver, answers the door, and serves the tea? Or am I the macho bloke who carries a gun and is trained to take a bullet for Miss Conrad? Be honest."

"You think I look down on you because you're her butler? If you must know, I'm a little intimidated by that fact. The closest thing I ever had to a servant when I was growing up were Rubbermaid products."

"Rubbermaid?" He looked at me blankly.

"You wouldn't understand."

"Do you know what I think? I think you're too class-conscious to want to go to bed with a mere butler. So I think you do need a bodyguard, no matter what you said this morning."

"Look, I came in here to apologize. I don't remember saying anything about wanting to go to bed with you." I'd said variations on those words to other men and had meant them, but now they sounded hollow.

"What's this all about, if it's not about the fact that you and I desire one another?"

"You met my ex-husband. How different are you from him? Okay, he's not a butler and he's not English. But I'd like to desire a man who doesn't carry a gun. I'm sure there must be one around."

A slight smile played on his lips. "Don't you find it odd that now that you carry a gun you want to meet a man who doesn't?"

"Look, what I'm trying to say is that I don't think it's the best thing for us to get involved. I'm feeling very insecure right now."

"Insecurity. The last refuge of the American woman."

The doorbell rang. He reached for his vest and jacket.

"Don't bother," I said. "I'll get it. It's the police. They want to talk to me. It seems I left the scene of a crime. God knows how that happened."

He moved toward me with the gun in his hand.

"You're going to shoot me and put me out of my misery."

"Take this." He handed me the gun.

"You want me to shoot you?"

"It's empty." He reached around me and closed the door. "I want you to hold the gun. I want you to know that I am unarmed and disarmed in your presence."

He put his hands on my shoulders and ran them down my arms. He bent his head down and rubbed his cheek against my hair. I put my arms around his neck. I could feel the back of his starched collar, his hair soft against my wrists, his chest hard against my breasts. His mouth found my mouth.

The doorbell rang again. He stepped back. His lips wet from mine.

"McGuire and Alvarez are not going to be so easily swayed by your charm." He opened the door for me. I gave him back his gun.

As I walked to the foyer, I tried not to smile. I tried not to notice that the earth had tilted ever so slightly. I was a mature woman who knew that this was just another kiss and, God knows, I had had my share of kisses and the men that went with them. I tried to pretend I was not just another deliriously happy besotted lemming. But God, this kiss was ripe with possibilities.

McGuire and Alvarez had been at me for about a half hour. I was sitting at my desk. McGuire, a large, barrel-chested man with legs so thin they looked like a rock star's, stood near the window. Alvarez leaned against the fireplace mantel. I, of course, had told them the first thing that came into my head and now I was stuck with it.

"Let me get this straight," Alvarez said, as his long tan fingers stroked his glistening black mustache. "You're looking down at this dead man and Claire Conrad asks you to run to Bergdorf's to pick her up a few things."

" 'Gloves,' the little lady here said 'gloves,' " McGuire added testily, glaring at me. He rubbed his chin. I could hear his hand scratching against the stubble.

"Gloves." Alvarez's voice was smooth and patient. But his black eyes were disturbingly unreadable. "Just like that. You're looking at a corpse and Claire Conrad wants a new pair of gloves?"

"She's eccentric," I explained.

"Claire Conrad's full of shit," McGuire snorted.

I thought it best not to respond.

"If it weren't for her knowing this Sitwell, she'd be in jail and you along with her," McGuire threatened. His powder blue jacket pulled at the seams.

I said nothing. Boulton came into the room and stood near the double doors. Alvarez ignored him. McGuire's body tensed.

"You armed?" he demanded.

Boulton nodded.

"Lay off," Alvarez warned McGuire.

"I don't like this. Three flakes coming in from L.A. and giving us the runaround. Gloves, my ass. My ass!" The last was said, I believe, to impress Boulton. I'll never understand men. Want their big arms around me, yes, understand them, no.

"Tell us," Alvarez said, his opaque, possibly dangerous eyes confronting mine. "Did you find the gloves you were looking for?"

"No. You see she can only wear black gloves or white gloves, depending on which day of the week it is."

I thought Alvarez was going to bite through his lower lip but he restrained himself. "Why does she only wear white or black?"

"I can't believe you're going along with this shit," Mc-Guire snapped.

"Answer the question," Alvarez said to me.

I took a deep breath. I always do when I don't know what in the hell I'm doing. "You see it has something to do with the light side and the dark side of life."

"You mean skin color?" Alvarez's eyes narrowed.

"Jesus Christ," McGuire muttered.

"Nothing to do with race," I assured Alvarez. "It's the two different worlds Claire Conrad works and lives in, not unlike you. One is the honest world, the world of light, of answers, of truth. The other is the world of lies, of murder, of evil." I couldn't look at Boulton. McGuire was getting perilously red in the face.

"Yeah?" He bellied up to my desk. "Let's see these gloves."

I got up and went into Claire's room. The drapes were drawn. A small lamp glowed dimly on her dresser. She was lying on her bed, staring up at the ceiling. Her strong profile etched against the dusky light.

"Comfy?" I asked.

"Third drawer on your right," she said. "Even in the best hotels the walls are thin."

"Sorry to disturb your nap."

I opened the drawer and took out the package of gloves I had picked up two days ago. A lifetime ago.

"Miss Hill?"

"Yes?"

"I liked what you said about the gloves. Use that when you write about me, when you remember to write about me, that is. It creates myth. Myth is good."

"But is it true?"

"In 1948 I was ten years old. My family and I were in England." The dark blue eyes never looked away from the ceiling. "It was a summer evening. Still light. My mother was wearing the most beautiful white evening gown. My father had on a black tuxedo. They each kissed me good-bye. I gave her a bouquet of wildflowers. They got into the Bentley and the chauffeur drove to the end of the long gravel drive. I waved. The Bentley exploded into a thousand pieces of metal and flesh. As I ran to them I was cut by the flying shrapnel that had once been their car. I never felt it. I only felt the absolute terror of not being able to find them, to help them. I can still hear Mother screaming, even though I know she had no time to cry out. I'll always hear it."

I said nothing. I knew she wouldn't want me to.

"I wear white on one day, black on the next, as a reminder of the one murder I have not solved. My parents' murder."

I took the gloves out of the package and stared at them. A white pair to go with a white evening gown. A black pair to go with a black tuxedo.

"But your version is not bad, Miss Hill. I rather like it. It has style."

I walked quietly out of the room and laid the gloves on my desk. McGuire picked them up. I didn't like him touching them. I jerked them out of his hands. He grabbed my arm. Boulton moved toward him. "Let go of her."

McGuire smiled. "You gonna use your gun?"

"Back off," Alvarez warned Boulton.

McGuire let go of me.

"I don't see anything that says Bergdorf Goodman on these gloves. Where's the receipt?" Alvarez asked me.

"Bergdorf's didn't have what I wanted. So I went to this little store run by a Frenchwoman." I gave them her name and address. She had never looked up from her glove-making. She wouldn't know what day or time I was in there. She'd only know what kind of gloves she made and I bought.

"And then what?" he asked.

"I came back here and waited for Claire."

We went around and around for another fifteen minutes. But my heart wasn't in the battle. They abruptly left, not without a lot of threats. Boulton showed them out. He came back into the living room and leaned against the fireplace.

"What's wrong, Maggie?"

I stared down at the gloves. "She just told me why she's a detective." I leaned back in my chair. We stared at each other across the room. "Who was driving the car, Boulton?"

"My grandfather."

The phone rang, startling me. My hand jerked out and grabbed it.

"Conrad Suite."

"This is Sheridan Reynolds. I'm in the lobby. I want to see Claire Conrad."

"Just a minute." I looked at Boulton. "Ask Claire if she wants to see Sheridan Reynolds."

Claire appeared in the doorway. Her tall, lean body tilted slightly toward the hand that rested on her ebony walking stick. Her silvery white hair caught the light. Her keen eyes glistened. I wondered who she looked like. Her mother? Her father? Can a ten-year-old girl's sunshine blond hair—or was she brunette—turn to white in one horrible moment? She nodded.

"Claire Conrad is receiving," I spoke into the phone.

Twenty

Claire was ensconced in the Queen Anne and I was still behind my desk when Boulton went to answer the door. We could hear Reynolds's angry voice, then the sound of scuffling. There was a crash. Glass shattered.

"Do you think that was the dreadful little green vase?" she asked.

"Yes."

"Mr. Desanto will be very upset."

"Yes." I smiled.

Sheridan Reynolds stumbled into the living room. Boulton, holding a gun in one hand and an ostrich leather briefcase in the other, was right after him.

"This is outrageous!" Reynolds's striped tie was pulled crooked and his wavy gray hair a little messed, but I didn't see any bruises. His wide handsome face was still heavy with fatigue, making his razor gray eyes appear even smaller.

"Sit down." Boulton shoved him onto the sofa, then placed the briefcase on my desk. "There is a gun and an envelope with approximately a hundred thousand dollars in here." He opened the case and handed Claire the envelope. "The gun has not been fired recently."

"May I at least have the keys to my case back?" Reynolds

asked peevishly. Boulton tossed them to him. He caught them easily, like catching the gold ring on the merry-go-round.

"What is the cash for, Mr. Reynolds?" Claire peered into the envelope.

"A business transaction," he said carefully.

"Do you always do your transactions in cash?"

"No." He smoothed his hair and straightened his tie. "It's for you."

"A bribe?"

"If you wish to call it that. I wouldn't use such a harsh word."

"And the gun?"

"Wouldn't you have a gun if you were carrying around that kind of cash?"

"And what do you want for your money?"

He leaned back and closed his eyes. "Peace." He rubbed his hand over his face. "Can you give me peace for a hundred thousand?"

"I think Mr. Reynolds could use a brandy, Boulton. Maybe we all could."

Boulton slipped his gun back into his shoulder holster and poured three brandies.

"I don't think I can give you peace, Mr. Reynolds, for any amount of money," Claire said. "A hundred thousand is not a large sum."

"There's more."

"Thank God for a wealthy wife," I observed.

He leaped to his feet. Boulton moved swiftly, jamming the edge of a silver serving tray into Sheridan's chest. The three crystal glasses tinkled. A little brandy spilled. But that was all.

"Your drink, sir," Boulton offered.

"How nice. The man who roughs me up serves me my brandy." He grabbed a glass. Boulton didn't move.

"Most of our guests show Boulton what he wants to see, avoiding unnecessary physical contact," Claire explained delicately.

"I wasn't expecting to be searched. I don't like it." This last was said to Boulton.

"I think you'll enjoy your brandy more if you sit down," the butler voice warned.

Reynolds sat on the sofa and swallowed half his brandy. Boulton served us, then stood behind Reynolds.

"What do you really want, Mr. Reynolds?" Claire swirled the brandy in her glass.

"I want you to leave my family alone. I want you to stop this investigation."

"Do you consider Paul Quentin part of your family?" She extended her long legs and took a sip.

"Of course."

"Miss Hill thinks he's a murderer." She could have been commenting on the weather.

"Because he patronized Peep Thrills? I'm sure he's not their only customer."

"When did Mr. Quentin tell you about Jackie?"

"After he talked to *her*." He jerked his head in my direction. "For God's sakes, it doesn't mean he's a murderer. I know the man. He's been with me for three years. And my wife has come to rely on him."

"And your daughter?"

"She's going to marry him."

"But if you thought there was just the slightest possibility of Mr. Quentin being involved in murder, I'd think you'd at least postpone the wedding," Claire offered. "For your daughter's sake."

"Well, he's not. Let me try to explain something to you. When I had a daughter and not a son, I thought my actions, my own private life, were separate from hers. Then one day

I looked closely at the man she wanted to marry. And guess who I saw? Me. Myself as a young man." He stared down at a thick gold Rolex on his wrist. He ran his finger over the face of the watch as if it were a woman's cheek.

"Maybe that's why I hired Paul in the first place. I used to be just like him. Poor but from good stock. All the right schools but no money. Ruthless. Didn't particularly care how I got wealth as long as I didn't have to work too hard for it." He spoke in a flat, nonjudgmental voice, as if he didn't want to offend anyone—especially himself.

"Why not charm a rich young woman in the right circle and marry her? I could always have a mistress. I did." He smiled. A ghost of Paul Quentin's smile. "And Paul will always have his cheap girls. Alison is marrying charm, and she's marrying betrayal. She's marrying what she's used to, what she grew up with. But she's not marrying a killer." He took a long swallow. "There's something else I want for my money."

"Yes?"

"Do you have any concrete evidence that Cybella's suicide was murder?"

"No, we have only Miss Hill's wish that for once a beautiful woman did not kill herself."

Sheridan stared at her incredulously, his mouth slightly opened. "You don't have all your ducks lined up, do you?"

"Ducks?" she repeated.

"You don't know what you're doing!" he said angrily.

"How did ducks get into the conversation?" she wondered.

"He means," I said, "you can't shoot ducks in a gallery unless they're lined up. In other words, you have nothing to go on. No real information."

"But why shoot your own decoys?" Claire asked.

"Actually, madam," Boulton said, "I think it comes from the mother duck lining up her ducklings."

"And then you shoot them?" she asked.

"Could we forget the frigging ducks and concentrate on the fact that you're tormenting my family and me for no reason?" Reynolds stormed.

"I am never without reason, Mr. Reynolds."

"I suggest you take this money and go back to Los Angeles."

"I don't have a paying client and God knows I do have overhead." She gestured at me and Boulton as if we were the demented relatives she kept in the attic. "But alas, I can't be bribed. Of course it never hurts to ask. It builds the ego of the private detective, gives her confidence, makes her think she might be getting close."

He scrambled to his feet. "You don't know what harm you'll cause."

"Give the man his money and his briefcase, Boulton."

"If you continue to harass my family, you'll be hearing from my lawyers." He jerked the case from Boulton's hand and lunged out of the room. Boulton followed.

Claire leaned back in her chair and finished off her brandy. "I still don't understand how ducks got into the conversation."

I thought it best not to try to explain. Boulton came back into the room.

"Have a brandy."

"Thank you, madam."

While he poured himself a drink she walked out into the foyer. I could hear her moving the broken pieces of the vase around with her walking stick. She came back in and leaned against the fireplace.

"That was quite a tussle you had with Mr. Reynolds."

"Yes, madam."

"He didn't want you to check the contents of his briefcase?"

"Yes."

"But why? Since he was going to walk in here and offer me the money."

"Some people overreact to being searched, madam. They take it personally."

"Are you saying that money wasn't intended for you?" I asked.

"That's exactly what I'm saying."

"So who else does he want to keep quiet?" I wondered.

"Maybe it was just the gun, madam," Boulton said. "Maybe he didn't want us to see it. I'll check on the dinner." He downed the last of his drink and left the room.

"Somehow it always comes down to a gun." Claire gazed into the fireplace.

Boulton appeared in the doorway. "Dinner is served, madam."

We ate dinner while hotel engineering boarded up the broken window and replaced the green vase with an equally ugly blue one. I tried to pry more information about their past out of Claire and Boulton but got nowhere. Instead, an aloof silence replaced my rapport with her and the intimacy I had experienced with him. I still was not one of them.

When I got into bed that night I found myself waiting for Boulton. It was exactly what I did not want to do, did not want to feel. It was everything I had been avoiding since my divorce. And here I was waiting for my lover-to-be to *tap, tap, tap* on my door. I considered it a reactionary position. Waiting, always waiting. My mother waited for my father to come home. She waited for the nuns to visit her. She waited for the priest to bless her. She waited for me to return to her. Waiting was a sign of vulnerability, of weakness. Women didn't have to wait anymore and yet . . .

The phone rang. Someone answered it. Alison's picture of me leaned against the mirror on the dresser. I stared at my dark windblown hair. The lines were deep around my lips. Lines I never used to have.

I waited.

I thought of the young woman with her camera. I thought of her father carrying around a hundred thousand dollars and a gun. I reached for the light and turned it off.

I was acutely aware of my nakedness, my breasts, the curve of my hips. The sheet against my nipples. I wanted to run my hands down Boulton's naked back and over the curve of his buttocks. I wanted his arms around me. I wanted to feel him inside of me. Of course, I could put on my bathrobe and go knock on his door. *Tap, tap, tap.* He was only in the next room. Four steps away. It was just a kiss, Maggie. So why should I expect him? To *tap, tap, tap.*

Tap, tap, tap. I raised up. *Tap, tap, tap.* There *was* someone knocking.

"Come in?"

The door slowly opened. Boulton filled the door frame. The top buttons of his shirt were open, his sleeves rolled up. The light from the hallway cast half of his face into shadow. He stepped into the room. "Maggie?"

"Yes?"

"Linda Hansen is in the bar. She wants to see you. Only you."

Claire appeared in the doorway. "Ask Miss Hansen what she has to do for the hundred thousand dollars, and thank her for the tip about Goldie."

"Don't forget your gun." Boulton's fingers gently stroked the edge of the bed, then he moved back out of the room and closed the door.

Oh, hell.

Twenty-one

Once again I threw on my slacks and sweater and made my way down to the bar. Only this time I had a gun in my pocket and was wondering how Claire knew the money was for Linda Hansen. Desanto lurked near the entrance. He pounced.

"Miss Hill, I told you we don't allow those kinds of women in this hotel."

"She's not here to do business, Desanto. She's here about the case that Claire Conrad is working on."

"I don't want any trouble. Mr. Orita is in there." He peered nervously into the bar, then at me. "I heard she almost caused a fight the other night."

"There won't be any trouble."

"On the other hand, if Mr. Orita should find her attractive . . ." His voice turned low and intimate, as if he were going to ask me for a date. "Well, of course, I could look the other way." He nervously looked the other way.

"That's what I like about you, Desanto. You're a man who not only stands on his principles but walks all over them."

His chin was doing its disappearing act as I entered the bar. Linda was at the table near the window in a short black leather skirt and black leather bomber jacket. The indolent way she crossed her long legs still conveyed easy sex. In the corner booth was a chubby middle-aged Japanese man impeccably dressed in blue jacket and gray slacks. His eyes and hair were as dark as a Sony CD player. He was surrounded by a harem of young American men in gray business suits with big pale eyes and big feet. None of them was looking at Linda; all were staring intently at Mr. Orita.

"My thoughts exactly," one of the young men cooed to Orita as I sat down at her table.

"It's tough to compete with the Japanese." She put a cigarette to her lips.

"Don't you ever talk to people in the daytime?" I asked testily.

"What's your problem?"

"Nothing," I snapped.

"My, we're grouchy. Sounds like you're not getting any." She forced a smile and blew a ghostly ribbon of smoke. "I know where we can both get laid."

I sighed. "Great. This must be true equality when two fairly intelligent women can sit around and talk like two dumb jocks."

"You're so middle-class."

"Somebody has to be."

"The police have been around Peep Thrills asking a lot of questions. Police make me jumpy."

"What do you want, Linda?"

"You left the message on my machine. What do *you* want?"

"Claire Conrad wants to thank you for the tip about Goldie."

"I don't know what you're talking about." The gray eyes were steady. The mouth hard.

"Goldie's dead. She thinks you called us to let us know about his death."

"Why would she think it was me? She doesn't even know me."

"Through me, she does."

"She trusts your observations that much?"

Her question threw me. I just thought I was very good at remembering information and passing it on to Claire. I had never thought of it as trust. But in a sense trust was involved. Claire Conrad actually trusted me.

"Yes," I said with a certain pride.

"Must be nice to trust somebody that way."

"Why don't you try it?"

"Are you kidding?"

"Did you make the phone call?"

"I liked Goldie. He protected us. Women don't get much protection nowadays."

"What were you doing at the Duke?"

"Checking up on him," she said vaguely.

"Or were you giving him the money you took from Sarah Grange?"

"I don't know what you're talking about."

"We know you and Goldie were blackmailing her."

"Who says?"

"She does."

Linda turned toward the window. The BMW was there. The churches were still holding down their place on the avenue.

"Did you force her to do the video?" I asked.

"I didn't need to force her to do anything." She studied her cigarette. "She likes doing porno. Soft-core. Maybe it's the camera. Look, Sarah's got maybe five years. And then she'll be over. Let's just say that it's in my interest that she stay at the top as long as she can."

"Claire doesn't buy that excuse. Why did Sarah really do the porno?"

"Why don't you just come out and ask me if I killed Jackie and Goldie? That's what Claire Conrad wants to know, isn't it?"

"She didn't mention it. You're avoiding my question."

"But you think I killed them."

"I don't know what to think."

She smashed out her cigarette. "I came to say good-bye. Now I wish I hadn't."

"Where are you going?"

"Away." She turned and looked at Orita. "Maybe Japan. Maybe L.A. Open up a boutique there. Sell only sexy underwear."

"Just what L.A. needs. It costs money to open up a boutique."

"I'm very good at raising money. Good-bye, Maggie." She stood and swayed toward the entrance. Not one young American head turned. They were too busy having the exact same thoughts as Orita. I was right behind her.

"Are you getting paid to leave town?" I asked.

She didn't answer. I stayed with her through the lobby and out onto the street.

"Are you being paid to leave?" I asked again.

"I like you, Maggie." She headed toward Park and the BMW. "Let's part friends."

"I'm tired of people liking me. I want some answers. Who's paying you? Sheridan Reynolds?"

"I don't know any Sheridan Reynolds. Who's he?"

"He's a guy walking around with a hundred thousand dollars and a gun in his briefcase. He was Cybella's lover."

She pulled open the car door and got in. I stood on the curb.

"What do you have on him?" I asked.

"I don't know what you're talking about." She pulled away from the curb. I grabbed the side of the car and jumped, swinging my legs over the door and down in the front seat.

"This is embarrassing, Maggie. Get the fuck outta my car."

"Isn't it a little dangerous blackmailing two people?"

She swerved back toward the curb and double-parked next to a limo. "Get out."

"Talk to me."

"Get out!"

Cars honked. She gunned the car and took off. The wind began its tug-of-war with my hair.

"You're making this very awkward, Maggie."

The streetlights yellowed our faces.

"What do you have on Sarah Grange and Sheridan Reynolds?"

"I'm not a blackmailer."

"Okay, you did something for them and they're paying you off. What?"

She didn't answer. She drove with a vengeance, careening around corners. She swerved sharply into an alley. Inside my pocket I held my gun. The car jerked to a stop, motor purring. She stared straight ahead, breathing hard as if she'd been running. The headlights illuminated plastic bags of garbage, a fire escape, and the raw mortar and bricks of the two buildings flanking the alley. As she turned toward me, she reached for something under her seat. Before I could get my gun out of my pocket, her hand came up holding her own.

"Get out of the car, Maggie. Get out!"

"At least it's not a knife. The murderer used a knife."

"Get out."

"I don't believe you'd shoot me."

The explosion was deafening. The bullet missed me, but I don't know how. My ears rang. My eyes felt as if a flash from a camera had gone off in them. I blinked.

"Get out, Maggie!" Linda screamed.

I got out. What else was I going to do, take my gun out so we could shoot each other?

"Sorry, Maggie. Chalk my behavior up to a lack of self-worth." She threw the car in reverse and backed down the alley. "A lack of identity, a lack of self-esteem," she shouted at me.

Lack of self-esteem, my ass, I thought, taking the gun from my pocket. It was a self-centered act. I didn't have to kill her. There was something better. I walked down the alley carefully aiming for the hood of her car. I fired and hit it. *Ping!*

"A lack of love," she yelled back.

I got the shiny new grille in my sight and fired, hitting the left headlight. It cracked and splintered. She hit the brakes and leaped out of the car.

"What the fuck are you doing?"

I approached with my gun still aimed at the car.

"Chalk it up to a lack of patience. A lack of pity. A lack of stupidity. Chalk it up to being middle-class."

"I wasn't going to kill you, Maggie."

"I'm not going to kill you. I'm going to kill your car."

I fired another shot into the leather upholstery.

"Shit."

"I don't like these kinds of cars. L.A. rich kids and agents who haven't made it drive them. Who's paying you to leave town?"

"I can't tell you."

I fired another bullet into the backseat. "These cars are passé, did you know that?"

"Stop it. This is all I have to show for my life." Her lips quivered.

"You better tell me, Linda. Somebody may not like the sound of gunfire. Somebody may have called the police." I took aim again. "They make you nervous, remember?"

"All right. It is Sheridan Reynolds."

"What do you have on him?"

"Look, I don't have the money yet. Don't ruin it for me."

"When are you supposed to get it?"

"He's going to let me know. And I'm going to enjoy watching him give me the money. That's all I'm going to tell you, Maggie. You can empty your gun into my car or me. That's all I'm telling you."

Again, there was the sound of sirens. We stared at one another.

"And what do you have to do for the money, Linda?"

"Just leave town, that's all."

"It's the video, isn't it? You found out he's Sarah's father and now you're blackmailing him. How'd you find out?"

"Ask him."

She got back into the car, backed out onto the street, and threw the car in drive. "Coin of the realm, Maggie," she yelled, waving her long graceful arm in the air as she sped off.

The sirens were getting closer. I ran like any common criminal with a gun in her hand.

Twenty-two

"Why didn't you aim for the car's tires, Miss Hill?" Claire asked the next morning over breakfast.

"Maybe she was aiming for the tires, madam, but hit the headlight instead." Boulton poured her coffee.

"I was aiming for the car's grille and hit the headlight instead. Maybe I'm not cut out for this line of work."

"On the contrary, you have a knack for the profession. Doesn't she, Boulton?"

"A definite knack, madam." They smiled at me.

"She's not smiling, Boulton," said Claire.

"No, madam."

"When the two of you are being nice to me at the same time, I have this need to count the silver."

"The spoons are all there," she said.

"If I have such a knack, why don't I understand how you knew that Sheridan Reynolds was paying off Linda Hansen? I mean, I understand why, it's the video and he doesn't want any publicity about Sarah Grange. But how did you know that last night before I talked to Linda?"

"Process of elimination. Our beautiful model and Nora Brown have no reason to extort money from him. And Sheridan Reynolds paying off Linda Hansen has nothing to do with the video, Miss Hill." She sipped her coffee.

I tried to look intelligent. "It doesn't?"

"There is only one possible reason he'd be paying her off. Remember, it's his wife's money. He does what she tells him to. Bring the car around, Boulton. I want to go to Bedford Place."

I turned Cybella's key in the door. The dead bolt released. Claire and I stepped inside the apartment. The air was heavy in the living room. Dust had settled on the crystal paper-weights, the lamps, the objets d'art. The sterling silver picture frames were beginning to tarnish and the silk shades looked as dried and brittle as an old woman's bones. The bright yellow cushions on the sofa needed plumping.

"Decor was a necessity for Cybella." Claire surveyed the room.

She crossed to the fireplace and studied the blowup of mother and daughter. I stared out the window at the East River. A tugboat, which looked as if it had sailed right off the pages of a child's book, bumped along its dirty waters. On the other side of the river's bank a Pepsi-Cola sign smeared red letters across the landscape.

"Where is Sarah's bedroom?" Claire asked.

"The door next to you."

She opened it and we went in. The bed was unmade. Panty hose, like shriveled legs, were abandoned on rumpled sheets. On the dresser a couple of half-full bottles of water stood among small empty bottles of makeup. A dried mas-cara wand pointed toward a few discarded lipsticks. Tops off, the lipsticks had been smeared down to pink nubs. A pearlized blue plastic compact had been left open. The pressed face powder was rubbed away, revealing the tin lin-ing. Four small face sponges, soiled with layers of beige makeup, were scattered like chunks of dirty flesh on the floor.

Inside the closet, a cheap cotton blouse seemed to cling to its hanger for life. Navy blue gabardine slacks, shiny from too much wear, hung from a belt loop. A dress, burdened with bows and buttons, lay on the floor, as if in a swoon. Claire poked her walking stick into the corners of the closet.

"What are you looking for?" I asked.

"Linda Hansen told you that Sarah kept a box of fashion magazines in her closet. Sarah's only connection to her mother."

"Maybe Sarah took the box with her to Nora's."

Claire pulled the blouse off the hanger and looked at it. "Homemade, and washed over and over again until it's almost yellow." She checked the hem of the slacks. "Held together with tape. These are the clothes of someone with very little money. No, Miss Hill, I don't think Sarah took the box of magazines with her."

"Maybe she threw it out when she left Buffalo."

"People who are starving hoard the little food they have instead of eating it. It is the same if you are starved for a mother's attention. You hoard what little piece of memory you have and you don't give it up easily."

"But Sarah was with her mother," I said.

"No, Miss Hill." Her shrewd eyes stared into mine. "Where is Cybella's room?"

I showed her. She opened the door and we walked in.

Claire held up her hand, motioning for me not to move. We stood as still as the room. Her eyes took in the bed, the vanity lined with crystal perfume bottles, the small antique bookcase, the silver-framed photographs on the marble-top nightstand. All of it seemed to be fading under a fine layer of dust.

The mirrored closet held our images. Claire, tall and

poised, tilted her head to one side, listening to the pressing silence, her white pantsuit a stark contrast to the yellow tones of the room. I, in my beige slacks and beige and white plaid jacket, stood with my feet wide apart. My chin jutted forward, as if daring someone to try to knock me over. Claire raised her walking stick, pointed at our reflections, and smiled, then threw open the closet doors. Our images vanished.

Once again Cybella's perfume permeated the room. Its very power seem to crack the stillness and disperse the gathering dust. We stared at the designer clothes arranged so methodically in their clear plastic bags. I unzipped the bag containing the evening gowns. Empty bodices and limp skirts still waited for Cybella's body to bring them to life. The St. Rome dress wasn't much more than a slice of red fabric. It felt cool and slippery in my hands.

"Jackie must've loved the feel of this against her skin," I said.

Claire took her walking stick and poked it into the dark corners of the closet.

"The box of magazines is not here." Claire moved to the vanity and sat down on a stool draped in a gold-threaded fabric. "Cybella needed her clothes. She needed her perfume, her jewelry. She needed to be photographed. She needed to look at herself in the mirror. She needed its affirmation. She needed to be reassured that her guilt didn't show." Claire opened a drawer and stared at an array of makeup neatly arranged. "She needed to paint her lips red. Brush her cheeks with a youthful blush. Only then could Cybella convince herself that she would not have been a good mother. That giving up her child was the right thing to do. That her love for Sheridan Reynolds was all that mattered." She closed the drawer. "Then Cybella could put on her red dress and go out. Then she could pretend that, after all these years, it wasn't for nothing."

Claire stood and ran her hand along the gold damask cover on the bed.

"Cybella needed her possessions. She needed what could not hurt her. She needed a beautiful daughter."

"What do you mean?"

Claire turned and looked at the bookcase. She pulled a book from the shelf and opened it.

"Cybella did not seek enlightenment. She was afraid of it. Afraid it might reflect her empty, narcissistic life back at her." She read the inscription page then returned the book to the shelf.

"Why does the lover always try to transform the object of his or her desire into his or her own image?" she mused. "And why does a mother always want her daughter to reflect her?" She held up her hand and again we listened to the silence.

"Cybella's photographs were still. And a mistress, because of her precarious position, must be silent. Yet she reached out to Elizabeth Reynolds only to discover she had given up her child not for the man she loved, but because of his wife and her money. Then finally she reached out to her own daughter." Claire's eyes met mine. "Or so she thought. Close the closet doors, Miss Hill. Let her rest."

In the Bentley Claire told Boulton to take us to Linda Hansen's. She lived a couple of blocks off Central Park West. When we found a parking place Claire said, "Come in with us, Boulton."

"Are you expecting trouble?" I asked.

She didn't answer. The outer door to Linda's building was unlocked. Her apartment was on the first floor toward the

back. I knocked on the door. It was opened almost immediately.

"Oh, God, Maggie, go away." Linda tried to shove the
door shut, but Boulton was already halfway in, forcing her
back.

"Claire Conrad just wants to ask you some questions," I
said.

"I don't have anything to say." She moved restlessly
around the small room. A soft butter-colored leather sofa
looked like the kind you pull out into a bed. A kilim rug
covered most of the bleached wood floor. A telephone and
answering machine sat on an art deco–style table. Cigarette
butts filled an ashtray next to the phone, pink lipstick thick
on the filtered ends.

"Sheridan Reynolds hasn't arrived yet?" Claire asked.

Linda eyed her suspiciously. She looked younger, more
vulnerable in the daylight. Without the smear of pink lipstick, the shape of her mouth was softer. She had on a
T-shirt and her short tight leather skirt. Add a strand of
pearls and she would've made *Bonton*. Maybe not. There
were still the pockmarks.

"Ask your questions and get out of here." She planted her
hands firmly on her hips.

"Where is your bedroom?" Claire demanded.

"You're standing in it. It's what they call a studio apartment, something I'm sure you haven't experienced."

Claire threw open a door opposite the sofa.

"Just a fucking minute." Linda moved toward her. Boulton grabbed her. "What are you looking for?" Fear narrowed
her eyes.

It was a deep closet with built-in drawers. Provocative
dresses and a couple of short leather jackets and skirts hung
neatly on their hangers. With her walking stick Claire lifted
a blanket off the floor, revealing a cardboard box.

"Will you get this for me, Miss Hill?"

I picked up the box and carried it to the sofa. It was half filled with magazines. I looked at a copy of *Bonton* from the year 1966. A young Cybella, her lean figure clad in a gold sequined gown, smiled from the cover. Her eyes were heavy with black liner and false eyelashes, her lips a pale pink. The long dark hair was backcombed into a wild mane, her body curved seductively as if molded by an invisible lover's hands. I gave the magazine to Claire.

"Everything you told Miss Hill that night on the way to Cybella's apartment was true except for who you really are," she said. "These magazines are your only connection to your mother."

Claire methodically began to lay out the magazines on the floor.

"I'm keeping them for Sarah Grange." Linda's voice was flat.

"You made one mistake. In the car going to Cybella's, you told Miss Hill too much. A writer would enjoy the information. A detective might be suspicious of it. Most people say as little as possible to us. Even if they're innocent, they always have secrets they don't want discovered. But you needed to set the scene so when Miss Hill met our beautiful imposter, there wouldn't be any doubt."

"I'm not Sarah and I don't know what you're talking about."

The floor was covered with about twenty magazines, each with Cybella on the cover. Like a chameleon, she changed with every new dress, wig, makeup job. Each photographer saw her differently. She had never been just one woman. Only her dark haunting eyes declared a vulnerable individuality.

"Besides, I'd think Cybella would know her own daughter," Linda added.

"Motherly instinct is highly overrated," Claire replied. "Cybella had not seen you since you were a small child, maybe even a baby. She wanted to believe that giving up her daughter had not caused that child any damage. She wanted a daughter as beautiful as she had once been. That belief overpowered everything."

"A box of magazines proves nothing."

"True. And the last thing I want to do is go to Buffalo to prove I'm right. Miss Hill, Boulton, search the apartment for some kind of identification."

Boulton moved into the tiny kitchen, which was separated from the room by an imitation pink granite counter.

I ran my hands inside the pockets of her jackets. And patted down the linings. There was nothing. I went into the bathroom. It felt damp. I could smell the freshness of soap and shampoo. I opened a drawer. Her makeup was arranged as neatly as Cybella's.

"I found it," Boulton said. "A birth certificate and a Buffalo driver's license. Not so cleverly taped to the back of the refrig . . ." He stopped.

I came out of the bathroom. Linda stood there with a gun pointed at Claire. Tears streaked her face. Pockmarks glistened. "What are you looking at, Maggie?"

"You."

"Well, don't. You're not going to see any resemblance to Cybella."

"You have your mother's figure and your father's gray eyes," I said.

"That gun is more of an irritant than a threat." Claire perched calmly on the arm of the sofa. "If you were going to kill someone, you would have shot Miss Hill last night when you had the chance."

"I just want you to leave. Now!" Her hand trembled.

"Besides, Boulton can take the gun from you anytime he wishes."

Linda's gaze darted to Boulton. Claire swung her walking stick, knocking the gun from her hand. Boulton picked it up.

Closing her eyes, Linda leaned against the wall. "I used to walk down the street and pretend I heard a woman calling out my name. I'd turn and imagine Cybella standing there, holding her arms out. But I never once in my worst nightmare thought Cybella would mistake somebody else for me."

"What is the imposter's name?" Claire asked.

She opened her eyes and studied Claire. "If I tell, will you leave? I just want to see my father face-to-face for the first time, take his money, and get out of here."

"You can't run away. Three people have been murdered," I said.

"Yeah, and guess who's going to be blamed for it?"

"I don't think you killed anybody, Miss Grange," Claire offered.

"Don't call me that. I'm Linda."

"What's the imposter's name, Miss Hansen?"

"Marina Perry."

"You told Marina Perry you were Cybella's daughter?" Claire asked.

"A little more than a year ago, after my grandparents died, I came here. I needed money. I got a job at Peeps. It was the closest I'd ever come to being a model. I took the name Linda Hansen. Marina worked at this shop. We hung out together. Sometimes when Marina held her head a certain way she reminded me of Cybella. Just for a moment." She took a cigarette from the table and lit it. "I got drunk one night, told her the story of my life. She didn't believe me. All the girls at Peeps lie about themselves. I didn't want her to think I was like them. So I kept giving her more and more details. I was such a pushover."

"You told her about Nora Brown?"

"I showed her one of the few letters Cybella had written to me when I was a child. She mentioned Nora. Couple of weeks go by and Marina disappears. It happens, people disappearing. I didn't think much of it." She paused, staring at the magazines, at her mother's face. "I was glad Marina had left. I'd exposed myself. I don't know how long . . . four months later, I'm walking down the street past this news-stand and there on the cover of *Bonton* is Marina Perry. Only she's not Marina Perry. She's Sarah Grange. Cybella's daughter. She's me."

"You called Nora Brown?" Claire asked.

"No. I just told the secretary that Sarah Grange should call Linda Hansen. Marina agrees to meet me. She's driving this black BMW and says it's mine, says I can have a new apartment if I don't say anything." She looked around the room. "You like it, Maggie?"

"You paid too much for it."

"Marina Perry is very bold young woman," Claire observed.

"She had nothing to lose. If her scheme worked, great. If it didn't, so what. She'd be back selling cheap underwear to women like me."

"I assume the video was Goldie's idea."

"He saw the BMW, knew I'd moved into a better apartment. He thought I had some kind of action going that he wasn't in on. Goldie could protect you, he could also hurt you. He made me tell."

There was a knock on the door. All three of us turned in unison and peered at it. Boulton's gun appeared in his hand. Linda lunged. Boulton jerked her back.

"It's my father," she said frantically.

"Your father has a gun," Boulton whispered to her.

We stood, not moving. I was aware of the sound of traffic. The refrigerator groaned. There was another quick knock. Claire turned to me and mouthed the words: "Answer it."

I walked woodenly to the door. Put my hand on the knob. It felt cold. I opened it.

His smile was charming. But his eyes widened. He was surprised to see me. Of course he would be. I wasn't in my proper place.

"Paul Quentin," I announced.

He turned and beat it down the hallway, out onto the street. I was right after him. He ran as gracefully as a quarterback toward the park. I plowed between two women. Quentin kept on running, never looking back. He wouldn't. His kind never do. He crossed Central Park West. The light turned red, and I stopped hard at the curb. Quentin stood on the other side of the street, his hand in the air, hailing a taxi. I moved out into the street hoping for a break in traffic. Cars swerved. Horns blew. Middle fingers became erect. I stumbled back to the sidewalk. Quentin's eyes never once looked in my direction. I did not exist. Jackie did not exist. Soon Alison would not exist.

The light changed and I bolted. He turned on the balls of his feet, took a few long strides toward the stone wall that lined the park, leaped over it, and disappeared behind some trees. The people sitting on the wall watched him. Now they watched me crawl over it.

In the park, I stopped to catch my breath and to see if I could spot him. Fragile branches curled toward the sky. Two young men wearing studded leather jackets smoked and shared a bottle. Their dirty dark hair was carefully waved back. Elvis lives. A couple of joggers ran past them. A drunk staggered toward me, his face as battered as an old American car. Young girls in school uniforms carrying books giggled and gossiped. No Paul Quentin.

I moved deeper into the park. Squirrels darted. A bird sang. Twigs broke underfoot. Not my foot. I turned. The drunk with the battered face stood watching me. He staggered back, then forward, reaching out for me. "Betty? Betty?" he cried.

He grabbed at the air and fell.

"Betty, Betty," he moaned into the ground.

I stood surrounded by trees and a drunk slobbering in the dirt who thought I was Betty. Wonderful. I ran toward the sound of cars close by and came out onto one of the transverse roads. Paul stood, his broad-shouldered back to me, still trying to get that cab. I moved slowly toward him. Hands clutched my shoulders.

"Betty, Betty!" the drunk screamed in my ear.

Paul spun around. The drunk's hands slipped off of me.

"Betty, Betty," he cried desperately.

Paul turned and started to run. I reached, grabbing the tail of his coat. He stumbled sideways. The coat slid off his shoulders and an envelope fell out. The drunk grabbed my free arm, pulling me backward as Paul hurtled forward; the coat slipped from my grip. The drunk jerked me off-balance and we crashed to the ground, tumbling on top of each other. I caught a glimpse of Paul running. So smooth.

"Betty, Betty." His breath was foul.

"I'm not Betty." I shoved my hand in his face.

"Just let me look at you," he panted. He raised his ragged body up off mine like a spent lover. His hands pinned my shoulders down.

A woman with an evil-eyed dachshund walked by. "Why don't you two get a room?" she snapped, pulling the dog away from us.

I brought my right knee up hard into his groin. His eyes glazed. His mouth flopped open.

"Betty," he groaned. He fell onto his side, gagging.

I got to my feet and picked up the envelope. In it was Sheridan Reynolds's hundred thousand dollars. I shoved it into my pocket. My heart was pounding. My legs were killing me. So Sheridan Reynolds had sent his assistant to do a father's job.

"Betty, Betty," the drunk panted.

"Oh, shut up!"

"That's what you always said to me, Betty."

"I am not Betty. We don't all look alike. We don't all have short arms and short legs and big tits and long necks and thick beautiful hair and model clothes nobody can afford and sit on stools in Plexiglas cages. We are not fantasy! We die a little when you leave us and we die forever when you plunge a knife into us."

He cried into the dirt. Oh, God, I was losing it.

The Bentley, as quiet and as dark as night, pulled onto the edge of the road. The door opened and Claire leaned out. I could see Linda Hansen in the backseat with her. "What *are* you doing, Miss Hill?"

"I don't know."

"Who is that?"

"I don't know."

"Employing you is worse than owning a pit bull. Get in the car, please."

I stared down at the drunk who was pulling himself into a sitting position. I looked in the envelope. The smallest bill was a hundred. I shoved it in his dirt-covered hand.

"From Betty," I said.

"That's my money!" Linda yelled.

"Miss Hill!" Claire threatened.

I got into the front seat. I handed Claire the money and

leaned back against the seat. Boulton plucked a few leaves from my hair.

"Nora Brown's office, Boulton," Claire said.

"We're not going after Quentin?" I asked.

"He will only run as far as the Reynolds residence, Miss Hill. He has no place else to go."

"Who is Paul Quentin?" Linda asked.

I turned and looked at her. "You don't know him?"

"No."

"He's your father's assistant. Your half sister's fiancé," Claire explained.

"Father, mother, half sister, fiancé. Those words mean nothing to me."

"Mr. Quentin liked to go to Peep Thrills and watch Jackie," Claire added.

"That's doesn't mean I know him." She turned toward the window. "I wanted to see Sheridan Reynolds, look into his eyes like he was just another needy man and not my father. So he sends me his assistant. Men are bastards."

"How did you find out he was your father?" Claire asked.

"I was scared. I not only thought I could be blamed for the murders, but thought I might be next. I wanted to leave town but I needed more money. So for the first time I called Nora and told her who I was and that I had proof and I wouldn't say anything about Marina if she helped me out. Nora didn't have any money. She broke down. Cried. As if she already knew about me. She told me who my father was. After all these years I learn my father's not French and he's not dead. He's alive and wealthy and could care less about me."

"Why didn't you ask Marina for more money?" I wondered aloud.

"I was afraid. What if she killed Jackie? She still doesn't have anything to lose."

Abruptly we came out of the park. Traffic converged on us. Being swept out of the relative quiet of the park was as jarring to the senses as falling out of bed.

"I used to buy madeleines," Linda said. "I thought eating them made me very French. Except I never was French. Have you ever had one, Maggie?"

"Yes."

"They're very soft in the center."

Twenty-three

Boulton waited by the car.

The *Bonton* receptionist was putting her lipstick on from memory. Claire, Linda, and I walked right past her.

"Just a minute. You can't go in there," she yelled after us. The phone's demanding ring drew her back.

The racks of clothes were gone. The women labored in their cubicles. The two secretaries were standing when we reached Nora's office.

"Do you have an appointment?" the one with the hair the color of bad white wine asked. Her fingers twisted around an expensive pen.

"Miss Brown will see me," Claire said.

"She's not here."

I pushed around her and tried the door. It was locked.

"Where is she?" Claire asked.

"I'm not at liberty to say."

"Miss Hill, get the police on the phone," Claire commanded.

"Police?" the two secretaries responded in unison.

I hate it when she does that. I never know if she means it or not. I reached for the phone.

"Just a minute," the secretary said, taking the phone from

my hand and punching two numbers. "Ms. Brown? That woman, that detective—"

"Claire Conrad," I helped.

"—is here. She's threatening to call the police."

Claire took the phone out of her hand. "Miss Brown, I have Sarah Grange with me."

The two secretaries gaped at Linda.

Claire hung up and announced, "She's on the fourth floor."

We took the elevator down to the fourth where gray doors lined a white hallway. Claire opened the one marked STUDIO.

Except for lights shining on a backdrop of pink paper, curving down from the ceiling like a giant tongue lapping at the floor, the room was dark. A photographer, a silver chain bracelet on each wrist, peered through a camera on a metal tripod, two assistants behind him. Marina Perry stood in the center of the pink paper wearing a tight ankle-length black dress. Lights drenched her skin in a blaze of purity. A large fan off to one side blew her hair back from her carefully made-up face. Some kind of country-and-western rock blared from a CD player. The male singer cried out in twangy, sexy agony.

St. Rome and Nora sat in director's chairs at the edge of the pink paper, as if it were a lake and they didn't want to get their feet wet.

"I want the strap of the dress to fall off her shoulder," St. Rome said, unaware of our presence. "Like the entire dress is about to fall off her."

And this from a man who had never desired a woman.

A girl with dyed red hair and too much red lipstick tiptoed in stockinged feet onto the pink paper and pulled the strap down. She paused, peering out at St. Rome. Receiving no further instructions, she scurried back into the darkness of the room like an animal frightened by light.

"Move to the music, darling Sarah," the photographer coaxed.

She began to form various poses and facial expressions.

"Lean over," the photographer cajoled. "A touch more cleavage, darling. I said, lean over. Let us see the damn things."

She leaned over, revealing the plump curve of her small breasts. Her dark eyes widened with astonishment as if she'd just discovered she had them. Her lips parted, displaying white teeth and the tip of a pink tongue. It was almost the same color as the paper.

"Keep moving," the photographer told her. She obeyed. "Sexy. Sexy. Lick your lips. Sexy. Too much hip. Chin down, darling. I love it. Arms look awkward. Better. Hair is in her face. Darling, can't you see when your hair is in your own face, for God's sake? What happened to sexy? I want sexy. I want *sexy*," he cried. "Is sexy so difficult?"

Nora turned in her chair and saw us. Her face was as pale as a small moon in the darkness. She nodded and we followed her into a long, narrow, brightly lit room. A makeup counter and mirror ran the length of one wall. Electric hair rollers heated in their case. Blow-dryers lay on their sides like bloated guns. Jars and tubes of makeup were scattered on the counter. Pieces of tissue bearing lipstick traces littered the floor. The smell of hair spray and deodorant lingered. Bra and panties were tossed on a chair. St. Rome dresses were jammed together on a rack. A thin man with bleached blond hair sat chewing on the end of a brush and reading a magazine with Ivana Trump on the cover. She too was leaning over and looking as if she had just discovered her breasts.

"The fan keeps blowing the hair in Sarah's face. You should be out there with her," Nora said.

"She said she didn't want me lurking around," he complained, getting to his feet and grabbing a can of hair spray.

"Since when do you listen to the models?" Nora asked.

He made it to the door.

"And nobody is to come in here until Sarah needs to make her change. You got it?"

"Yes, Ms. Brown." He opened the door. The music wailed into the room.

"And close the door."

"Yes, Ms. Brown."

He said "Ms." as if he were playing a southern black servant in a 1930s movie. He closed the door and the music faded. Claire paced the room. I leaned against the closed door.

"Nora Brown, meet Sarah Grange. Sarah Grange, Nora Brown," she said.

Nora tentatively extended her hand. "Hello, Sarah."

Ignoring the gesture, Linda sat on the counter, her back against the long mirror as if she wanted to deny the reality of her own reflection. "I'm Linda."

"Linda," Nora repeated the name. "I was with your mother when she gave birth to you in Paris."

"I'm touched."

"I'm sorry, there's no reason you should be."

"Did I have pockmarks then?"

"What? No, you were a perfect baby."

"I wonder what happened." Linda spoke to the wall in front of her, never looking at Nora.

Nora glanced down at her blue sleeve; there actually was a piece of lint on it. She didn't bother to brush it off. As if suddenly exhausted, she slumped against the counter, her back to the mirror. I guess nobody wanted to look at herself.

"When did you know that Marina Perry was not Sarah Grange?" Claire stopped her pacing and leaned on her walking stick.

"I didn't know until you showed me the video and I confronted her. You have to believe me," Nora said.

"Miss Brown, if you believed she was Sarah, then why didn't you tell her that Sheridan Reynolds was her father? Because you knew she was an imposter."

"There were times when I wondered, but it was just a feeling. She was vague about certain things. I assumed she didn't want to talk about her past. She made Cybella happy." She turned to Linda. "I'm so sorry."

"You keep saying that." Linda's face was expressionless.

"I do, don't I? I'm usually not sorry for anything. Now I can't stop."

"Marina Perry also secured your job at *Bonton*," Claire reminded Nora. "Maybe that helped with any doubts you had."

"Sarah . . . I mean Marina was very good. The first time she called me, all she wanted was to see Cybella. She never mentioned anything about modeling. She let me discover her. When she walked into my office, I knew she had it. The hair needed work, makeup . . . but there was no doubt the camera was going to love her."

"And what about Cybella's love? Did that come as easily as the cameras?" I asked.

"When Cybella saw her," Nora continued, "she reached out. Marina took her hand and said, 'Hello, Mommy.' Cybella wanted to believe. I wanted to believe."

"In what? All this?" Claire raised her stick and took a swipe at the blow-dryers and makeup on the counter. A lipstick and a brush clattered to the floor. Linda laughed sharply—or was it a cry?

I felt the door handle turn and moved away. Marina rushed in. She stopped when she saw us. Her lips drew back, her nostrils flared slightly. She reminded me of a beautiful thoroughbred horse smelling fire.

"Marina, they know," Nora said.

Marina closed the door and locked it. "You can't let them tell anybody, Nora," she said. "You and your magazine will be destroyed. Everything you worked for. St. Rome wants me to change into the gold dress. He's wondering where you are."

"It's over, Marina." Nora almost sounded relieved.

"No." Marina faced Claire. "Don't tell St. Rome, please. I didn't kill anybody."

"You had every reason to," Linda said.

Marina turned on her. "Is that your way of getting back at me? Telling them I killed Jackie and Goldie? This all happened because you're a coward. You didn't even try to stop me. You could've told Cybella you were her daughter, but no, you just wanted to cry about your terrible life. At least you knew where your mother was—I still don't."

There was a knock on the door. "They're waiting, Sarah." It was the hairdresser's voice.

"I have to change." She grabbed a gold sequined dress from the rack and tossed it on an empty chair. She slithered out of her black dress. It crumpled on the floor around her feet like a broken shadow.

"When did Cybella know that you weren't her daughter?" Claire asked.

"She never did. She suffocated me, wouldn't leave me alone." Braless, wearing only panty hose, she leaned against the counter and peered at her face. Her breasts curved toward the mirror as if admiring themselves. "I would've moved out but I couldn't afford to. I was paying Goldie."

Somebody tapped on the door. "Sarah, what are you doing?" It was the hairdresser again.

"I'll be right out."

"Does St. Rome know about any of this?" Claire asked.

"No." With expert precision Marina ran a dark pencil back and forth across the bold line that already outlined her eyes. "He thinks I did the video because I'm a flake, a masochist." Marina threw the pencil down, picked up a soft brush, and stroked her cheeks with it.

"Sarah? Nora? We're waiting." It was St. Rome's voice.

Marina stiffened. "I'm coming." She quickly applied lipstick with a tiny pointed brush, blotted it, and threw the Kleenex on the floor. "I'm making money for Nora and St. Rome. I made Cybella happy."

"Is that why she supposedly killed herself—because she was so happy?" I asked.

"We're all responsible for her suicide," Nora said, then looked at Marina. "I wanted to believe you were making her happy but you weren't. I could see it in her face. And I did nothing because I didn't want to know the truth about your identity."

"All right, she was miserable." Marina took the dress off the chair and stepped into it, pulling it up around her. The sequins shimmered. "She'd just stare at me. I was afraid she'd see that I wasn't her daughter, see it in my eyes. I think she hated me. I didn't care. It was easier if she hated me." Unzipped, the dress hung loosely on her body. She held it to her like a golden shield, took a step back, and sank down awkwardly into a chair. She looked dazed. Her long legs jutted out. Away from the camera and the lights her shoulders looked bony, her hands and feet too large. Her body too thin. Her neck too long. Her make-up too thick. Her hair too wild. Every part of her was an exaggeration.

"I spent nights preparing how to be her daughter, looking in the mirror, remembering everything Linda had told me. But how can you be a daughter when you've never had a mother?" she asked plaintively.

"Nora? What's going on?" St. Rome demanded imperiously through the door.

Marina hurried to her feet. "I've got to get out there," she whispered nervously. "Zip up my dress, Nora."

"It's over, Marina."

"Nora, please," she begged.

"The clock is ticking, ladies," St. Rome persisted.

"Nora, please, I have nothing else in my life. Zip up my dress."

"Sarah, darling!" St. Rome commanded Marina.

She froze as if hypnotized by the voice on the other side of the door. The gold sequined dress shimmered, seeming to have a life of its own.

"Somewhere in these United States is a young girl admiring herself in the mirror this very moment and saying, 'I'm just as pretty as Sarah Grange,' " St. Rome derided. "She'll be strutting into town any day now. So get your ass out here."

Nora stared straight ahead. Linda looked down at the floor. Claire tapped her finger on the head of her walking stick. The lapis shimmered darkly.

"Sarah!" St. Rome pounded on the door.

"Coming!" Marina cried out.

She leaned over, adjusting her breasts in the dress. I thought of the gowns with their empty bodices waiting in Cybella's closet. Then Marina slipped on a pair of gold satin high heels. She turned to Linda. "Fasten my dress."

Linda shook her head.

She faced Nora. "Please."

"No, Marina."

Marina turned her back to me and held her long dark hair up off her shoulders. Her body trembled. "Help me. Help me."

I fastened her dress.

"Thank you." Tears welled, mixing with the eyeliner, streaking her face.

St. Rome knocked.

Twenty-four

"Hurry, Miss Hill." Claire strode quickly through the *Bonton* lobby. Linda ran after us.

"Wait a minute!" she yelled. "What about my money?"

"I thought if we understood why the model had done the video," Claire said, ignoring her, "we would understand why the murders were committed. But the murders have nothing to do with that silly video."

"But Marina Perry . . ."

"There's only one person who could have committed these murders. But I need proof. The police ignored the woman, Miss Hill. I've been avoiding her but I can't any longer."

"What woman? Who are you talking about?" I asked.

"I want my money!" Linda caught up with us by the Bentley.

"No!" Claire snapped. "And I don't have time to talk."

"It's mine, or am I still a suspect?" she demanded.

"You are not. But the police are going to want to talk to you, young woman. If I give you the money, you'll run away."

"So when do I get it?" Her tough demeanor was back.

"When the case is over."

"Marina Perry did it. The case should be over now. So give me my money."

"She is not the murderer."

"But she has a motive," I said.

"What is her motivation for following Jackie to our hotel that morning? If she'd wanted to kill her, all she'd have to do is call and arrange a meeting with her in some out-of-the-way place. I will call you, Miss Hansen."

"Don't worry, you'll be hearing from me." She tossed her head back and managed a sardonic smile. "Coin of the realm. See you around, Maggie." She turned and headed down Madison. Her body swayed with sexy abandon. Two men deep in conversation swiveled their heads in unison, watching her. Linda had her audience, her own version of being on the cover of *Bonton*. At least she had it for a while.

"I hate to say this," I said, settling in my corner of the car, "but I'm beginning to think Cybella did kill herself."

"You'll be happy to know that for once a beautiful woman did not die by her own hand. The Duke Hotel, Boulton."

He turned to look at her. "The Duke, madam?"

"She didn't open the door. That's what was disturbing me when we discovered Goldie's body."

"The Woman Who Cries?" I asked.

"She sits alone in her room, crying out for help, listening for the footsteps that might bring it." Claire's voice was concentrated and precise, as if recalling a dream. "And when she hears them she pushes open the door, and clutching her torn garments to her naked body, she screams out for that help."

"Just because she didn't open the door when we walked by doesn't mean . . ."

"Miss Hill, it's a ritual, a compulsion. She must scream

for help, she must open the door. But the afternoon we discovered Goldie's body, something overpowered her compulsion."

"But what?" Boulton asked.

"Is she a reliable witness?" I asked.

"I don't think you should do this, madam."

But Claire had stopped talking and had closed her eyes, leaving Boulton and me to look with concern at one another in the rearview mirror.

Twenty minutes later we were walking down the side street next to the hotel. Claire stopped at the alley. "I'd like to avoid the desk clerk. Let's see if the back door has been locked," she said.

In the alley the smell of urine and garbage mixed with the aroma of Chinese cooking. I thought of the flies circling over the thick red meat. Claire rested her white-gloved hand on the handle of the hotel's back door.

"If I am unable to question her, Miss Hill," Claire instructed, "I want you to. I doubt she'll be coherent, so you must listen to her words carefully and take them literally. Do not project your own feelings onto her."

"I understand," I said.

"It's the shattering of all logic, the shattering of the intellect by one violent act. It is chaos I abhor. The chaos of helplessness, of weakness. You know I could do nothing for my family, or yours, Boulton."

"I know, madam."

She pulled at the door. It opened; a broken chain dangled from the handle. "The tenants still rule," she commented as we stepped into the alcove.

Boulton let the door close quietly, easing us slowly into the darkness of the hotel.

We moved to the dim light at the top of landing. The woman whimpered in her room. Her door remained closed.

Claire tapped it with her walking stick. It swayed open, re-vealing the woman crouched on her bed, clutching ripped clothes to her half-naked body. The room smelled of dirty hair, unclean sheets, and soiled flesh. Light from a brass lamp shaped like a genie's bottle cast a weak glow over the woman's tormented face. Wrinkles as thick as bird's claws pulled at her colorless eyes and twisted the skin on her chin and neck. Tears stained her face and breasts. Elizabeth Reyn-olds cried in much prettier isolation.

Claire walked slowly to the bed and looked down at her. The woman drew back, cowering. Claire's shoulders grew rigid. I felt Boulton move behind me. The woman threw her arm over her face as if to ward off an imaginary blow. Claire flinched and stepped back. The woman let her arm fall to her side. She stared at Claire with eyes that could see only horror.

"I've come to help you," Claire said, her voice hollow.

"Yes?" The woman's voice was raspy but childlike.

"Yes." Perspiration had formed above Claire's lip. The hand on the walking stick trembled. She looked down at it and willed it into stillness.

The woman peered around at us. Her body began to shake. She raised a swollen finger and pointed at Boulton.

"No, no, no," she cried out. "Don't hit me."

"It's all right," Claire said.

The woman's mouth fell open like an old empty purse and she screamed. The suddenness of it made my body jerk. Somebody pounded on the floor above but she continued to scream, and for a moment there seemed to be nothing else in the world but her cry.

Claire turned on Boulton. "Leave the room."

"Miss Conrad, I don't think . . ."

"Boulton!"

He stepped out, closing the door. The screaming stopped.

I let out my breath. The back of my neck was damp with sweat. My hair clung to it like wet fingers.

"I helped you," Claire said soothingly. "He's gone."

"There are others." The woman's eyes searched the room. "With their car lights and their heavy dirty boots."

"They're gone too."

"They always come back. Always."

"Did they come back yesterday?" Claire clenched the handle of her walking stick so tightly that her hand drained of color.

"Yesterday?"

"Do you remember yesterday?"

"Always. Always." Her words turned into a whimper.

"Do you remember Goldie?"

She nodded. Claire's eyes grew distant. And again it was as if she were seeing beyond the woman into another room, another world. I walked toward her. The woman sucked in her breath at my sudden movement.

"No! No!" she gasped.

"Claire?" I murmured.

"I cannot help her." Claire stared at the woman, unseeing.

"Did you see Goldie yesterday?" I asked the woman. The sweat ran from my neck down my back like a sharp fingernail.

"Car lights, surrounding me. I can't see because of the lights. But I can see their boots on the ground. They laughed. One grabbed my hair. The other my legs. The lights are so bright."

"Let's go," I said to Claire. When she didn't move, I put my arm around her and guided her toward the door. I reached for the knob but the head of her walking stick stopped me.

"Not yet, Miss Hill." She turned quickly and confronted the woman. "Were there lights yesterday?" The sharpness in her voice was back.

"Always."

"And the light blinded you?" Claire demanded.

"They wanted it that way."

"So you couldn't identify them?"

"Yes, yes." Her dead eyes searched the room once more. "Handsome young men. Bright lights. I just wanted them to want me."

"And Goldie. Did you see him? Hear him?"

"He moaned."

"Did he moan after you saw the light?"

She nodded. "I was afraid. I didn't open my door any-more. They'll come with their car lights." She let out another piercing cry. The woman put her hand over her mouth. Yellow nails curved. The screaming stopped. Her hand dropped from her lips.

Claire opened the door and moved out into the hall.

"I wanted to feel beautiful," the woman said to me in a little-girl voice, trying to cover her sagging breasts with the thin shreds of her clothes, of her decency.

Gently I closed the door.

Shadowed by the dim light at the top of the landing, Boulton waited. Claire walked past him and down the stairs without speaking.

"Is Miss Conrad all right?" he asked.

"I think so."

"Anything?"

"Not that I could tell."

He moved from the shadows and his eyes searched mine. "What's wrong, Maggie?"

I needed to know that it was all right between men and women. I reached out my hand. He took it.

The woman screamed.

Twenty-five

"The Reynolds residence, Boulton."

"Who did the woman see, madam?" he asked, pulling out onto the street.

"Not who, Boulton. It's what she saw. Light."

I looked at her. "She always sees lights. Car lights in her mind."

"And yesterday she saw a light and it wasn't in her mind. It was real and it shattered her compulsion. I want you to come with us, Boulton."

The doorman at Avenue 8000 was behind his granite console controlling his monitors. "Mr. Reynolds and his daughter are both out," he informed Claire.

"What about Paul Quentin?" she asked.

"Does he expect you?"

"Tell him he will either expect me or he will expect the police."

He picked up the phone and discreetly repeated Claire's threat.

In the elevator Claire instructed me: "Miss Hill, I want you to steal the film in Alison's camera. The camera she carries in her tote bag. If there are any used rolls of film, take those too."

"She always has the bag with her," I said. "But I'll take a look. I don't know anything about cameras. She has state-of-the-art equipment. How do I get the film out?"

"I assume there's a button to push."

"Why?"

"Because there's always a button to push. Isn't there, Boulton?"

"Always, madam."

"I mean, why steal the film?"

"The bright light, Miss Hill."

The elevator doors opened, and Paul Quentin stood there, all clean and pressed after our run in the park. He had a death grip on a glass of scotch. The blue eyes shone like ice, but he was still able to give us one of his exquisite smiles.

"You didn't need to threaten me with the police. I have no reason not to see you."

"You finally caught a cab," I said. "Why'd you run?"

"I always run. I hate to be tacky, but the money . . . ?"

"We have it, Mr. Quentin," Claire informed him. "How long has the family known that the woman who said she was Sarah Grange is an imposter?"

"They didn't know until the real Sarah, I believe she calls herself Linda Hansen, informed us yesterday. Elizabeth was suspicious. She couldn't figure out why the model never contacted us. Of course, Elizabeth is always suspicious."

"Mrs. Reynolds also wanted to draw my attention to the model and away from her own family. That's why she met with me, why she told me the model was Sheridan's daughter. Isn't that true?"

He smiled inappropriately, then gulped some more scotch.

Claire strode into the living room and sat impatiently in one of the black velvet chairs. "Where are Sheridan Reynolds and Alison?"

"I don't know."

"Are they together?"

"Yes."

"A wedding is much better than blackmail, isn't it?" she asked.

"What are you talking about?" he asked.

"It's so much more respectable. It assures that what you know about the deaths of Cybella, Jackie, and Goldie will all be kept in the family. That would please Mr. and Mrs. Reynolds, wouldn't it? And you would be guaranteed a life of wealth."

"I've made no attempt to hide the fact that I am interested in money. But that doesn't mean I know anything about these deaths."

"Tell me about Jackie."

"I already told your assistant everything I know."

"Listen to me carefully, Mr. Quentin." Claire's voice was strangely calm and menacing at the same time. "I am a woman who abhors violence. So is Miss Hill. But Boulton has a vicious streak. Don't let his careful studied appearance fool you. I would hate to see you harmed in any way."

"Are you threatening me?"

"With physical violence. Yes."

His eyes brought Boulton into focus. "I'm a nonviolent person myself." He took a quick sip, listed toward the window, and stared out at the heavens. "I was utterly captivated by Jackie. I couldn't get enough of her. At first I'd meet her at the Duke but I didn't like the surroundings. So we began to meet in elegant hotel suites. She was so exquisitely trashy. So perfectly common. I loved watching her in those rooms. I was fascinated by the contrast. She would do anything I wanted. Anything." He faced us. "I adored her. I didn't kill her. And I have positioned myself so that no matter what

happens in this family I will survive. Even if it's just Elizabeth Reynolds and me."

"Just like a cockroach," I said.

"Alison knew about Jackie, didn't she? She knew about
the hotel suites." Claire stood and began to pace.

"I might have told her."

"She followed Jackie. She thought Jackie was meeting you
at the Parkfaire. But she wasn't," Claire said to no one in
particular.

"You'll have to ask Alison," Quentin replied primly.

She stopped pacing and demanded, "Where is her darkroom?"

He hesitated. "Why?"

"Tell her," Boulton warned.

"Second door down the hall off the foyer."

Claire nodded at me and I headed down the hall. The
darkroom was as clean and as inviting as an operating room.
I looked through cupboards and drawers. There was no tote
bag, no cameras. I went down the hall opening doors: a den,
a man's bedroom, bathroom. A dark, musty room with dust
sheets thrown over the bed and the chairs. Elizabeth Reynolds's, I assumed. A pale blue bedroom with an open shoe
box on the bed. White peau de soie high heels nestled in
their white tissue paper. Shoes to match a wedding gown.
The tote bag rested on the floor next to her dresser. I took
the camera from the bag. I hated cameras. People smiling.
Smiling even if they're miserable. Immediate revision of the
moment. Smile if you're having a terrible vacation. Smile,
then get divorced. Smile . . . my finger slipped, pressing a
button. The flash went off in my eyes. I froze. I couldn't see
a thing. Gold rings shimmered. Depression crawled through
me. I put the camera back and carried the tote bag out to
Claire.

"I don't like where this case is going. What do you expect to see on this film?" I handed her the tote bag.

"The woman at the Duke Hotel. Car lights can momentarily blind the vision, Miss Hill. So can a flash of light. The kind of quick dazzling light that comes from a camera. It was a defensive move. So the woman could not identify anybody. Isn't that right, Mr. Quentin?"

"I wouldn't know."

"What happens when you get that film developed and find out there is nothing but chimney pots, hinges, and door knockers on it?" I asked.

"I don't think that will be the case, do you, Mr. Quentin?"

He didn't answer. He was between smiles. Not a pretty sight. She handed the bag to Boulton. "Use her darkroom. How long will it take to develop the film?"

"A half hour, forty-five minutes at the most."

Claire studied the tote. The lines deepened around her mouth. "Just a minute, Boulton. Doesn't Alison always take this with her?" she asked Quentin.

"I guess she forgot it. Why?"

"Where is she? Where have they gone?" she demanded urgently.

"I told you, she left with her father. That's all I know."

"You've been waiting here, drinking. You said even if it's just you and Elizabeth Reynolds. What are you waiting for?"

"For Sheridan and Alison to return." The hand with the drink trembled. Ice tinkled.

"I don't think so. I think you're hoping they don't return. Break his fingers, Boulton."

"Jesus Christ!" Quentin staggered back, dropping the glass. It shattered on the limestone floor like a small star colliding with the earth. Boulton gripped his arm. Before he even touched his fingers, Quentin's knees buckled.

"They've gone to Cybella's. Sheridan wanted to see her

apartment for the last time," he whimpered. "That's what he told me."

"This is very important, Miss Hill. I want you to go to Bedford Place. I want you to keep them there, if we're not too late. Wait for my call."

"Be careful, Maggie," Boulton warned. "Remember he has a gun."

"You're wrong about Alison," I said.

"I'm never wrong, Miss Hill," she said, sadly.

Twenty-six

Sitting in the back of a cab racing down Park, I thought of Alison taking my picture.

Don't move, Maggie.

Smile, Maggie.

Expensive apartment buildings gave way to expensive office buildings.

Alison was creative. She had a chance to survive, to be something other than an angry woman, a needy, desperate, rejected woman. A woman who waited. A woman who killed. Claire had to be wrong.

I left the cab, and the cold spring wind blew right through me, as if my existence didn't matter.

The dead bolt clicked, and once again I pushed open the door to Cybella's apartment. Before walking in, I listened. No sounds. I took the gun out of my purse, stepped quietly inside and closed the door. The living room showed no signs of visitors. Dirty face sponges were still strewn across the floor in Marina's room. Her clothes from another life remained sheltered in the closet. I went back and stood outside Cybella's bedroom, listened again. I pushed the door. It swung back, banging against the wall, the ruffles on the linen pillows billowing with the movement of air. But that was the only reaction to my grand entrance. I moved toward the bathroom. I peered inside at marble walls and a marble tub the color of flesh.

Maybe Sheridan and Alison had come and gone. Maybe they weren't even coming. I sat on the vanity stool and waited. In the mirrored closet, I looked at myself holding the gun. I held it like I almost knew what I was doing, but my eyes and mouth took on a humorous, ironic look as if I were going to tell a witty story. The silence creaked. I waited. The silence creaked some more. A door opened and closed.

Heavy footsteps.

I moved swiftly into the bathroom and positioned myself behind the half-open door.

Sheridan Reynolds came into the room. He looked like a man peering over the edge. Removing his overcoat, he tossed it on a chair and stared down at Cybella's bed. Gently, he touched the silky damask cover. His fingers tightened around the fabric. Slowly he pulled the cover to him as if he were pulling Cybella into his arms. He buried his face in the spread, then dropped to his knees. He stroked the bed poignantly as if stroking her naked body. His mouth opened and a deep dry sob escaped. Still on his knees, he leaned against the end of the bed and cried.

Again the sound of a man crying left me feeling uneasy. It is the sound of our fathers losing control. It is the sound of the world cracking apart. I wanted to stay where I was. I wanted to leave him with his pain, his loss. Then Alison appeared in the doorway, her arms folded against her breasts, her lips pressed in a tight line. She watched her father through eyes filled with bitterness and hurt. She looked like her mother. I moved into the room with my hand tight around the gun.

"Claire Conrad wants to see both of you," I said.

Sheridan stumbled to his feet and faced me. His eyes were swollen from tears. Alison didn't move.

"What are you doing here?" her father managed to ask me.

"We're going to wait for Claire," I said. "Sit on the end of the bed, Alison." She did as she was told.

"Take the gun out of your pocket and place it on the floor," I told Sheridan.

"I don't have a gun on me."

"You had a gun on you last night."

"Well, I don't have one now."

"Then take off your jacket."

"I will not. You going to shoot me? And her?"

"If you give me any trouble, I'll shoot you in the arm or the leg. Then I'll have to call the paramedics and they'll call the police. Wouldn't you rather talk to Claire Conrad? Now take off your jacket and drop it on the floor. Slowly."

He finally did.

"Now sit on the end of the bed."

He slowly sat down. I grabbed the jacket and pulled it to me. The gun was in the right-hand pocket.

"You must understand, Cybella's death was an accident," he said. His hand softly stroked the coverlet. "Oh, God. I thought I could handle it, take care of everything." He stood.

"Sit down."

"I just want to wash my face."

Still able to see Alison, I stood in the bathroom doorway. He wet a towel, then buried his face in it. His shoulders jerked convulsively. "I never had a chance to mourn for Cybella properly."

I would have felt more for him had he left out the word *properly*. There was something self-righteous about it. He stepped from the bathroom wiping the back of his neck with the towel.

"Sit back down on the end of the bed," I told him.

"Let me go away with my father." Alison finally spoke.

The phone rang. Sheridan leaped to his feet.

"Sit down!" I yelled, grabbing the receiver.

"Miss Hill?" It was Claire. "I'm holding a photograph of the Woman Who Cries. Are they with you?"

"Yes."

"We're on our way."

I hung up the phone.

"This is ridiculous. You have no right to hold us. Where is Claire Conrad anyway?"

I wasn't listening to him. It was Alison I wanted to hear. "It's a waste, isn't it? All your talent? All your hope and promise?"

"Hope and promise?" The hazel eyes blinked.

"Tell me about Cybella. You remember her, your muse?"

"Don't say anything, Alison," her father warned.

Her eyes lost their alertness. She took on the look that abused children sometime have, the look that says, I am no longer a part of this moment, this situation. I am in my own world where no one can touch me or hurt me. "I pushed her over the railing."

"Let us go," he said. "Please."

"I looked over the railing," Alison continued, as if he had not spoken. "I saw all the doormen rush to her. I took the elevator down. There was so much commotion, I just walked away without anyone noticing me. I wish someone had."

"Let me take care of this myself," Sheridan pleaded.

"Like you've taken care of all your women?" I demanded.

He leaped to his feet, snapping the towel at my face. The heavy wet end bit like a whip under my right eye. He snapped it again. I thrust out my arm to block it. My gun fell from my hand. The towel stung my neck. He bent over and reached for his coat jacket. I kicked at his side. He rose, swinging his jacket hard against my head. I took the weight of the gun in his pocket full force. Alison's small delicate face was frozen in time like a cameo. He swung again. My knees buckled. Sheridan must have been a popular guy in the men's locker room. The white carpeting turned dark.

Twenty-seven

I opened my eyes. The darkness spun. I closed them. Quiet.
No distant sound of traffic, no car horns blasting their one
long *fuck you*. Too quiet. I missed those horns. I opened my
eyes. Stomach turned. Mouth dry. I licked my lips. Pain shot
through my cheekbone. I raised my hand to my face. The
right side was swollen. Not to worry. I had use of my arms.
My legs? Maybe. I was flat on my back. The bed was soft.
Would my legs work if I stood on them? That was the question. Bed? Cybella's? I slowly sat up. The darkness dipped.
I got my feet to the floor. Uncarpeted. Not Cybella's. I sat,
panting like a dog, trying to keep my stomach down, my
body upright.

A door opened somewhere in the blackness. Light slashed
a path right to me. Alison walked along the ray of light like
an angel on a golden tightrope.

"Maggie?"

I looked down the golden path and saw her father in the
next room sitting at a desk. Men are always sitting at their
desks. Rome burns. Maggie dies. Men sit at their desks.

Alison peered down at me, then walked back to the door
and shut it. We were plunged into darkness. Panic seized me.

"Close your eyes, Maggie, I'm going to turn on a light," she said.

Not on your life. I kept them wide open. Light blasted the room. I was blinded. My eyes closed all by themselves.

"Are you all right?" she asked.

I balanced myself on the precipice of the bed and opened them. Blinking, I adjusted to the brightness. My right eye ached.

Alison sat in a chair across from the bed, her small face colorless and strained. In contrast, her hazel eyes had an unnerving brilliance. The abused child had disappeared. "I want to talk to you."

I became aware of the room. The walls were papered in some kind of ivy print. The floor was dark oak planks with a red and green needlepoint rug. The bed was all goose down and pillows. She sat in a chair that was covered in a green trellis-print fabric. Everything was perfectly mismatched. Another expensive room.

"Where am I?"

"Our country home."

"Any particular country?"

"Near Greenwich. This is my bedroom."

"What time is it?"

"Around seven."

"In the evening?"

She nodded, and curled her legs under her. One girlfriend getting ready for a long chat with another. "I want you to understand what I did. I care what you think about me."

"Is that why you brought me here? Alison, I don't know what I look like but I bet I'm not looking too pretty."

"I'm sorry, Maggie. My father was desperate." She adjusted a tortoiseshell barrette that held back her unruly hair. She uncurled her legs, stood, opened a dresser drawer, and pulled out a pink sweater. She threw it over her shoulders. "Are you warm enough?"

"Yes."

When I looked the room over again, this time it wasn't for decor but for escape routes. There was one large draped window. Besides the bedroom door, there were two other closed doors. I assumed one led to a closet, the other a bathroom.

She moved back to the chair and sat down. "Paul would tell me about Jackie, tell me how he liked to watch her, how he liked taking her to different hotels. He enjoyed telling me about her."

She leaped up quickly, as if somebody had called her name, and began to move restlessly around the room. With the pink cardigan pulled around her shoulders, she looked like a teenager waiting for the phone to ring. She looked like any mother would want her daughter to look.

"My mother's pain, her hurt didn't allow for anyone else's. I'd cry, she'd cry. Her tears would overpower mine. One day I just stopped crying. I stopped feeling. I started following Jackie and Paul. I began to feel again. I felt anger."

"Did you plan to kill Jackie before or after you killed Cybella?"

Her head jerked back as if I had slapped her. Even now she couldn't think of herself as a murderer. She was just a daughter trying to work out her problems with her mother.

"After." Her voice was a whisper.

"Killing Cybella made it easier to kill Jackie, didn't it?"

She couldn't answer; instead she said, "Maggie, I did tell Cybella about studying her pictures in the library. She put her arms around me, and I couldn't remember my mother ever embracing me like that. I got all confused. I said terrible things to her and ran out onto the landing. She followed me." She picked up a silver-framed picture from her dresser and handed it to me.

"My first really good photograph."

A young, almost-pretty Elizabeth Reynolds stood next to a young, handsome Sheridan Reynolds. Her smile was wary, her eyes riveted on her husband. He was looking away as if something beautiful had caught his eye.

"How old were you when you took this?" I asked.

"Ten."

She returned the picture. "I like the composition of it. Even then I could understand the importance of space and distance between objects." Her eyes searched my face for some kind of recognition. "You liked my pictures, didn't you, Maggie?"

"Yes."

"I know my work needs refinement. But the more I do it the better my pictures will . . ." She stopped.

We stared at one another. "Your work isn't going to get any better. You're never going to have the refinement that comes with years of practice." Anger filled my voice.

"I know, Maggie. I tried to tell you that."

The door opened and Sheridan Reynolds stood there with a gun in his hand. It almost pointed at me.

"Claire Conrad will be looking for her, Alison. We don't have much time." His body leaned heavily against the door jamb. His eyes were two small cavities in his face.

"What are you going to do?" I asked.

"There's a letter on my desk explaining our deaths."

I struggled to my feet. "Don't do this." I started toward them. "You can't." He pointed the gun at me. I stopped.

"Killing you won't matter to me now." He looked like a man who meant it. "It's best this way."

"Alison, don't let him do this."

She turned and looked at me. Her eyes were no longer

bright. Sheridan looked at her with a mixture of love and regret. I had a chilling feeling that his wife and mistress had received the same look.

"Good-bye, Maggie," she said.

"Wait! Please, don't."

He guided her out of the door, his fatherly hand pressed tenderly on the back of her pink sweater. I heard the door being locked, then the sound of something heavy being pushed against it.

Still woozy, I moved toward the large draped window. I pulled the curtains open and peered out. The moon aimed a coldhearted glare across the tops of black trees. The window was either stuck or bolted. I tugged at it again. Nothing. I grabbed a heavy brass lamp off the nightstand and swung its base at the glass. It cracked. I swung again. The window glass shattered. I knocked away at the jagged edges, then leaned out. The cold air hit me. I was on the second story about fifteen feet from the ground. There was no latticework on the side of the house, no convenient tree limbs, nothing but a drop that might break only one leg and an elbow. If I was lucky.

One of the closed doors opened into a closet. The other opened into the bathroom. I found the light switch. No windows, only my reflection in the mirror.

Blood matted my hair near my left temple. A welt had formed under my right eye where he had got me with the towel. No woman should look this way. I ran the water and splashed it on my face. I leaned over the sink and let the water drip off me. My hands gripped the curve of the white porcelain bowl. I waited. No sound. No gunfire, only my breathing. I waited until a gunshot cracked the silence. That was one. It would take a few moments. Even minutes. He would have to look at her. Cry out for the loss, for what might have been. I ran more water and splashed it on my face. He had to be holding the gun to his head, or neck, or heart, and wondering about the pain. His hand would shake. He didn't want to flinch, didn't want to merely wound himself. I turned the water off and peered into the mirror. My eyes were dilated with fear. There was no second shot. He couldn't do it. It was easier to kill someone else, even your daughter, than to kill yourself. He was a man who could handle it all, a man who had all his women tucked safely away. He was a man with a gun in his hand. And I was another woman.

A door opened and closed somewhere in the house. I turned off the bathroom light. Heavy footsteps. On the stairs. I moved across the bedroom, grabbed the lamp I had used to break the window, switched off the overhead light. I waited by the bedroom door where the footsteps stopped. I held the lamp like a baseball bat. The heavy barrier was being pushed away from the door. I had one swing. One chance.

The key turned. The door opened slowly. He took one step in. I swung. His arm shot up, blocking my swing. The lamp was knocked from my hand. The weight of his body crushed me against the wall. His free hand grabbed my throat. Fingers pressed. No air. I kicked. No breath. He shoved his leg between mine.

"Maggie." The fingers loosened their hold.

"Jesus Christ, Boulton."

Twenty-eight

Claire sat on the edge of Sheridan Reynolds's desk going through his papers.

"You look terrible, Miss Hill."

"Thank you."

"Mr. Reynolds has left a suicide note for himself and his daughter."

"There was only one shot. It came from outside the house."

Her sharp eyes held me for a moment, then she moved swiftly. Boulton and I followed her down some stairs and into a large colonial-style hallway. The walls were lined with pictures of mallards.

The light from the porch spilled down brick steps and pooled onto the cobblestone drive. The Bentley was parked at an angle. The dark figure of a man inside.

"Who's that?" I asked.

"Paul Quentin," Boulton said. "Handcuffed to the steering wheel."

"He guided us to the house reluctantly," Claire explained.

I could see our breath curling in the cold night air. It was as if our souls were escaping, as if they couldn't take any

more. I stared at Quentin. He looked quite at home in the
Bentley, in the perfect box at last.

"Here, Maggie." Boulton handed me my gun. "We found
it in Cybella's bedroom."

"Could you tell which way the shot came from?" Claire
asked.

"No. But not too far from the house."

The moon followed us like an aloof lover as we made our
way around to the back. Boulton held a flashlight he'd taken
out of the car. We came to a large terrace overlooking a
tennis court and swimming pool. The flashlight shone on it.
Looking like reclining old men, empty Adirondack chairs
waited for summer. We moved toward the tennis court. The
flashlight's narrow beam traveled over the surface of the
court. Leaves were piled in one corner. There was no net.
Beyond the tennis court was a phalanx of trees. We headed
for them.

Just where the civilized garden ended and the woods began was Sheridan Reynolds. The moon seemed even more
remote, as if it were trying to put a great distance between
itself and the man kneeling on the grass. The flashlight bore
into his raised distraught face.

"I couldn't do it. Alison stood there waiting. I raised the
gun and fired into the air. I couldn't even turn it on myself."
The circle of light slipped from his face and moved on the
ground near him.

"Where's the gun?" Claire asked.

"She grabbed it and ran into the woods."

"Get Paul Quentin, Boulton. And call the Greenwich Police and have them come here." He ran back toward the car.

I stared at the thick bank of black trees. "Has there been
another shot?"

He shook his head and got to his feet.

"What is she doing out there?" I wondered.

"Shadow Hills is on the other side," he answered.

"Sometimes mother's milk, even if it's mostly tears, is better than nothing," Claire observed, looking at Sheridan. "I want you to wait with Paul Quentin until the police arrive. Then bring them to Shadow Hills. Do you understand me, Mr. Reynolds?"

"Yes."

"How do we get to the sanitarium from here?" Claire asked.

He gave her directions. Boulton and Quentin hurried across the lawn. "Are they dead?" Quentin asked. "Are they?" He was unable to keep the eagerness out of his voice. His arms were handcuffed behind his back. He stumbled to a stop when he saw Sheridan.

"Oh, thank God, you're all right," he said, quickly adjusting. "Tell them to take these things off me."

"I don't understand," Alison's father mumbled. "He hasn't done anything."

"He killed a man known as Goldie," Claire offered.

"Goldie?" Sheridan repeated the name.

"I swear I didn't. Alison's photographs prove I didn't do it," Quentin blurted. "Alison killed him. She killed all of them."

"Mr. Quentin." Claire spoke impatiently. "You've been with Jackie at the Duke. You had to know about the back door to the hotel, and more important, you had to know about the Woman Who Cries. If Alison were going to kill Goldie, she would not have had her camera ready to take a picture. But you would. Because you knew the woman would open the door."

"It was Alison!"

"Boulton!"

Boulton moved behind Quentin and jerked his elbows straight up, forcing him down to his knees. Quentin screamed.

"Stop it," Sheridan demanded weakly.

"He'll break your shoulders, Mr. Quentin," Claire said.

Quentin groaned. Boulton released him. "Goldie thought I killed Jackie. He was going to kill me. Alison hadn't slept." Quentin was breathing hard. "She came back to the apartment yesterday on the early morning train. She wanted to confess to you about killing Cybella and Jackie, but her parents wouldn't allow it. She went to her room and slept. I took her camera and a knife from the kitchen, and went to the Duke Hotel." He looked up at Sheridan. "She'd murdered two people, for God's sake. What's one more?" His lips quivered into a feeble line. I hoped he was permanently between smiles, the equivalent of purgatory for Paul Quentin.

Alison's father turned from him and moved hesitantly, like an old man, toward the house. Boulton jerked Quentin to his feet, and we made our way back around the house to the Bentley. Quentin and Sheridan walked up the steps to the house. They paused between two Jeffersonian columns.

We sped down the drive and onto a dark road. The Bentley's lights spread the blackness apart.

"Tell me what Alison and her father said tonight, Miss Hill," Claire said.

As I spoke, I could hear her ring tapping against the handle of her walking stick. When I finished, the tapping stopped. "Miss Hill?"

"Yes?"

"I'm going to let this come to its natural conclusion."

"What does that mean?"

"It means I want you to do as I say."

A few minutes later Boulton stopped the car in front of

a gate across the sanitarium driveway. We got out and walked around the gate, which only blocked the drive. We followed a dirt path onto the grounds and up a slight ridge. Bungalows dotted the landscape beyond. A few glowed with light. We went down the other side of the ridge and stopped. A female figure kneeled in the path. All I could make out was long hair. I slipped my hand into my pocket and gripped my gun as we moved closer. Boulton's flashlight found her. Frantically searching for something on the ground, she jumped up, transfixed by the light. I remembered her from our last visit to Shadow Hills. Thin as death, defiantly refusing her fattening pink drink.

As we approached she hid her hands behind her back. I wondered if we looked as desperate as she did.

"Could you tell us where Mrs. Reynolds's cabin is?" Claire asked, as if we were all taking a Sunday afternoon stroll.

"What are you people doing out here?" the girl whispered. "You're supposed to be in your rooms."

"What are *you* doing out here?" Claire demanded.

"Collecting rocks." She brought her hands from behind her back. She held smooth flat pebbles. "I only need a couple more."

I leaned over and picked up a rock and handed it to her. "Where is Mrs. Reynolds's cabin?"

"That's too big. It won't stay." She twisted her long blond hair up from her skeletonlike face till it formed a bun on her head. "I have to hide them in my hair. They're going to weigh me tomorrow morning. I was supposed to gain three pounds," she said anxiously.

I found some smaller ones for her.

"Thanks. You won't tell anybody, will you?"

"Not if you tell us where Mrs. Reynolds stays," I said.

"Why do you want to know?"

"Because," Claire said testily, "I'm a private detective."

"You mean like Sherlock Holmes?"

"The comparison has been made."

"Her cabin's over there."

We looked in the direction she was pointing. A small structure stood apart from the group of low buildings.

"Thanks," I said.

"Do you think you're Sherlock Holmes, too?" she asked me.

"Worse," I said. "I think I'm Dr. Watson."

She gave me a sympathetic nod. We left her searching for more pebbles and headed toward the bungalow. I took my gun out of my pocket.

We curved around and came up alongside the cabin. It was dark. We edged toward the front of the small building. Boulton pointed to the door, meaning he would go in first. I grabbed his wrist.

"Don't kill her," I whispered.

His eyes bored into mine. "That will depend on Alison, will it not?"

He moved toward the door. I was right behind him. Claire was behind me. He turned the handle and it opened.

Mother and daughter sat on the side of the bed. The dregs of a fire burned in a flagstone fireplace, dimly lighting the small square room. Alison held a gun. Elizabeth Reynolds stared at it as if her daughter had picked up the wrong fork.

"Drop it," Boulton said.

"She won't," Elizabeth Reynolds said. "You've caused this! Don't hurt her."

Claire stepped into the room. "Hello, Miss Reynolds."

Alison watched her. Claire stood by the fireplace, warming her hands while we all pointed our guns at each other.

"I'm chilled to the bone." Turning and warming her backside, she faced Alison. "You had me fooled for a while."

"I don't think I meant to fool anybody," she said simply.

"I could understand why you killed Jackie. But I could never figure out how you knew she was going to be at our hotel that morning."

"She didn't kill anybody!" Mrs. Reynolds said.

Claire ignored her. "That is, I didn't understand it until Paul Quentin told us he had met Jackie at different hotels."

"I followed her sometimes."

"And you followed her the morning you killed her."

"Paul was away all night."

"And in the early morning you went to the Duke Hotel."

"Yes, I thought Jackie and Paul had spent the night there. I wanted to confront him. When I arrived I saw Jackie walking away from the hotel. She caught a bus. I got on too. She didn't know me so I wasn't worried if she saw me. We got off on Madison near the Parkfaire. I watched her talking to Maggie. I followed them to the hotel."

"And you waited across the street in the basement stairwell. Why didn't you kill Jackie before Maggie returned to get her?"

"I thought Jackie was waiting for Paul. I wanted to see them together. Then Maggie came back out. I thought she was a contact. I thought she was taking Jackie up to Paul."

"It was an accident!" her mother cried. "She only wanted to talk to her."

"With a kitchen knife in her tote bag?" Claire demanded angrily.

"When Jackie came out of the hotel, she crossed the street and came by the stairs." Alison spoke quietly. "I walked up a few steps and told her I wanted to talk to her about Paul. I just backed down the stairs and she followed me."

"And after you stabbed her, you took the money from her purse to make the murder look like a mugging, and in doing so found the newspaper clipping of me."

"Yes. That's when I told my parents."

I looked at Mrs. Reynolds. "You knew all this?"

"I tried to be a good mother. I tried." She rocked back and forth, a new set of tears beginning to form.

"Please, don't cry," Alison said in a tired voice, stroking her cheek. "I just wanted to say good-bye." She stood.

"And now I want to go outside," she said. "Let me go outside."

Whimpering, Elizabeth crawled back into a corner of her bed.

"No, Alison," I said.

"I won't run away. It's best."

"No, it's not."

"I'll fire the gun at Miss Conrad." She looked at Boulton. "You'll shoot me, won't you?"

"Yes," he answered calmly.

Elizabeth cried.

"Let her go, Miss Hill," Claire spoke softly.

"You have no right," I said to Claire. "It's not our decision."

"It's mine." Alison slowly backed out of the cabin. "Good-bye, Maggie." The door banged shut.

Elizabeth Reynolds cried louder. I whirled around and aimed my gun at her. "Stop it! Stop it!"

Her crying stopped.

"I want you to hear this," I raged. "I want you to remember it."

She stared at me. Face wet. Lips trembling. Eyes glazed against the world. In the silence, Boulton leaned against the screen door, examining the weapon in his hand. Claire turned and peered into the fire. The explosion of Alison's gun split the night apart. Elizabeth Reynolds screamed.

Twenty-nine

Four days later we had finished breakfast and I was at my desk at the Parkfaire. Claire, all in white, seethed in her chair as she watched McGuire strut around the living room. Alvarez leaned against the fireplace, petting his mustache.

After Alison's death, Claire and I had stood outside the bungalow. The Shadow Hills patients waited in clusters, their faces as pale and as tight as a bunch of straitjackets. They watched the outside world intrude on their tormented isolation in a swirl of red lights and a parade of police cars. Elizabeth Reynolds stayed in her closed cabin, sobbing. A psychiatrist held her hand. I had watched the coroner's men put Alison's body into the ambulance. Somebody had to watch.

We had spent the rest of that night into the early morning answering questions and giving information to a Detective Jacobs of the Greenwich Police Department. The next three days were spent talking to the heads-that-be at the NYPD. Paul Quentin, Sheridan Reynolds, Marina Perry, Nora Brown, and Linda Hansen née Sarah Grange were all brought in for questioning. Quentin was the only one held. Nora and Marina Perry were all over the tabloids. St. Rome was suing anything that moved.

Now McGuire strutted. Alvarez petted.

"Where are they?" McGuire demanded.

"My new gloves are not pertinent to this case," Claire said, watching him as if he were a pigeon on the sill.

"Listen, lady, you withheld that video from us. Now I want the gloves. They're evidence."

"I had no way of knowing the importance of the video until I found out who the real Sarah Grange was," she said self-righteously.

McGuire leaned over her. "That's a lie and you know it."

"Prove it." She took the handle of her ivory walking stick and shoved it against his chest. "Do not swarm over me."

Alvarez chuckled. McGuire shot him a look. He stopped chuckling. Boulton carried some luggage into the hallway. McGuire saw it and threw a tizzy.

"You're not leaving. There is no way you're leaving!"

Gerta came out with some more cases.

"I have had an early morning conversation with Graham Sitwell and your commissioner," Claire continued. "They both assured me I may return to Los Angeles. If there are any more questions to be asked, there is the telephone and the fax. I'm confident that you know how to use both."

"I want the gloves." His voice was mean. "You withhold evidence and you don't leave town."

"This is harassment."

"The gloves."

She closed her eyes for a moment. "The gloves, Miss Hill."

I got up and went into the hallway. Gerta opened one of Claire's traveling cases and took out both pairs.

"Such a shame. Never been worn." She shook her gray head sadly.

I handed them to McGuire, who jammed them in his coat pocket. Claire cringed.

"You'll be hearing from us," McGuire said.

Alvarez stopped petting his mustache and they left.

Claire continued to seethe. The phone rang.

"Conrad Suite," I answered.

"Maggie? Linda Hansen. I'm at Cybella's. Marina gave me the keys to the apartment." She sounded as if she'd been drinking. "I've been here all night. I need to talk to someone."

I had time. The plane didn't leave till four. Why did I always have time? Oh, hell.

"Linda Hansen wants to see me at Cybella's," I told Claire, hanging up the phone.

"Miss Hill. Nothing, I repeat nothing, is going to prevent us from leaving."

"I understand."

Her eyes narrowed. She didn't look as if she believed me. "Boulton and I will be at the glove shop."

For the last time, I entered Cybella's apartment. Linda, wearing jeans and a white cotton shirt, sat on the yellow silk sofa. A bottle of Jack Daniel's—the only date that's left for some women—stood on the coffee table. A cigarette burned in an ashtray.

"I'm scared to go into Cybella's bedroom." The gray eyes were misty with booze.

"Come on."

She followed me but remained on the threshold, the bottle in her hand. She took a quick swallow. "Oh shit, I don't belong here. Marina was right. I'm a coward. I let my mother be used just because I couldn't face her." She staggered, then regained her balance. "I'm tired, Maggie."

"It's the booze, Linda. It has a way of making you feel tired and sorry for yourself."

"I'm no better than Jackie. I'll get myself knifed in the belly one night. I know it. Some bastard who won't want to pay. I know it."

"You're smarter than that. Two years of college smarter."

She looked at me and smiled. It softened her face, and again I was amazed at how young she really was. "Only one year," she corrected me, "and you're so fuckin' middle-class, Maggie."

"That's why you called me. I could use some of that." I held out my hand for the bottle.

She paused, then cautiously moved into the room, handing it to me. I took a swallow. It burned all the way down. She looked furtively around like a little girl who isn't allowed in her mother's room. She staggered and sat down on the end of the bed. I stood and opened the closet doors. The aroma of Cybella's perfume was barely discernible. It had already begun to fade.

"Can you smell that?" I asked.

She sniffed the air. "I'm not sure. I think so."

I pulled out the expensive suits and the evening gowns and threw them on the bed. They cascaded around her. She pushed them away. "What are you doing?"

"Look at them, feel them, smell them—they're your mother," I said.

I opened the drawers to Cybella's vanity table, grabbed some costume jewelry, and threw that on the bed.

"Here are some books given to Cybella by Nora Brown. Did you know Nora loved her?" I tossed a couple of the books on the bed.

"No."

"Your mother never read them. Now you, on the other hand, would probably enjoy them."

"Stop it." Her head swayed. "Stop it."

"Get to know her. She was only flesh and blood. Not too

intelligent, but clever. Superficial, but she was in a superficial business. She loved a man she shouldn't have loved. He loved her. She ruined her own life long before she died. Maybe you can do better. Somebody has to do better. Get to know her, Linda, the best you can, then let her go."

Tears glistened on her pockmarked cheeks. "Oh, God, Maggie." She fell back onto the bed amid Cybella's clothes and jewelry. Turning on her side, she brought her long legs up toward her body. She was quiet. Passed out.

I tried to walk out of the room but I couldn't. I picked up the phone and called the Reynolds residence. A maid answered. I told her who I was and to put Mr. Reynolds on. I waited a while but he finally took the call.

"I'm at Cybella's. Your daughter is passed out on the bed. She's trying to get to know her mother but she needs help. I thought maybe you could . . ."

"My daughter's dead." His voice sounded empty as if there was nothing left inside of him.

"This is your other daughter."

"How much more money does she want?"

"I'm not talking money. I thought you might come over here. Get to know her."

"Elizabeth wouldn't like that." He hung up.

I tried to walk out of the room again, but I knew I wasn't going to make it to the front door. I dialed another number. I was put through to the two female guard dogs.

"Maggie Hill for Nora Brown." They put me on hold without a word. Nora came on the line.

"What do you want?"

"Linda Hansen is passed out in Cybella's apartment. She needs help."

Silence.

"She's Cybella's daughter. The woman you loved, remember?"

"I'm in a meeting. The board of directors fired me."

"I have the feeling you'll bounce right back."

"Is she all right?"

"No."

"I'll be there as quickly as I can."

I took one last look at Linda curled among her mother's beautiful clothes and sparkling jewelry. Everything that belonged to Cybella was there on her bed. I took the hundred thousand out of my purse and placed it on the vanity. I laid the keys to the apartment on top of it. I hoped Linda didn't wake up before Nora arrived. I hoped she wouldn't take the money and skip town. I hoped.

I stared at my spectator pumps. The black patent leather curved around the white leather and glistened crisply in the morning light. Wing tips. I thought of Jackie. Her mother had dreams. I thought of Alison with her camera. Her mother had tears.

To observe. To witness.

A female arm with a lot of silver bracelets reached in and plucked the shoes out of the window. They were replaced by a pair of black satin shoes with gold, knifelike heels. I watched in horror. I couldn't adjust. My heart broke. My spectator pumps. Gone. Oh, hell, Maggie, let the soul yearn.

"Thinking of buying a pair of stiletto heels, Maggie?" Boulton moved next to me. "So you can stomp all over my heart?"

I gave him a slow, sly look and patted the gun in his shoulder holster. "Your heart is protected, Boulton."

"Miss Conrad has ordered her gloves. She awaits," he said in his best butler voice, gesturing down the street toward the glove shop.

———

Our plane glided downward, skimming L.A. Its giant bird-like shadow reflected over all the flat-roof houses, the baby blue swimming pools, the tops of the shaggy palm trees where the rats lived, and the freeways where the commuters inched closer to home.

Boulton sat across the aisle, next to Gerta. He brought his fine fingers to his somber lips and blew me a kiss.

"Is Miss Hill going someplace, Boulton?" Claire asked.

"I hope not, madam."

Yes, I thought, watching him, it's good for the soul to yearn.

"There will be work for Miss Conrad," Gerta said, peering out the plane's window. "I can feel it."

The sun was as round as a pregnant woman's belly in the southern California sky and it burned with life. I put on my sunglasses.